RAYMOND HAIGH

---◆---

KISS AND KILL

Complete and Unabridged

ULVERSCROFT
Leicester

First published in Great Britain in 2007 by
Robert Hale Limited
London

First Large Print Edition
published 2008
by arrangement with
Robert Hale Limited
London

British Library CIP Data

Haigh, Raymond
   Kiss and kill.—Large print ed.—
   Ulverscroft large print series: mystery
   1. Lomax, Paul (Fictitious character)—Fiction
   2. Private investigators—England—Fiction
   3. Detective and mystery stories 4. Large type books
   I. Title
   823.9'14 [F]

   ISBN 978–1–84782–210–9

Published by
F. A. Thorpe (Publishing)
Anstey, Leicestershire

Set by Words & Graphics Ltd.
Anstey, Leicestershire
Printed and bound in Great Britain by
T. J. International Ltd., Padstow, Cornwall

This book is printed on acid-free paper

Raymond Haigh was born, educated and has lived in Doncaster, South Yorkshire, all his life. He is married with four children and six grandchildren.

KISS AND KILL

Private eye Paul Lomax expected trouble when Velma Hartman said she needed a big, strong man. But it's hard to say no to a woman alone. And the formidable Mrs Pearson is demanding intimate pictures of her husband with his lover: another unwanted case when all Lomax wants to do is cultivate his relationship with the irresistible Melody Brown . . . The police are interested in what Lomax knows. Two killings later, Lomax makes the connection between Velma and Mrs Pearson and the corruption that blights the town. But then he's staring death in the eye himself, and there seems to be no way out.

1

The dark-haired girl strolled past the paintings, her skirt brushing against the barrier rope. She gazed up at Monet's *Forest of Fontainebleau* for all of two seconds, then turned towards a life-sized statue of Venus on a low pedestal in the centre of the gallery.

I sat, motionless, on the blue sofa, head down, catalogue on my knee, watching her over heavy horn-rimmed spectacles. Her bored gaze took in white marble breasts, then dropped to plump thighs. Her oval face was clearly visible. She wasn't pretty, but a youthful freshness stopped her looking plain. Thick eyebrows arched over brown eyes and almost joined above a nose that was a little too large. Her small mouth had full, almost pouting lips. Even without make-up, they were startlingly red against the paleness of her face. She was tall for a woman, maybe five foot nine or five-ten, and slender. I guessed she'd be in her twentieth year.

It was her. I was sure of it. After a while you develop an instinct. You just know. And the short-sleeved black and white summer dress, the black and white clutch bag, and the matching shoes, gave her away. They looked expensive. She was dressing to impress; to please a man. And anything smarter than jeans and a T-shirt, or track-suit bottoms and trainers, would have marked her out. Round here it usually takes a wedding or a funeral to persuade a woman to wear a dress.

The tiny camera was hidden in a void cut into the pages of a notebook. I turned the notebook on to its edge, slowly manoeuvred it into position, then pressed the shutter release button beneath the cloth spine. The girl hadn't looked at me. She was gazing up at the statue's face. I took another three shots, each time shifting the position of the camera a little before pressing the button. At least one should produce a clear picture.

Indifferent to Canova's handiwork, the girl turned and ambled over to a big painting of a couple of droopy-eared dogs. She had her back to me now, and the animals were interesting her in a way that Venus never could. Adjusting the horn-rims, I took a last glance at her through the plain-glass lenses, then headed out into the entrance area and began to examine art books and prints in a display opposite the stairs. I looked back, beyond bronzes of a girl with wide hips and a youth with big feet, making sure I still had a clear view into the gallery. She was leaning over the barrier rope, studying some gloomy Grimshaw streetscapes hung low down on the wall. I picked up a copy of *Watercolours From the Leeds City Art Gallery*, slid the specs down my nose, and pretended to read while I watched and waited.

Behind me, entrance doors opened and swung shut, footsteps echoed, and then a tall, prosperous-looking guy, his greying hair neatly barbered, strode past the book display. He was wearing a biscuit-coloured summer suit and carrying a brown leather briefcase.

A sudden expression of joy transformed the girl's face when he entered the gallery. He snatched a quick backward glance. The receptionist was sitting behind her counter, staring out through the glass entrance. I was almost hidden behind bookshelves, head down, still pretending to read. He must have thought they were unobserved. He slid an arm around her waist and she clung to him while they exchanged a lingering kiss. Holding the notebook camera steady against the display shelving, I snatched a couple of pictures.

He whispered something, and her laughter, happy and excited, fluttered up to the high ceiling. Then they were walking, arm in arm, out of the gallery, moving past massive columns at the foot of the stairs, heading for the entrance. Lines of age and experience were deeply etched into the man's tanned, smiling face. It was a handsome face; very masculine, very distinguished. She was gazing into it adoringly. They were completely absorbed in each other. If the place had been on fire they wouldn't have noticed. As they approached and moved past, I took more pictures, then slid the book on watercolours back on to the shelf and followed them through the vestibule.

Out in the square, the noise of the traffic seemed loud after the quiet in the gallery. Leaning against the haunches of a Henry Moore reclining woman, I waited until they reached the bottom of the access ramp, then strode after them. They ran, hand-in-hand, across Cookridge Street, dodging between cars, then disappeared through an opening between the Radisson Hotel and Brown's restaurant. Horns blared when I tried to do the same. I held back. When I passed through the opening, they'd vanished. I checked a juice bar and a pizza parlour on my right, then climbed steps and glanced around an enclosed square, but couldn't see the girl and her companion.

Moving back down the steps, I pushed at a glass door and peered across the cool vastness of the Radisson Hotel's foyer. The couple hadn't joined the sprinkling of guests sitting around low tables, and the staff at the reception desk weren't attending to any newcomers. For a moment I thought I'd lost them. Then, when I stepped inside, I saw them, standing by the lifts, watching the illuminated numbers change as the car descended. His arm was around her waist, her head was resting on his shoulder. Plucking a leaflet from a rack, I unfolded it, held it on top of the notebook camera and pretended to read while I snapped a couple of pictures.

Lift doors rumbled open. As soon as they were inside the brightly lit compartment, her arms slid around his neck. He dropped his briefcase, cupped big hands under her buttocks and pulled her close. I managed to press the shutter a couple of times before the doors rattled shut and they were whisked upwards.

The job was almost over. I was glad. Spying on lovers leaves me feeling soiled, but when you come highly recommended by an old client, when you know he wants you to do him a favour by taking the case, it's not easy to say no.

Back on the street, I made for the multi-storey where I'd parked the Jaguar. The sun was blazing out of a sky that was painfully bright, and I toyed with the idea of finding somewhere cool for lunch. I decided not to. I wanted to get back to Barfield, print the photographs, hand them over and wash my hands of the job. With any luck I'd be in the office by 2.30, and there was more than a chance Melody would have sent one of her girls to get me a sandwich or a take away.

★　★　★

The office is a couple of attic rooms and the use of a toilet built for a dwarf. They're at the top of a big Georgian town house in a nameplate-studded terrace that faces the parish church. Walking up the pedestrianized area that borders the churchyard, I found myself searching out the dark-haired, dark-eyed young teenagers amongst the groups of schoolgirls heading for the town-centre comprehensive. Kathy would have been fourteen in a few days' time; Susan would have been thirty-six. Another stolen year. Another lonely year. And when the memories are only pleasant ones, the feeling of loss is all the more intense.

I took the worn steps at a run, collected the mail from the box behind my slot, then glanced through Melody's reception window. Miss Melody Brown is the blue-eyed blonde

6

who owns the typing and printing agency on the ground floor. Her girls direct clients up to me, type reports and take phone calls when I'm out, which is most of the time. Melody was leaning over one of the desks, discussing something on a computer screen with a tiny brunette called Rachel.

Cord carpet covers the first two flights of stairs. Ancient brown linoleum protects the final flight to the attic. I've kept it that way. When you're up there on your own, and the building's quiet, you can hear the tread of feet on the hard surface. There are times when it's good to be warned that someone's paying you a call.

I clattered across the top landing and stepped into the waiting room. The leather chairs and coffee table had come from the lounge of a hotel. The copies of *Yorkshire Life*, the glossy fashion magazines and the copies of *House & Garden* had been supplied by Melody. She needn't have bothered. Clients who read that stuff don't hang around in waiting rooms; they expect to be called on.

The smell of old papers and dusty brown carpet, the festering remains of yesterday's lunch in the waste bin, hit me when I stepped into the office. It was furnace hot. The rooms are just below the slates, and the sun had given the trapped air a morning-long baking.

I flung the dormer windows open, let in the rumble of downtown traffic, the aroma of coffee beans roasting in the deli on the corner, and a breath of fume-laden air that was so tired it could barely waft over the sill.

Footsteps were tapping up the stairs and across the landing. I got behind the desk just as Melody stepped through the half-glazed door, holding a tray.

'Thought you weren't coming in.' She balanced the tray on the piles of papers stacked on the desk.

'Had to drive over to Leeds. Surveillance job for a worried wife who'd . . . ' My throat had gone dry. Melody's curves were sensational, and some artist of a seamstress had made the black suit, with its tiny jacket and pencil skirt, fit like a second skin. Suddenly realizing I'd been staring too hard, I made a heroic effort and raised my eyes to her face. There were two spots of colour high on her cheeks, and her generous mouth was shaped in that half-pleased, half-reproachful little smile she always gives me when she knows I'm ogling her.

Swallowing hard, I said, 'Gorgeous suit. Looks new.' And then I had to give in and allow my eyes to wander all the way back down to the high-heeled satin and suede shoes.

'You like my outfit, then?' Her husky voice was whispery with pleasure. She was smiling broadly now. 'How does it make me look?'

I was losing the plot. I couldn't figure out what she wanted to hear, so I shrugged, and said, 'Sexy.'

Her smile faded. 'Sexy? Is that all you can say: sexy?'

I knew I was being tested in some way, but I still didn't know what she expected. I watched her wrap a napkin around the handle of the coffee pot and begin to pour. Giving up the struggle, I grinned, and said, 'Very sexy?'

She let out a sigh, and her big blue eyes held me in a disapproving stare. 'You've a one-track mind, Paul. Sometimes I think you're a throwback; a Neanderthal in a crumpled suit. It's supposed to make me look businesslike and sensible. A woman who can't be trifled with. A woman who's . . . who's . . . '

'Formidable?'

Her face brightened. 'That's the word: formidable.'

'And very sexy.'

She tut-tutted, poured milk into the coffee, then spooned in sugar. 'Janice tried to get you some raw mammoth meat from the deli, but she had to settle for ham rolls.'

'Ham rolls are fine.' I reached for one,

paused with it halfway to my mouth, and asked, 'Why do you want to look formidable?'

'Business meeting. Someone wants to buy out my lease.' She flashed me a bright little smile.

I tossed the roll back on to the plate. 'You're selling up? Packing in the business?'

'I might, if the offer's attractive enough.' She was still smiling. She'd dropped her bombshell and she was enjoying the effect it was having on me.

I wanted to blurt out, 'What about me, what about us?' But that would have sounded childish and pathetic, and I didn't want to reveal how much the news had upset me. So I tried to sound indifferent when I asked, 'Who wants to buy out the lease?'

'Don't know. I've been contacted by valuers who've been hired to approach the tenants and negotiate. They've been talking to the accountants on the second floor. I understand they're interested. They were thinking of relocating out of town anyway.'

I gazed at her across the cluttered desk. Slender fingers reached up and tucked a stray curl behind her ear. She'd pinned up her hair. She looked younger when she did that, and vulnerable in a very attractive way. It wasn't the thing to do if she wanted to appear formidable. Diamond studs were flashing on her ears. They looked real, not paste.

Swallowing hard, I said, 'Who are the agents?'

'Allot and Jones. They have offices in Leeds.'

'When's the meeting?'

'Tonight. Over drinks and dinner with the senior partner. He's picking me up at six. He said we could explore possibilities together tonight, then his people could negotiate with my valuer if I was still interested.'

Her smile had widened. I could see traces of lipstick on very white teeth. *Explore possibilities together tonight*: she'd lobbed in her second bombshell, and she was revelling in the devastation. The gentle sex. They know how to goad you; how to inflict emotional pain. She hadn't bothered to ask me if I'd been approached. She probably knew the accountants sub-let the attic to me on a six-monthly basis. If they went, I'd have to go.

'Aren't you going to eat your rolls?'

'I'm not hungry.'

Her smile widened. A cloud of some expensive fragrance had reached me across the desk. The room didn't smell of sun-baked dust and old carpets any more.

'At least drink the coffee,' she insisted huskily. 'You can get dehydrated in this heat.'

Dehydrated! I felt as if I'd been wrung out

11

and hung up to dry. I managed a dismissive shrug, then muttered, 'Have a pleasant evening.'

'I'm sure I will. Charles sounded charming over the telephone.'

'Charles?'

'Charles Allot, the senior partner. Nice cultured voice, very gentle, very professional.' She was almost laughing now. Beaming at me, she said, 'I'll let you know how I get on,' then turned and headed for the door.

'Yeah, do that,' I growled after her. The provocative sway of her pert little posterior only intensified the pain. It was as if she was using her body to mock me.

When she reached the door, she paused and turned. 'I almost forgot. You had a visitor, a Miss Hartman. She wants you to give her a ring. The number's on the slip of paper on the tray.' She smiled. 'This one's definitely not your type.'

'Not my type? What's my type?'

'She's no longer young, rides an old sit-up-and-beg bike with a basket on the front, wears a headscarf and muddy boots and a dirty raincoat. In this weather! And she's got back problems.'

'Back problems?'

'She reeked of rubbing oils. And she asked if you were big and strong. She didn't mention clever, wise, sensitive or tender. She just asked for big and strong, so I said you'd fit the bill perfectly.' Melody giggled. 'The address is on the paper: Branwell Farm, Hawthorne Lane. She said it was just outside Moxton.'

Hips, sheathed in black, swayed as Melody crossed the waiting room. I listened to the tap-tap of her heels as she descended the stairs, then glowered at the ham rolls. On a sudden impulse, I hurled them through the open window. They hit the parapet wall and dropped into the gutter.

The phone began to ring. I groped for it amongst the piles of papers, lifted the handset and muttered, 'Lomax.'

There was a brief delay, then the line opened and a refined voice announced, 'It's Mrs Pearson. Have you any information for me?' I guessed she was calling from a public phone.

'I have, Mrs Pearson. Would you like to come into the office, or would you like me to visit your home?'

'Are your findings positive?'

'I'm afraid so, Mrs Pearson. Positive and conclusive.'

'Oh dear. Mmm . . . I have to visit my sister. Could you meet me at the railway station?'

I glanced at my watch. I had to get the memory chip out of the camera and print the images. 'What if I meet you there at three? Would that be convenient?'

'Perfectly, Mr Lomax. I'll be in the Travellers' Friend snack bar: the one on platform four.' The line went dead.

Cradling the phone, I picked up the notebook camera and went over to a table beneath the sloping part of the ceiling. I loaded paper into the printer tray and switched it on. By the time I'd got the camera out of the compartment in the notebook and withdrawn the memory chip, the 'ready' light was on. I slid the chip into the slot, punched keys, then returned to the desk and opened that morning's mail. A fatuous tax demand, a cheque from the DHSS for obtaining evidence on the last batch of benefit cheats, and a couple of circulars.

Pocketing the cheque, I crossed over to the printer. Glossy photographs were emerging and dropping into the tray. They were clear, sharp, and incriminating.

2

Emma Pearson was waiting in the snack bar on platform four, a yellow silk handkerchief bursting like an exotic flower from the top pocket of her saffron-yellow trouser suit. She was sitting at a table beside a window, long legs crossed, her face frozen in a deathly stillness, her carefully made-up eyes staring sightlessly at an information display hanging from the ceiling. She didn't notice me until I pulled out the chair facing hers.

'I hope I've not kept you waiting long, Mrs Pearson.'

Stylishly cut, silvery-blonde hair brushed the shoulders of her jacket as she straightened up. 'I got here early, Mr Lomax.' She was pulling herself together; bracing herself for the sordid little details she'd hoped never to hear. Lacing her fingers together, she rested her arms on the table and leaned towards me.

I handed her a manila envelope. She just stared at it, her lips pressed in a hard line. Maybe she was thinking that, once she opened it, things would never be the same again.

A train moved noisily into the platform.

Carriage wheels rumbled, then metal began to screech on metal as it juddered to a stop.

Emma Pearson took a deep breath, lifted the flap, and pulled out the glossy ten-by-sevens. I'd printed them all. Every image was there, arranged in shooting sequence. She looked down at the picture of the dark-haired girl in the summer dress standing by Canova's *Venus*, then glanced up at me and let out a little laugh. Her body had relaxed and a sudden relief sounded in her voice as she said, 'I'm afraid you've made a mistake, Mr Lomax. You've been following the wrong person. This is — '

I interrupted her with a shake of the head. 'Keep leafing through, Mrs Pearson. There hasn't been any mistake.'

She glanced down and began to flick through the pictures of the girl alone in the gallery. When she reached the shot of the grey-haired man and the girl exchanging a kiss, she let out a shocked gasp, and trembling fingers reached up to her throat. Out on the platform, a whistle blew, the distant roar of revving motors grew louder, wheels groaned and began to rumble.

Her voice was little more than a whisper; I could hardly hear it above the din, but I thought she moaned, 'Dear God, not her. The fool. The bloody fool.'

16

She stared down at the image for quite a while, then leafed through the shots of them walking, arm-in-arm, out of the gallery. The last picture, the one of them in the brightly lit lift, their bodies framed in the narrow gap left by the closing doors, was the clincher. She spent some time studying that one: the girl hanging from the guy's neck, his mouth crushing hers, his big hands curved around the top of her thighs, rucking up her dress.

She shuffled the photographs together, tapped them into a neat bundle on the table, then slid them back into the envelope. When she glanced across at me, the look in her huge grey eyes was chilling. She gave me a humourless smile and said, 'Thank you, Mr Lomax. I must say, I'm impressed. And more than a little surprised.' The top-drawer voice was strained. She was fighting for self-control.

I kept quiet, just raised an eyebrow.

'When I gave you the job, I couldn't understand why you'd been so highly recommended. I thought you were rather like my husband: tall, dark, handsome and stupid.' She laughed mirthlessly, gesturing towards the photographs. 'How wrong I was. Just three days later, and look what you've brought me.' The smart remark, the laughter; she was building a dam to hold back the tears.

'Where were they when the photographs were taken?' she asked.

'Leeds City Art Gallery. The lift is in the Radisson Hotel. It's just across the road from the gallery.'

'How very convenient for them.' She let out another bitter laugh.

'Could I get you a coffee, or a drink? I think they sell alcohol.'

'You're very kind, but I'd rather not.' She clicked open her bag and slid the envelope inside. 'Do you know who the girl is, Mr Lomax?'

Shaking my head, I braced myself. She'd joined the bleeding hearts brigade and she was going to tell me whether I wanted to know or not. It's always the same, and it's one more reason why I usually avoid jobs like this.

'She's my daughter's best friend. She almost lived at the house until my daughter went to university. The girl's grades weren't good enough, so she didn't get a place. Now we know why they weren't good enough, don't we?' Bleak eyes stared at me across the table.

I just gazed back at her and said nothing. Her lipstick had leached into the fine lines around her mouth, and the backs of her hands and the deep V of tanned flesh between the lapels of her jacket were whispering secrets about her age. But she was still a very attractive woman; immaculately groomed, expensively dressed.

The silence was making her edgy. She said, 'How much do I owe you, Mr Lomax?'

'I've kept a record of the hours. I'll tot it up and let you have a bill. If you'll give me your address . . . '

'I'd rather you didn't do that. I'd much prefer to settle with you now.' She suggested a figure, then said, 'Would that cover your time and expenses?'

It was twice what I was going to charge, so I said, 'The bill's going to be less than that. Why not let me — '

'No, Mr Lomax. No bills, no records.' She clicked open her bag again, slender fingers dipped inside, and she began to flick through the contents. She produced a wad of notes, folded it, then discreetly covered it with her hand as she slid it over the table.

I pocketed it. Taking cash from clients makes me uncomfortable. A bill and a cheque through the post distances you from the process; makes it painless.

'Are you married, Mr Lomax?'

'I was.'

She sighed. 'Dear God, everyone's divorced these days. No one respects marriage vows any more: to love and cherish, in sickness and in health, until death — '

'I'm a widower.'

She closed her eyes to hide her shame. 'I'm sorry, Mr Lomax. That was unspeakably thoughtless of me.' Her lips were trembling now. She was losing her battle with the tears. The dam was about to burst.

'That's OK,' I said softly. 'I understand.'

'I don't think you can possibly understand, Mr Lomax. It was my silver wedding anniversary last month. I've spent the best years of my life helping a rather stupid man become successful. I've given him a child, I've made him a beautiful home, and he betrays me by having an affair with some plain-Jane young enough to be his daughter.' She glowered at me across the table while a train roared through. I was another member of the loathsome sex. 'Say something to me, Mr Lomax. For God's sake, say something to me,' she demanded, when the clatter had faded.

Say something? Bleeding hearts weren't my territory. I'd not the faintest idea what to say. I wanted to get away from her; to be finished with the job. I swallowed hard. 'This sort of thing's not uncommon, Mrs Pearson. Men of a certain age, they realize time's passing. They no longer feel invincible and begin to doubt themselves. When they look for reassurance, they sometimes behave irrationally.'

Her mouth had curved into a sneer. I knew I wasn't handling it very well. What I was saying sounded pathetic to me. Heavens knows what it sounded like to her.

'It's probably just a fleeting thing,' I rambled on. 'A kind of madness; a rush of blood to the head.'

'A rush of blood to the head!' she snorted. 'I think you need an anatomy lesson, Mr Lomax.'

Ignoring that, I said, 'Your husband won't be doing this to hurt you, Mrs Pearson. You'd be the very last person he'd want to hurt. Infatuation's just leading him like a bull with a ring through his nose.'

'I really don't know what you're trying to say to me, Mr Lomax.' Her voice was frosty.

'I'm saying he's being stupid. He'll come to his senses. Might be best to just watch and wait rather than start something you could regret.'

'He's always been stupid, Mr Lomax. If I hadn't guided and encouraged him, he wouldn't have the biggest architectural practice in South Yorkshire. He'd still be a pathetic little nobody scribbling away in the council offices. And it's him that's started something he's going to regret. You don't know the half of it.'

I shrugged and managed a sympathetic smile. She'd demanded that I say something, and now she was giving me grief about it. All she'd wanted to do was have an argument. I pressed my hands on the table and began to rise.

'Do you have the negatives, Mr Lomax?'

'Digital camera. No negatives. The images are stored on a memory chip.'

'Of course. I'm forgetting how things have changed. Do you have the chip?'

I nodded.

'I'd like it. May I purchase it from you?'

Reaching inside my jacket, I groped in the small-change pocket, withdrew the square of plastic and handed it to her. 'On the house. If you take it to a photo shop they can print out more copies for you.'

'Do you have any more copies?'

I shook my head. 'I don't keep copies, Mrs Pearson. On paper or on disk. My only records are a copy of the bill I send the client and the receipt for payment. You've not been billed. You won't get a receipt.'

'And you'll be discreet; if anyone comes asking?'

'We've never met, Mrs Pearson. I stay in business because I'm discreet.'

She managed a bleak little smile. 'I'll let

you go. I've got to catch the Sheffield train. I'm visiting my sister.'

Rising, I held out a hand. She slid hers into it. It was ice-cold, and I could feel rings with big stones when I shook it.

The Jaguar was parked in one of the short-stay spaces that face the station entrance. I climbed inside, wound down the window to let out the heat, and waited. I didn't have to wait long. Five minutes later, a tall woman in a saffron-yellow trouser suit emerged from the opening. Her eyes and half her face were hidden behind big sunglasses with yellow frames. She glanced around, then crossed over to the short-stay bays and unlocked a bright-yellow Mini Cooper. She clearly had a thing about yellow. A starter whined. I hunched down behind the wheel, watched her motor across the forecourt and join the line of cars waiting on the feed to the inner ring road.

She'd avoided giving me her address, she'd contacted me by public phone, she'd been uptight about records, and she'd told a porky about visiting her sister. When she merged with the flow of traffic, I followed. She led me to a big detached house in a leafy suburb to the south of town. After driving on a hundred yards, I pulled over and reached into the glove compartment for a pad. As I was noting the address, my mobile started bleeping. I keyed it on and muttered my name.

'It's Miss Hartman. Your secretary said she'd leave a message for you to call me. It's been hours and I'm getting scared. I wondered if you'd forgotten.'

'I've not forgotten, Miss Hartman.' The lie came effortlessly. 'I had business not far from Moxton. I'm going to call in. How do I find Hawthorne Lane?'

'Are you coming from Barfield?'

I said I was.

'Just drive through the village, then turn left at the first crossroads. Hawthorne Lane's about half a mile along. You'll see the farm when you turn into it. You'll get here before dark, won't you?' Fear was threading its way through the soft voice.

I promised her I'd be there within the hour.

★   ★   ★

Branwell Farm was isolated; hidden in a dip in rolling countryside about ten miles out of town. When I turned off what passed for a main road and headed down the lane, I could see its slate roof and tall chimneys through gaps in a hawthorn hedge.

I parked down the side of an old corrugated-iron shed and looked over at the

24

house. An estate agent would have described it as a picturesque property in need of some refurbishment. Moss and lichen spotted its limestone walls, paint was peeling from window frames, and the old iron gutters were sagging. Blue slates swept down over a single-storey extension that formed a large windowless porch.

Picking my way between nettles and rusting machinery, I crossed a sun-baked yard and gave the door a pounding. It was a heavy, iron-bound door; low but unusually wide. After a few seconds, a breathless voice said, 'Who is it? Who's there?'

'Lomax, come to see Miss Hartman.'

'Thank God.' Bolts slid and chains rattled, and the door swung open.

She wasn't wearing a dirty raincoat and headscarf now. Pale freckled face and arms, vivid-green eyes, red hair falling over her shoulders: in the white muslin dress she looked like a Pre-Raphaelite's muse.

Relief softened her features as she looked me over. 'Come in, Mr Lomax. I was getting worried.'

She didn't seem to have any qualms about inviting a stranger into her home. Maybe things Melody had said about me had reassured her, or perhaps she needed help so badly she was beyond caring. She led me past an old bike and along a short passage. I couldn't smell the rubbing oils; just perfumed soap and clean linen and the shampoo she'd used on her hair. Riding over it all was the fragrant aroma of a meal cooking.

'Do you mind if we sit in the kitchen? It's a bit cluttered, but I've got to get the vegetables on.'

I ducked through a low opening, into a kitchen with a stone-flagged floor. Spindly Windsor chairs were arranged on either side of an old iron cooking range, and a big table in the centre of the room was strewn with the jars and utensils she'd used for preparing the meal.

She pointed at a chair. 'Sit down while I finish off.' Picking up a big cook's knife, she began to slice carrots and parsnips. Her movements were quick, deft, without effort. The knife must have been razor-sharp. 'You'll stay for dinner, won't you, Mr Lomax?'

I hardly heard what she said. She was bending over the chopping board and her pale freckled breasts were heavy against the low-cut bodice of her dress, quivering slightly as she wielded the knife.

She glanced up. 'You'll stay for dinner?' she repeated.

I tried to concentrate on what she was saying. Dining with clients, especially female clients, was best avoided. It blurred the boundaries of what should be a purely business relationship. Then hunger kicked in, reminding me I'd skipped breakfast and thrown my lunch against the wall in a fit of jealous pique.

'It's beef stew. My own recipe, with brown ale.' Her voice was coaxing.

She didn't have to coax me. I said, 'I'd be pleased to have dinner with you, Miss Hartman.'

She scooped the vegetables into saucepans, splashed in water from a brass tap above a chipped stoneware sink, then slid them on to the cooker. A pipe snaked from the cooker to a gas cylinder under the draining board. The cooker and a fridge were the only modern things in the room. She struck a match and lit the gas, then gestured towards a battered Welsh dresser. 'Could you open the wine, Mr Lomax? We'll have a drink while we're waiting. Won't be long now.'

I uncorked the bottle and filled a couple of glasses. When I turned I found her sitting in the Windsor chair facing mine, pale legs stretched out and crossed at the ankles. Her shoes were startling: scarlet suede, with ankle straps and pointed toes and Cuban heels. They were the last things I'd expect a farming woman to wear. 'Maybe you could tell me why you want to see me?' I was hungering for

27

the meal, but I wanted to get the business over with. And I was curious.

Ignoring the question, she smiled and said, 'I told your secretary I wanted a big strong man. A man with a lot of physical presence. She said you matched the description.' Miss Hartman ran her eyes over me, sipped at her glass, then added, 'She was right.'

'She's not my secretary, Miss Hartman. She just looks after callers for me. She has a printing firm on the ground floor. My offices are on the top floor.'

Understanding dawned. 'That explains things,' she said, and took another sip from her glass.

'Explains things?'

'The stunning designer suit, the fabulous shoes: not the sort of things a private investigator's secretary could afford to wear. She made me feel dowdy in my headscarf and old mac; I wear them to protect me from the sun. I burn in seconds. And I couldn't believe your offices filled the entire building.'

I pictured my frowsty attic rooms, and smiled at her.

Miss Hartman took a generous sip from her glass, then went on. 'The firms I checked out before I came to you were pretty seedy. A bald-headed little man had one, a chain-smoking consumptive ran the other. Like I

28

said, Mr Lomax, I need someone with physical presence; someone who can be threatening.'

'Threatening?' I watched her drain her glass, then asked her again what her problem was.

Ignoring me, she said, 'Would you pour me another?'

When I reached for her glass, I noticed the remains of paint — white, black, red, yellow, blue — in her nails and on her hands. They weren't the hands of a girl, but they weren't the hands of an old woman, either. They were soft and white. It was quite a while since she'd ploughed the fields and scattered the good seed.

While I was over at the dresser, filling her glass, she said, 'She's very glamorous.'

'Who's very glamorous?'

'The woman who does reception for you. And that husky voice! Is she a heavy smoker?'

'She doesn't smoke.' I handed her the glass, then tried to sound firm when I said, 'Miss Hartman, we really must talk about your problems, not the woman who does reception for me.'

Pans began to boil over and water hissed in the flames. 'Scuse me.' She took a good swallow from her glass, rested it on a trivet projecting from the old cooking range, and dashed over to the cooker.

When she'd turned down the gas, I said, 'Your problems, Miss Hartman. Could you tell me how I can help you?'

'It's Velma, Mr Lomax. Please call me Velma. I feel ancient enough without you calling me Miss Hartman all the time. What's your first name?'

'Paul.'

'May I call you Paul?' She took a sip from her glass.

'I'd like you to.'

The wine had driven some colour beneath the freckles on her cheeks. There was a softness to the flesh around her mouth; creases at the corners of her eyes. She was slender. That made her breasts all the more striking. I couldn't guess her age. It could have been anything between thirty and forty. Dragging my attention back to the business in hand, I said, 'Perhaps you could tell me — '

'I'm so glad you're here,' she interrupted. 'It's the first time I've been able to relax in almost six months. You don't know what a relief it is.' She drained her glass and held it out. 'Do the honours for me, Paul. And take both bottles through to the parlour; I'll serve the meal in there.'

Wandering across the gloomy passage, I found myself in a room about the same size as the kitchen. Two big rooms down, and probably two big rooms up, arranged on either side of the passage and stairs. Perhaps it was a standard farm-house plan. Shelves sagged under the weight of large books, there were ashes in the grate of a black marble fireplace, and rugs covered the stone-flagged floor. A white cloth had been smoothed over a table.

Cuban heels tapped across the passage, and Velma Hartman swirled past carrying a tureen and holding some place mats under her arm. She began to set the table.

'Can we talk about what it is you want me to do?' I demanded, after she'd served the meal.

'Later, Paul, please. After we've eaten. You're with me now, and I just want to enjoy the feeling of not being scared.' She held out her glass. 'Open the other bottle and give me a refill.'

More than a little uneasy now, I did as she asked. It was almost as if I was being held prisoner by a crazy woman. Crazy or not, the woman with flaming red hair in the high-waisted Regency-style dress wasn't unat-tractive. After a second glass of wine, I got to thinking I could get used to being imprisoned by Velma Hartman. I might even get to like it. Having given up pressing her about the job, I had to keep the conversation going, so I said, 'What do you grow?'

She stared at me, her face blank, her lips pressed together while she chewed on a mouthful of stew. She ate like she drank; enthusiasm overlaid by just the right amount of refinement. She swallowed. 'What do I grow?'

I gestured with my fork. 'On the farm; in the fields.'

'I don't grow anything,' she laughed. 'I just live in the farmhouse. It was my uncle's. He left it to me. He never married; just lived here alone. There was no one else for him to leave it to. The fields are rented out. More than a hundred acres. It doesn't bring in a fortune, but it leaves me comfortable enough to do what I want.'

'Which is?'

'I'm a painter. My studio's upstairs.'

Suddenly remembering a poster over an archway, I said, '*The* Velma Hartman? You've an exhibition at Leeds City Art Gallery.'

She beamed at me. 'You know about that? I'm incredibly flattered. Are you interested in the visual arts?'

For some inexplicable reason, when she said that my gaze dropped to freckled breasts nestling in white muslin. I closed my eyes to shut out the view. When I opened them, I was looking into her face again. 'A little,' I said. 'I've spent quite a lot of time in art galleries. You pick things up.'

'You go to exhibitions?'

'Not exactly.' I let it rest there. I didn't want to explain that galleries were places I lurked around, watching the middle classes conduct amorous liaisons.

'Did you enjoy *my* exhibition?' She laid her knife and fork on a cleared plate and reached for her glass. 'Top me up, will you, Paul? And then I'll go and make coffee.'

'It was impressive,' I said. I hadn't seen it. My business had been in another gallery.

'They're mostly paintings I did a few years ago.' She began to stack dishes. 'I've moved on from landscapes and still lifes. Shan't be a minute.' She picked up the dishes and headed across the passageway. While I listened to her bustling around in the kitchen, I wandered over to the floor-to-ceiling shelves that covered a whole wall. They were filled with glossy art books, fashion journals, books on art techniques. When she returned with the tray of coffee things, I said, 'We really must talk about why you need to hire me Velma.'

'Sit down.' She nodded towards a huge settee. Its tapestry covers and the silk ropes binding its corner posts were tired and faded, but when I leaned into the high back, its softness enveloped me. She handed me a cup, held out the milk and sugar, then relaxed into the other end of settee, her body turned towards me, her feet in the scarlet shoes reaching towards mine.

'There are some men.' She gulped at her coffee. 'I think there's two, but there could be three or four. They come after dark, always on Thursday and Friday, and sometimes on other days. They bang on the side of the tractor shed and make scary noises and yell things.'

'Yell things?'

'Suggestive things, sexual things. I've heard worse, but when you're a woman living alone it's very threatening.'

'What about the police? Surely you've — '

'They've been. Three times. They sent a policewoman to sit with me while policemen hid in the outhouses. The men seemed to know they were here. Whenever the police came, they never turned up.'

'Couldn't you call them out while the men are here?'

'It's so isolated, Paul. And they have to come from Sheffield. The police house in Moxton was sold off years ago.'

'And what is it you want from me?'

'I want you to confront them, scare them off.'

I tried to hold back a smile. 'Two men, maybe four. They might not scare so easily.'

Her body sagged when I said that. Disappointment was making her mouth droop. Maybe she was beginning to think I wasn't worth the wine and the meal. 'Can't you just go out and be fierce; hit them if you have to?'

She could see the smile. I was almost laughing. 'Acting fierce wouldn't work, Velma. And violence could land me in court; maybe put me out of business.'

Her eyes were desolate now. When she put the cup on its saucer, her shaking hands made them rattle together. She said, 'Then I don't know what I'm going to do. It's not right; men coming here and frightening me out of my wits and no one being able to do anything about it.'

'Stay with the police,' I said. 'Get them out again.'

'They think I'm mad. After the third visit they as much as said I was a neurotic time-waster. They'll not come out again.' She put her head in her hands. 'God, I'm so scared. I can't cope with it any more, and I don't know what to do. I was hoping . . . '

'It's Thursday today,' I said.

She nodded. 'That's why I wanted you here.'

35

'What time do they arrive?'

'Varies a little, but it's always getting dark. Ten or half past.'

'I'll wait with you,' I said, tossing common sense to the winds. 'Let's see what happens and play it by ear.'

'At least that's something,' she said frostily. It was obvious I was a big disappointment. 'Where's your car?'

'Parked across the yard.'

She rose to her feet. 'You'd better hide it in the tractor shed. I'll get you the keys.'

3

A faint tapping on the glass told me they'd arrived. They seemed to have refined the torment; turned it into a kind of ritual. Barely audible rubbings and scrapings on the window were followed by a rapping on the door.

Switching off the light, I parted the curtains and peered into the darkness. The night was hot and overcast, heavy with the threat of rain. The tractor shed, the heap of rusting machinery, were no more than indistinct shapes. I let the curtains fall back, reached for the switch on the reading lamp, and clicked it on.

Velma Hartman was pressing herself into the huge slab-sided settee. More than a piece of furniture, it was like a room within a room, and she seemed to be trying to hide herself in it. Her face was grey. In a shaky little voice, she said, 'You hardly ever see anything. It's just noises. I used to get angry and yell at them, tell them to go away, but they just laughed and said filthy things.'

A metallic clatter rattled across the yard. Someone was dragging a stick along the side of the corrugated iron shed. Velma's body was trembling now. Shoulders hunched, she was squeezing her legs together, concealing the flesh above the bodice of her dress with spread hands. Perhaps she saw the torment as a sexual threat. Across the yard, someone was laughing; it was a gasping sound that ended in a fit of coughing.

'What would you do if I weren't here?' I asked

'Go upstairs, lock myself in the bedroom and crawl under the bed.'

'I think you should go up there now and lock yourself in.' I held out the keys she'd given me. 'Tractor shed, front door. Where's the key to the back door?'

'There is no back door. The ground floor of the house runs into the side of the hill at the back.'

'Is there a phone in the bedroom?'

She shook her head and tried to lever herself out of the vast softness of the settee. 'There isn't a phone in the house. My uncle wouldn't pay for the landline.'

Taking her hand, I helped her to her feet. 'What about a mobile?'

'It's in the kitchen. I forgot to charge it.'

I reached inside my jacket and handed her mine.

She took it, picked up a torch from the

mantelpiece above the fireplace, then said, 'What are you going to do?'

'Something,' I said grimly. I was angry now, wondering what kind of sick bastards would take pleasure in tormenting a woman in this way. And I don't need you to tell me I was being stupid. I know I should have walked away the minute she told me what her problem was. I should have known it was a no-no when she told Melody she needed a big strong man. But when pride walks in, common sense flies out of the window.

I followed her into the passage. She was shaking badly, and the dim light of the torch was wavering over the walls and floor. 'Do you want me to see you up to the bedroom?'

'Please, oh please,' she whimpered. She held out a hand. I took it and followed her up the steep uncarpeted stairs. She led me through a doorway. 'The house wants rewiring. The lights in the passage and up the stairs won't go on. I'll have to get an electrician in.' She was talking to hide her fear.

The curtains hadn't been drawn in her bedroom. Taking the torch, I swept the beam of light over a bed, a chest of drawers and a dressing table that made up a suite of furniture her uncle's grandmother must have used. Then I went over to the window.

Leaning into the embrasure, I got my eyes close to the glass and peered out.

A stick suddenly clattered over corrugated iron, and more wheezing laughter drifted up from the yard. No moon, no stars, no wasted city light: it was crow black out there. Sheds and undergrowth, the trees beyond, were no more than dark shapes. It was starting to get to *me*. God knows what it was doing to Velma Hartman. I drew the curtains, groped my way back to the door and switched on the light.

She was sitting on the high Edwardian bed, her eyes locked on mine, her hands squeezed between her thighs. 'What are you going to do?' she whispered.

'Go downstairs, check out the situation, take it from there.' I glanced at the bedroom door. Crude iron bolts had been fixed to it, top and bottom. 'Lock yourself in. Call the police on my mobile if you need to.'

'If I need to?' She stared across at me. Inane laughter was coming up from the yard and someone was rapping on the door. She slid from the bed. 'I've got to use the bathroom. Don't leave me until I've been to the bathroom.' Picking up the torch, she ran out on to the tiny landing, and a door slammed.

'Yoo-hoo, Velma.' The voice was a mocking, sing-song falsetto. 'We know you're in there.

Are you going to invite us in?' I couldn't place the accent. It sounded Eastern European; Romanian, maybe, or Albanian.

Two men were laughing now. There was some more banging on the corrugated-iron shed, then the sing-song voice chanted, 'No knickers, no knickers, you've got no knickers on.' The laughter was raucous. 'I know you've not, cos they're in my pocket. Six pairs. Let us in, Velma, and I'll give them back to you.' The rapping on the door turned into a pounding. 'Yoo-hoo, Velma. Let us in. You know you want to.'

I switched off the light, crossed over to the window and stared into the darkness. I could just make out a hand banging a stick on the shed, and the blurred shape of a face; nothing else.

There was a movement behind me. I let the curtain swing back, and Velma switched on the light. She was dabbing her face on a towel, and I could smell the perfume in the soap she'd been using.

'Have they started saying things?'

I nodded.

'They stole my underwear from the clothes line a couple of weeks ago. They haven't stopped making juvenile remarks about it.'

'Bolt the door,' I said grimly. I handed her the torch, then felt my way down the stairs and along the passage. When I moved into the big windowless porch, I tripped over something, groped around, and felt an iron boot scraper.

Close up, the pounding on the door was deafening. Suddenly it stopped and a mocking voice was chanting, 'I know you're in there, Velma. I know you're dying for it, Velma.' There was a sudden burst of gutteral laughter. 'Have you got the boy in there, Velma? Is the boy giving you one? You need a man, Velma, not the pretty boy.'

Boy? I was old enough to feel flattered, but pretty boy was a hot needle on a nerve. They must have seen me at the window. Or maybe they'd been watching the house and seen me arrive.

The pounding on the door was rhythmic now. On the far side of the yard, the other guy was playing a tune on the tractor shed. I slid the bolts on the massive old door, unhooked the chains, then felt for the lock and turned the key. When I released the Yale latch, the pounding began to push the door open. I stood back.

The blurred outline of a face appeared through the gap, and a surprised voice yelled, 'Silly girl, Velma. You've left the . . . '

I hurled myself at the door, swinging it shut, felt his body shudder as his head was

42

crushed against the frame. When I stood back, he slumped down on to the stone flags. He didn't even groan.

Boots began to tread across the yard and a voice called, 'Alia? You there, Alia?' followed by some talk in a language I still couldn't place.

Stepping clear of the door, my heel caught the boot scraper. I crouched down and wrapped my hand around the blade. He was standing on the threshold now, staring down at his friend. I came up, swinging the heavy mass of metal, and smashed him in the face. The force of the blow sent him reeling back. He dropped in the yard.

I peered into the darkness. There were no more voices, no sounds of movement; just the distant hooting of an owl to disturb the silence of the summer night. The two men lying at my feet were the only intruders. I stepped over the bodies and ran to the tractor shed, fumbling for the key as I went. I got the door open, reversed the car up to the house, and took a torch from the glove compartment.

The intruders surprised me. I was expecting youngish men; late teens, twenties. But these guys were thick-set and heavy, moving into middle age. One had greying hair, the other a shaved head. Blood was oozing from the nose of the guy who'd had his head crushed in the door. When I knelt down and checked for the beat of a pulse in their throats, the smell of beer was strong.

I tugged a wallet from the back pocket of the jeans on the grey-haired guy. It held about a hundred pounds in notes, a Romanian driving licence and some papers issued by an agency that arranged temporary employment. They gave his name as Petre Roman and listed bricklaying jobs around the town. Gripping the torch under my chin, I noted down the details, then squeezed the wallet back into his pants.

Heaving the body aside, I patted the pockets of the other guy, felt keys for some transport and a handful of loose change. I rolled him over, unbuttoned pockets on the front of his shirt, and found a summons requiring Alia Fatos to attend court for a motoring offence. There was also a packet of tobacco, cigarette papers, a cheap plastic lighter and a mobile phone. The summons had been sent to a house in Steelyard Street, Ashford; a suburb of Barfield popular with immigrants.

I pocketed the keys and mobile, then dragged the still comatose intruders over to the Jaguar and lifted them into the boot. Their legs were dangling over the fender; the boot lid was resting on their thighs.

Shining the torch into the darkness, I went inside the farmhouse and climbed the stairs. A chink of light showed under the bedroom door. I put my face close and said, 'Velma? You OK, Velma?'

Bolts rattled, then light was spilling out on to the landing. 'What's happened? Is everything — '

'Everything's been taken care of. Two Eastern European guys. Not young, both heavily built, one's a Romanian. Do you know anyone like that?'

She shuddered, stared at me wide-eyed and shook her head.

'Could they have been working around here; on a farm, perhaps?'

'I only ever see the tenant farmer and his cow man, and I don't see them very often. I don't think they employ casuals. It's not that kind of farm. Have they gone away?'

'I'm going to take them away. Probably be about an hour. When I get back, we've got to have a serious talk.' As I headed down the stairs, I called back, 'The big key's in the lock. I'll secure the door on the Yale.'

★ ★ ★

A white transit van had been reversed into Hawthorne Lane, and the keys I'd taken from

45

the bald-headed guy fitted. Tugging on a pair of driving gloves, I lifted the boot lid on the Jaguar. The one called Petre was muttering and letting out the occasional groan. His bald friend, the one with the nose bleed, was making snoring noises. Taking Petre first, I got them over my shoulder, staggered the half-dozen paces to the van, and heaved them into the passenger side of the cab.

I shone the torch into the back. Sheets of plasterboard were leaning against one of the sides, held in place by bags of plaster. Shovels had been laid in a mixing bath, and packs of canned beer were piled behind the seats. Invoices for materials and fuel, made out to a firm called Strathmore Developments, littered the cab. I took a couple.

Thunder rumbled closer and the first drops of rain began to patter on the roof of the van. Slipping my jacket off, I put it in the boot of my car. There would probably be a long walk back, and there was no point letting the rain soak the jacket as well as the pants.

When I climbed into the driver's seat of the van, I saw the guy with the shaved head had slid into the footwell. He was jerking around and the snoring noises he was making sounded angry. I pulled out into the road and made a left, heading away from Moxton. Lightning skittered across the sky and thunder was loud above the drone of the engine. An old iron railway bridge loomed up ahead. I slowed to about twenty and raked the side of the van along its rivets and plating. Beyond the bridge, the road dipped steeply, then curved away between overgrown hedges. Braking hard, I jumped down from the cab, slammed the door, and let the van roll on down the incline. It was travelling fast when it bounced over the verge and smashed into an old stone wall.

Rain pelted down and the air was heavy with the smell of moist earth as I ran towards the wreck. The passenger door had sprung open and the guy who'd been sprawling on the seat had fallen out. I climbed into the cab, heaved the bald one called Fatos up, and got him behind the wheel. After making sure his prints were all over a can of beer, I pulled the tag and let the contents spill over his shirt and pants. Then I used his mobile to dial 999. When the female voice said, 'Which service?' I growled, 'Ambulance. Hurt. Been a crash.'

'Where are — '

I let out a groan. 'Three miles past Moxton. In the dip after the railway bridge.' I gave her another groan. 'Hurt. Hurt bad. Send ambulance. Please send . . . '

Leaving the phone switched on, I pressed it into the hand of the guy behind the wheel, then climbed down from the cab and began the long jog back through the pouring rain.

* * *

I knocked on the heavy old door and called her name up to the window. Seconds later, I could hear her approaching along the passage and crossing the porch.

'Paul? Is that you, Paul?' When I said it was, bolts rattled, the big key turned and the door opened. As she led me into the parlour, she was asking, 'Have you dealt with them? They won't come back, will they, Paul? Tell me they won't come back.'

'They won't be able to come back; not for a while, anyway.'

She got a good look at me. 'God, you're soaked. Let me . . . '

'I'm OK. Just sit down. We've got to talk.'

Lowering ourselves on to chairs, we faced each other across the table where, a few hours earlier, we'd had the meal together.

'What's wrong? There's something wrong, isn't there?' She'd sensed my concern.

'Have you any enemies, Velma; someone you've upset pretty badly?'

'Upset?' She was sitting up straighter now, her eyes flickering nervously over my face. 'I . . . I don't know what you mean.'

48

'It was men making the commotion outside, thirty-five, fortyish, not young louts tormenting you for the hell of it.'

'I just live here alone, minding my own business. How could I upset anyone?'

'Have you had problems with a man? Made some man or woman jealous, perhaps?'

She swallowed hard. 'I . . . I'm not involved with any men.' Her voice became more forceful. 'And anyway, I don't know anyone who'd do a sick thing like that.'

'People will do all manner of things, Velma. And that includes so-called respectable people. People who are moneyed and educated and ought to know better. Some incident makes them angry, the hurt starts to fester, and after a while they get to a pitch where they'll do crazy things.'

'But I don't know any Romanians or Bulgarians or whatever they are. I've never met any. I've certainly never upset any.'

'They could have been paid to harass you. Someone may have hired them.'

'Hired them?' She let out a jittery laugh and green eyes flickered over my face. 'That's preposterous. I just spend the days painting. A farmer takes me and my bike into Barfield on his lorry once a week, and sometimes I cycle to the village shop in Moxton.' She frowned. 'Perhaps they saw me going down the lane to the farm.'

'And how did they know you didn't have a man here? Have any tradesmen been to the house?'

She shrugged. 'A joiner came to fix bolts on the bedroom and studio doors, but that was after the trouble started. The mail's left in a box at the top of the lane. Models sometimes come to the house. I had one who cycled here, but they usually come by car.'

'Models?'

'I use models for my painting. And people sitting for portraits come occasionally, but that's rare. I don't do many portraits.'

'Where would the models come from?'

'Mostly people I know from working at the college. I used to teach fashion design, and I took some of the life classes. There's an agency in Leeds, but I usually hire people I know.'

'Female models?'

'Some, but I mostly use men. I've tended to specialize in the male nude.'

'Could one of their wives or partners — '

'No they couldn't,' she snapped. Her sudden anger surprised me.

We gazed at each other across the table. Her trembling fingers were picking at the frayed hem of a napkin. I decided to stop questioning her. She clearly found it inconceivable that someone could hate her enough to have her tormented. After a while, I said, 'Do you have a friend or a relative who could stay with you?'

'What are you trying to say to me, Paul?'

'I'm worried,' I said earnestly. 'Those guys weren't a couple of stupid kids; they were mature men. If you can't get someone to keep you company, you should think about getting a dog. Something big and vicious. Failing that, you should seriously consider leaving.'

'I don't care for dogs. A fierce dog would scare me more than it would scare those men. And I'm not leaving. If I'd been prepared to leave, I'd have done it weeks ago.'

I decided to call it a day. She wasn't listening to me. I'd chased the men away, and she thought everything was fine again. Rising to my feet, I said, 'If the police call, just tell them what you know. Say we waited together, the men came, and I saw them off. And bolt the doors, even during the day. And keep your mobile in your pocket.'

'Your phone,' she said, suddenly remembering. 'It's in the bedroom.' She took the torch and disappeared into the passage. When I heard her feet clattering back down the stairs, I went over to the parlour door. She handed me the phone.

'There was a call. I thought I'd better answer it in case it was you. It was a woman: Melody Brown. I told her you'd be back in a while, but she said it wasn't important. Is she the woman who does reception for you?'

I nodded.

'She sounded very offhand. Just cut me off when I asked if she wanted you to ring her back.'

4

Some appalling accident had given nature a helping hand. He was the ugliest man I'd ever seen. And tall, maybe six-three, with too much weight spoiling the look of his dark suit. Thinning grey hair and a certain stiffness of movement said he was well into his fifties. A much younger, pasty-faced guy, with black hair that emphasized his unhealthy pallor, was following him into the office. Wrap-around shades hid the younger man's eyes. They hadn't bothered to knock.

'You Lomax? Paul Lomax?'

I nodded.

The ugly guy reached into his jacket and produced a blue wallet. He let it drop open. 'I'm Detective Chief Inspector Foster.' He inclined his head. 'This is DI Hogan.' His deep voice was like a warning growl. He stepped over to the desk and flopped down in the visitor's chair. The one called Hogan closed the door and leaned against the filing cabinet, his arms folded across his chest.

Foster nodded at the piles of papers on the desk. 'Busy?'

'I get by.'

The black-haired guy was grinning. Not being able to see his eyes was hassling me.

'Were you busy last night?'

'I was out on a case.'

'What case?'

'My client might not want you to know.' I smiled affably.

'Your client's already told us.'

I gazed at him. His face was so repulsive it was compelling. You just had to stare. The two halves seemed misaligned, parted by a deep scar that crossed from left brow to right cheek. Forcing my eyes to meet his, I said, 'And who's my client?'

'Hartman; Velma Hartman.'

'And what did Miss Hartman say?'

'I'll ask the questions, Lomax. Don't smart-arse me. Last night, between ten and midnight, where were you?'

'Branwell Farm, just beyond Moxton.'

'And what were you doing at Branwell Farm?'

The guy in the shades was still grinning. His oiled hair was fixed in that spiky style young posers seem to go for. I looked back at Foster and said, 'Dining with Miss Hartman.'

'Friend of yours, is she?'

'Client.'

'Why did she hire you?'

'She's troubled by rowdies. They pay her a

visit after dark; make noises, yell things. It scares her.'

'We know that, Lomax. Half the force sat it out for three nights. Didn't hear a thing.' He scowled at me. 'Didn't get dinner, either.'

I glanced from his big misshapen features to the smiler in the wraparound shades. They were expecting me to say something, so I said, 'They came last night.'

'They?'

'I think there were two.'

'Make trouble, did they?'

'Hammered on the shed, banged on the door, yelled things. Miss Hartman was scared half to death.'

'And?'

'And what?' I demanded.

'Don't slow-time me, Lomax. And what did you do?'

'Went to the door and checked it out. I was scared, too. It was dark; really dark. Couldn't see a thing. They left after ten or fifteen minutes.'

Thick lips curled into a sneer. 'I've heard all about you, Lomax. You don't scare easily. And if it was so dark you couldn't see a thing, how did you know there were two?'

The dark-haired guy's grin widened.

'Someone was hammering on the shed while someone else was banging on the door.

Unless there's a guy out there with very long arms, that makes two.'

'Miss Hartman says you fronted them up; scared them off.'

I smiled. 'That's what she expected. That's what I let her believe.'

'She said you went out, came back an hour later, soaked to the skin.'

'I checked things out: sheds, outhouses, the bushes and trees that enclose the place. And I walked to the end of the lane.'

'See anything?'

I shook my head.

'What's your real involvement in this, Lomax?'

'Involvement? The woman was scared. She couldn't keep you interested, so she hired me. It's just a job; a case. That's all there is to it.'

Foster said, 'Show me your hands.'

I held them up, palms out.

'The knuckles, Lomax. The knuckles,' he growled irritably.

I obliged.

He sniffed. Something had disappointed him. 'Did you hear a crash while you were looking around?'

'I was out in a storm: thunder, pouring rain. That's all I could hear.'

'Emergency services got a call around 11.15, from some guy who'd crashed his van

56

about a mile along from Hawthorne Lane. Almost went through a wall.'

I said nothing, just glanced at the grinning cop leaning against the filing cabinet, then returned my gaze to Foster sitting on the other side of the desk.

'Romanians in the van,' he went on. 'Two Romanians. Didn't fully regain consciousness for a couple of hours. Blood test showed they were well over the legal limit. One said they'd lost their way. The other kept babbling, 'The bitch stitched us up. I'll get the bitch for this.' '

'He was a Romanian. How did you know what he was saying?'

'One of the porters speaks the lingo. The nurse got him to the bedside.'

I shrugged. 'Drunk, concussed; he could have been talking about anything.'

Foster made himself more comfortable in the chair, then said, 'Doctors were puzzled.'

'Doctors?'

'At Accident and Emergency. The X-rays showed injuries they couldn't have sustained in the crash.'

The black-haired cop had stopped grinning. The ugly guy was giving me a searching look. The distant rumble of traffic, and the quieter sounds of pedestrians in the street below, drifted in through the open windows.

57

After what seemed like an age, Foster said, 'I'll ask you again, Lomax, what's your involvement in all this?'

'A woman hired me because she was scared. When I checked things out, I heard intruders, but didn't see — '

'Velma Hartman's going to be even more scared now, Lomax.' He gave the guy in the wraparound shades a glance, then rose to his feet. 'She's going to need all the protection she can get.' Turning, he ambled through to the waiting room. His sidekick followed: he hadn't said a word. Foster looked back through the open doorway. 'Ever heard of Strathmore Developments, Lomax?'

I remembered the invoice I'd taken from the white van. 'Rings a bell,' I said. 'Guys fingered for benefit fraud. Three are pleading not guilty. I'm in court tomorrow to testify. Some of their pay cheques were traced back to Strathmore Developments.'

Foster smiled at me. His face was still the ugliest I'd ever seen, but the smile transformed it; made him look human. His friend was clattering down the stairs and Foster was turning to follow.

I called out, 'What's Barfield's finest doing on traffic duty?'

He glanced back. 'This isn't traffic duty, Lomax. And you'd better get your arse over to Branwell Farm. Miss Hartman's going to need you.'

Melody suddenly swirled into the waiting room, holding a tray. When Foster turned and faced her, she let out a shocked little scream. Foster laughed.

'I . . . I'm sorry. You startled me. I didn't expect . . . '

'It's all right, love. I've learned to live with it. I give kids nightmares and housewives have been known to faint when they open the door.' He looked back at me. 'Phone me, Lomax. Phone me if you come up with anything.' And then he was thudding down the stairs.

Melody slid the tray on to the desk. 'I'm sorry I screamed, but it's gloomy in your waiting room and he shocked me.' She wrapped a napkin around the coffee-pot handle and began to pour. 'What a dreadful disfigurement.' She added milk and sugar, then reached over and put the cup in a gap between the piles of papers.

I relaxed back in the chair. 'How was dinner with your charming valuer friend?'

'He was very pleasant, almost too pleasant, but halfway through the meal I began to feel uneasy.'

'Uneasy?' I was relieved. I know it's juvenile and stupid, but imagining Melody having dinner with some other guy really upset me.

'He was putting a lot of pressure on me. He kept saying his client wouldn't argue with any reasonable valuation for the outstanding term of the lease, and I'd be wise to accept. Anyway, like I said, I began to feel uncomfortable, so I told him my partner was picking me up and went to the powder room and phoned you.' She laid a plate on one of the piles of papers. 'I did you some toast. I don't suppose you had breakfast?'

I shook my head and reached for a slice.

'God knows why I bothered calling. You're never there when I need you.'

'You should have warned me.' I felt smug. The day before she'd been winding me up with all that talk about a cosy dinner for two. I bit into the toast and gazed across at her. Blue eyes were vivid against tanned skin, and blonde hair was bouncing around on her shoulders. She was giving a lot of shape to a dress that was identical to the one the girl in the art gallery had been wearing: black and white with a bold zigzag pattern.

'Gorgeous dress,' I mumbled while I chewed. I was giving my eyes another joyride. 'Looks special.' I tried to remember a word Velma Hartman had used. Suddenly it came back. 'Looks like a designer dress.' I took another bite at the toast.

Crimson lips parted in a surprised smile. 'How did you guess?'

I shrugged. 'It looks so . . . unique.' I knew I was saying all the right things.

The smile widened. 'Balenciaga. Found it in a little boutique in Leeds. Manageress said it was the only one she'd bought in. And it was my size.'

I let my eyes browse over her tanned arms; the forms beneath the fabric, then said, 'Stunning. Absolutely stunning.' I didn't tell her I'd seen another just like it. That was something she wouldn't want to hear.

'Did you finish the mucking out?'

I raised an eyebrow.

'Miss Hartman: she wanted a big strong man? I presumed you were shovelling out the cow shed. And what was she doing answering your mobile in that breathless girlie voice?'

'Rowdies have been scaring her. I left her my mobile while I went outside to check things out.'

Melody frowned down at me. 'You're going to get yourself killed. You should tell her to call the police in.'

'She did, but they got tired of her.'

'Had her aches and pains gone?'

'Aches and pains?'

'Embrocation: she reeked of rubbing oils.'

'Turpentine,' I said. 'She's a painter, an artist. She must have spilled some on her clothes.'

'She's an artist?'

'Famous. Got an exhibition on at Leeds City Art Gallery.' I bit into the second slice of toast.

'Abstract daubs?'

'She specializes in the male nude these days.'

Melody was sucking in her cheeks to kill a smile. 'Male nudes? I'll have to sew you a posing pouch.'

I started to laugh. She managed to keep her face straight. A feeling of contentment had settled over me. Some worry, some irritation, had left me. And then I realized it was relief at being told the cosy dinner for two hadn't amounted to anything. Smiling up at her, I said, 'Marry me Melody.'

'I'd rather you didn't start that again.'

'I'm serious,' I said softly.

She took the cup and plate and stacked them on the tray. 'You know I don't like it when you get serious. And what makes you think I'd want to marry you?'

That floored me. I thought hard, then said lamely, 'We get along. We'd make a good team.'

She laughed. 'I get along with the man in

the delicatessen. I get along with the girls in the office. And Barfield Wanderers might make a good team in a hundred years.'

She gathered up the tray and headed out. The sway of her hips was making the hem of her dress swing. I closed my eyes, trying to capture the vision. And then I got round to thinking about Foster's warning; a warning I didn't need. I was already worried about Velma Hartman, and angry with myself at the way I'd let pride make me do a stupid thing, a thing that could have put her in danger.

* * *

The documents I'd found in his shirt pocket had given me Alia Fato's address and I was searching for it in an area of grimy terrace housing about a mile from the town centre. Built right up to the pavement, the dwellings faced one another across a narrow roadway. Some had been treated with cement grooved to look like stone, a few had been painted bright colours, most had plastic front doors. I cruised past a gap in the line of parked cars, braked hard and reversed into it.

Net curtains were hanging across the windows of Number 35 Steelyard Street. I put my face close to the glass, but all I could see was the reflection of sunlit houses on the far side of the road. I gave the door a pounding, then waited and listened. Two women in long black dresses and black hijabs, one pushing a pram, the other leading a couple of kids, walked past. When they'd moved on I turned back to the door and hammered it again.

An angry voice was muttering, 'I'm coming, I'm coming.' Then the door swung open and I was looking at a swarthy young guy with curly black hair. He needed a shave.

'Alia Fatos,' I said. 'I'm looking for Alia Fatos.'

'He's not here.'

'What about Petre Roman? Does he live here?'

'He lives here, but he's gone away.' Scowling, he said, 'Why do you want them?'

'A job. I need men for a job.'

'They've gone away. They won't be back for a week, maybe two. Fatos maybe longer.' He yawned and scratched at the hair above his vest.

'Where can I get hold of them? It's urgent.'

He was waking up. Coal-black eyes were looking me over. 'There are other plastering gangs. Ten builders live here. I talk to them. Come back later. I find you another plastering gang. Zelco and Goran, perhaps. They're good workers, very — '

'I want them for a *job*,' I growled. 'Not a plastering job.'

His eyes became wary. He began to close the door. I jammed a size nine across the threshold. 'I can find you plasterers, bricklayers, electricians,' he said. 'They're the only jobs we do.'

'Fatos and Roman; where are they?'

'Hospital,' he muttered. 'Alia is in Barfield General. They've taken Petre to Sheffield. Both got head injuries.'

'Where's the van they were using? Where's Strathmore's van?'

'Police had it towed away. I don't know where — '

'Police?' I snapped, trying to wind him up, 'The police are involved?'

He was really agitated now. 'They were here this morning, early. Questions, questions, questions. They wanted to see everyone's papers. Alia and Petre are stupid. I told them this is England, not Romania.'

'*He's* not going to like this,' I said ominously. 'They were told to be careful.'

★ ★ ★

Patches of woodland, flecks of dark-green between fields that were golden after the long hot July, broke up the rolling countryside to

65

the south of town. I cruised through Moxton — an old stone church, a dozen cottages, a pub and a corner shop — then wound my way between open fields for another mile or so before turning into Hawthorne Lane.

A small red Fiat was parked close to the farmhouse. I left the Jag down the side of the rusty metal tractor shed, crossed the yard and knocked on the door. Birds twittered in the hedges, insects buzzed, and the sun was making the coverings on the shed roofs so hot you could smell the tar. I knocked on the door again; harder this time.

Footsteps scraped in the porch and Velma Hartman said, 'Who is it? Who's there?'

'Paul,' I said. 'Paul Lomax.'

The big key grated in the lock, the door opened and she was smiling at me. 'Come on in. I'm working, but the session's almost over. Ten minutes: could you give me ten minutes?'

'Sure,' I said. 'No problem.' After she'd led me into the room she called a parlour, she dashed back up the uncarpeted stairs. I heard women's voices, then a door slammed, and footsteps began to patter across the floor above.

I sank into the huge settee, closed my eyes and tried to make some sense of the Velma Hartman situation. The ugly cop had only warned me about what I already feared: that it was more than rowdies making a nuisance of themselves. The enigmatic conversation I'd just had with the guy in Steelyard Street came close to confirming that Fatos and Roman had been hired to make Velma's life a misery. Velma was keeping secrets. She'd upset someone pretty badly: someone who knew how to organize a little retribution.

My mobile began to bleep. I reached for it, keyed it on and announced my name. After a few seconds' delay, a very refined voice said, 'You're rather elusive. I've phoned you at your office three or four times. In the end, your secretary gave me your mobile number.'

'I'm almost always out, Mrs Pearson. How can I — '

'I need to talk to you, but not over the phone.'

'I'll be back in the office around one. Would you care to — '

'No, I wouldn't,' she interrupted. 'Where are you now?'

'About a mile south of Moxton.'

'You're not too far from the M1, then?'

'It's about five miles to the nearest junction.'

'What junction would that be?'

I tried to picture the map. 'Thirty-eight, maybe thirty-nine.'

'There's a motorway services place at

junction thirty-seven. Could you meet me there in about an hour?'

'I'm on a job, Mrs Pearson. Make it two hours. What if I meet you there at 1.30?'

'1.30 is fine. I'll be waiting in the main cafeteria.' The line clicked. She hadn't wasted a goodbye on me.

Upstairs, a door opened and women's voices grew louder as feet descended the stairs. Glancing around the end of the settee, I saw a dark-haired woman of around thirty, in jeans and a red cotton top, pass by the open door. She looked back at Velma and said, 'Will you want me again?'

'Not until I find a man. Would you mind posing with a man?'

The woman laughed. 'So long as he's professional and I don't know him too well. And so long as he's OK about it.'

'It's finding the right one,' Velma said. 'Is Jeremy still working at the college?'

'He packed it in when he got married. He's a postman now. He could give you an afternoon, I suppose. Do you want me to ask?'

'Mmm . . . No, I don't think so. He's not quite right. He's too small,' Velma said. I heard the door open.

'How about Tarquin?'

'That's out of the question,' Velma

snapped, her voice icy.

The woman laughed. 'Well, when you find someone, give me a call.'

They exchanged goodbyes, the door slammed and Velma stepped into the parlour. Rising from the settee, I said, 'I'd like to talk with you, Velma.'

'Is it about the police? They were here, early this morning, asking questions about some men in a van.'

'Not really. We just need to talk.'

She gave me a worried look, then glanced down at the faded green cotton dress she was wearing. It buttoned up the front, and her fingers must have got tired before they reached the top. Something black and lacy was contrasting with the milky-whiteness of her skin.

Turning her back on me, she headed out into the gloomy passage, fastening buttons as she went. She called over her shoulder, 'Come on up to the studio. We can talk while I clear up.'

The studio was the only really light room in the house. The ceiling had been removed, and the slates on the north-facing side of the roof replaced with glass. Velma worked on a heroic scale. Big canvasses were stacked against the walls, and the easel was a massive affair: an arrangement of big timbers that could be moved around on castors. A Japanese screen enclosed a small area in the corner of the room. Buttoned red leather on an Empire-style couch clashed with some green velvet that covered a low dias.

Velma gestured towards the easel. 'Would you like to see the painting? I don't usually care to show work in progress, but I can make an exception.' She smiled at me, then led the way round to the front of the canvas. 'No, not there. You're standing much too close.' She linked her arm in mine and walked me back to the wall. 'Stand over here.'

It was the woman I'd just seen leaving the house. The index finger of one hand was touching lips shaped in a coy smile; the other hand was outstretched and holding an apple. Completely naked, she was gazing at the vague outline of another figure that hadn't been painted in.

'Adam and Eve,' I murmured. Standing against the wall, nine or ten feet from the canvas, the individual brushstrokes, the tiny flecks of colour, seemed to coalesce and create an image that was vividly real. The woman had broad hips, plump arms and thighs, heavy pointed breasts. And Velma's technique was masterful. The picture had that elusive quality that separates the magical from the mundane. Groping for something appropriate to say, I suddenly remembered an article I'd read in a Sunday supplement and murmured, 'You paint flesh better than Lucian Freud.'

She let out a peal of laughter and squeezed my arm. It was still linked in hers. 'No one paints flesh like Lucian Freud,' she said, 'but you're very sweet, Paul. It's a commission: Martin Walton. He imports sanitary fittings from China, owns Barfield Wanderers. He's refurbishing Norby Hall and this is for the dining room. I've kept him waiting. I can't find an Adam.' She looked me up and down. 'You wouldn't consider — '

'No,' I interrupted. 'It's not something I'd care to do.'

'Don't be shy. You shouldn't be embarrassed about your body.' She looked me over again and tested my upper arm with another squeeze. 'And you'd be perfect; absolutely perfect.'

I laughed softly. I couldn't help it. I mean, would you want your private parts dangling over some guy's dining table?

The laughter seemed to annoy her. I sensed she was a little disappointed in me. She let go of my arm and moved over to a table covered with a sheet of white glass she used as a palette. Taking a long-handled brush, she caught up some pigment, stepped up to the canvas and altered the highlights on the apple. Her movements were swift and deft; effortless, like they had been when she'd sliced vegetables with the big cook's knife. She was engrossed. I might as well not have been there.

'If I could do that,' I said softly, 'I think I'd do it night and day and never stop.'

She wrenched herself away from the painting and dropped the brush in a jar. 'You understand obsession,' she said. 'If only my husband had.' She began to scrape the daubs of paint from the palette and wipe them on to a sheet of newspaper.

Husband? She'd begun to tell me secrets.

She unscrewed the cap on a can, poured fluid on to a rag and began to wipe the glass plate clean. The aromatic smell of turpentine drifted over to me.

'You said you wanted to talk,' she said.

I moved closer to her and sat on a battered old Windsor chair that had lost its back. 'I'm worried about you, Velma.'

She stopped wiping and looked up at me. 'I'm not leaving the farm.'

I ignored the protest. 'Those men: they weren't hassling you for the hell of it. They'd been hired. Somebody wants to get at you. Maybe someone you've upset in some way, perhaps without even realizing it. Like I said the other night, the most respectable people can go a little crazy.'

'And like *I* said the other night, I just work and mind my own business. I don't see many people to upset.' There was irritation in her voice. She didn't want her life to change and she was in denial about the danger she was in.

'You mentioned a husband; is he still alive?'

She laughed. 'He's very much alive. And don't get any ideas about him. He's a dear sweet man. We parted very amicably about four years ago. We got divorced later, when he wanted to marry again. And his new wife's the kind of woman he should have married in the first place.'

'You didn't get on?'

'I neglected him. I was lecturing at the college all day and painting halfway through the night. He was holding down a job as well as doing most of the cooking and cleaning.'

'What is his job?'

'He teaches maths at Sycamore Street Comprehensive. He's neat and ordered and unimaginative. He never understood the creative urge.' She laughed. 'He never understood obsession.' She gestured around the cluttered room, at the paint-encrusted floor beside the easel, at the discarded rags and newspaper she'd used to wipe her

73

brushes and palette clean. 'You've seen the house. I don't dust, I don't do much cleaning, I just paint. His new wife's called Charlotte. She cooks and cleans; sits knitting while he marks exercise books. She's there for him.'

'She wouldn't — '

'You're being ridiculous, Paul.'

'You say you lectured at the college. What about colleagues, former students, someone who couldn't take criticism, perhaps?'

'Having your work criticized is part of the learning process. Students understand that.' She let out an exasperated little sigh. 'This is all so . . . so far-fetched, Paul.'

'Trust me, Velma. Nothing's far-fetched. In my business you meet a lot of people who don't think straight. Guys who'd kill you if they thought you were giving them a funny look; anonymous letter writers who set out to destroy lives; people who poison pets, scratch cars; educated, moneyed people who should know better. It's not ridiculous, Velma.'

I watched her pour more turpentine on to the rag and begin to clean her hands, then said, 'What about colleagues? You're talented and becoming successful; academics can be very bitchy.'

'Sending men to scare me to death?' She laughed. 'No, Paul. But if you must know, I didn't get on with the dean, Dr Faulkner.

Pompous old idiot — he just talked about art and wrote about art. Never practised it. On committees for this, committees for that. It was mutual loathing in the end.'

'Could you have upset him so much he'd arrange a little retribution?'

Velma laughed helplessly. 'If you'd met old Faulkner, you wouldn't be suggesting that. He's a small man in every sense of the word. Arrogant, humourless, no talent, no imagination. The last thing he'd do is hire louts to harass me.'

I smiled at her. Small, humourless, arrogant, no talent; these were the usual ingredients. And she'd no idea how mean and crazy people could get. Sighing, I said, 'What about partners? Has there been anyone since you left your husband? Someone you dumped; someone who could be jealous?'

'You asked me that the other night, Paul. The answer's still no.' Glancing down at her hands, she began to scrape the paint from the cuticles of her nails. I sensed she was trying to avoid my gaze, that she was holding something back, something she might not want to admit, even to herself. She poured turpentine on to a cleaner piece of rag and started rubbing again. 'Could it be a woman you've upset, Velma? Someone who's tormented by jealousy?'

Her head jerked up and her green eyes were wary. 'You're like the police,' she snapped. 'You just sit there, asking the same old questions over and over again.' She looked down at her faded cotton dress, the scuffed down-at-heel shoes. 'Who'd be jealous of me?' she demanded. Her red hair was drawn back and tied with a green ribbon. A few strands had broken free and were floating around pale freckled cheeks.

'A lot of women would be jealous of you, Velma. You're very attractive; beautiful in a rather unusual way.'

She didn't go all coy and argue with me, but her voice shook a little when she said, 'Thank you, Paul. It's a long time since a man said things like that to me. I've been called old. I've even been called smelly, but . . . ' Her voice faded and her eyes became wary. It was as if she realized she'd let her guard down; that she was saying too much.

'If you aren't open with me, Velma, I can't help you.'

'I've told you once, now I'm telling you twice, I don't know anyone who'd hire men to harass me. And you've already helped me. You've got rid of the men. That's what I asked you to do, and you did it.'

'I didn't do you any favours, Velma. I

should have left it alone; told you to call the police again. They won't be in hospital for ever, and whoever was doing the hiring can always find someone else.' I eyed her steadily for a while, then asked, 'Who's Tarquin?'

'How do you . . . '

'I heard you talking to your model, when you were showing her out.'

'He used to be a student of mine for fashion design. Sometimes he modelled for me. He's in London now. He abandoned his course and went to work in a fashion house.' She tossed the rag down. She seemed close to tears. 'Questions, questions,' she moaned. 'You've given me a migraine. I'd like you to leave. I'm going to take some aspirin and lie down.' She turned her back on me and hunched her shoulders. The conversation was over.

'I'm sorry, Velma.'

'Go. Please go. Show yourself out. I've got to lie down in the dark.'

From the doorway, I said softly, 'Phone me if you need me. Day or night. You've got my mobile number.'

I'd touched a raw nerve and she'd reacted by revealing more than she intended. Perhaps if I'd handled it better, she'd have told me everything.

When I climbed into the car I checked the

dashboard clock. It was almost one. I only had half an hour to find the motorway and get to the services at junction thirty-seven: and Mrs Pearson wasn't a client who'd take kindly to being kept waiting.

5

Mrs Pearson glanced at her watch and gave me a scathing look when she saw me approaching between the tables. I didn't apologize for being late. I didn't even ask her if she'd been waiting long. I just slid on to the chrome and crimson chair facing hers and smiled. The last thing I wanted to do was give her the idea the training techniques she'd used on her husband would work on me.

'You said you wanted to talk,' I opened.

She sniffed. 'I've had some time to think about my husband's sordid little affair, and I've reached a decision. What I need now, Mr Lomax, are photographs that are more incriminating.'

I looked her over. She was wearing a grey suit with white lapels and cuffs. Her tan seemed to have deepened a little, and she'd brushed her silvery-blonde hair away from her face. Cold grey eyes were meeting mine in an unblinking stare. I was looking at the engine that had propelled a stupid husband to success. I was beginning to feel sorry for Andrew Pearson.

'Could pictures get any more incriminating

than the shot of them in the lift?' I asked.

'Do you always try and talk clients out of engaging you, Mr Lomax? I could tell you were reluctant the first time I approached you, and I can tell you're even less interested now.'

'I don't care to take people's money when I'm pretty sure they're wasting it.'

'Surely they're the best judge of that?'

'Not always, Mrs Pearson. Often they're angry, or scared, or just too upset to think straight.'

Thin but shapely lips twitched into a smile, and the cut-glass voice said, 'So, you think I'm too upset to think straight?'

'I think you're pretty angry,' I said. 'In fact, I think you're as mad as hell.'

She laughed. 'You know what they say, Mr Lomax? Don't get mad, get even. I've always tried not to become emotional. One can so easily lose sight of one's objectives.' Andrew Pearson was getting all my sympathy now. She was giving me her haughty look. I was a mere man and she expected a man to toe the line.

'So you want more photographs?' I said, to end the silence.

She stopped challenging me with her eyes, dropped her gaze to her coffee cup and began to toy with the spoon. Sunlight was flashing off some big stones in the rings on her hand. When she said, 'I need a picture of them making love,' her voice was calm and matter-of-fact. She could have been asking me to pass the sugar.

'They were kissing in the gallery,' I said softly. 'They were kissing passionately in the lift.'

'Are you utterly naïve, Mr Lomax? Do I really have to spell it out for you? I want a clear picture of them in the act of coitus: having sex, copulating.'

'That's not my territory, Mrs Pearson. I could recommend — '

'You've already been recommended to me, Mr Lomax. Recommended because of your discretion and integrity by someone I trust. This is a far more delicate matter than you realize. I want you. I don't want someone else.' She suddenly looked beyond me, her eyes ranging nervously across the sea of tables, at travellers snatching quick meals.

'You need a specialist, Mrs Pearson. Someone who knows the hotels, knows the staff. Someone who . . . '

'I'm surprised you make any money at all,' she snapped. 'The way you turn work away. And you don't need to know any hotel staff. He's meeting the girl at his offices.'

'What about the Radisson in Leeds?'

'A one-off. She's going to his office, out of hours.'

Stalling for time to dream up a convincing excuse, I risked a question. 'Did you mention the photographs to your husband, Mrs Pearson? I mean, if you show them to him, he could hardly deny — '

'I considered it, but decided not to. I talked to him.'

'You asked him about the . . . liaison?'

She smiled her superior little smile. 'You don't have to try to avoid hurting my feelings, Mr Lomax. Apart from anger, I don't have any. And I wouldn't be so unsubtle as to just ask him.' Her breathing had quickened a little, and hard-looking little breasts kept pushing against the triangle of white silk between the lapels of her jacket. She was kidding herself. She was distressed in the same way I'd be distressed; the same way you'd be distressed. I didn't speak; just watched her.

Presently she went on, 'I asked him if he still found me attractive. When he said he did, I asked him if he missed the way I was when we were first married, if he missed being with someone young. He didn't answer that. And then I asked him if we could go away on holiday, go on a second honeymoon. He just laughed and said I knew how busy he was, that it was out of the question. That night he didn't stay up working. He came to bed and made love to me. It was the first time in . . . ' She pursed her lips and looked up at the ceiling. 'More than eighteen months. If you could call it making love. It was what I once overheard some young lout describing as a quick shag.' She smiled. 'You're blushing, Mr Lomax. Have I shocked you? Do *you* think I'm just a middle-aged woman whose looks have faded: if you're desperate, she'll be all right for a quick shag provided you keep the lights out?' Her eyes were bright with unshed tears and her parted lips were trembling. Her small teeth were well cared for; her lipstick was still leaching into the fine lines around her mouth. Jealousy, loss, rejection, were all bubbling away in a seething cauldron of emotions. It was bitterness and anger that had made her want to shock me.

'I wouldn't think of any woman in that way, Mrs Pearson. And most women half your age would be grateful if they looked half as good.'

'You don't have to be kind because you think I'm upset, Mr Lomax. One should have the courage to face reality. The biggest fools are the fools who deceive themselves.' She dragged in a deep breath. 'This isn't getting us anywhere.' Clicking open her bag, she rummaged around, then fished out a couple of new-looking keys on a ring. 'You'll need these.'

'Why would I need keys?'

She held them out. 'My husband's architectural practice. Key for the outer door and the key for his own office.'

I didn't take them. 'Why do you want more intimate pictures, Mrs Pearson?'

Shaking the keys, she said, 'Humour me. Just do as I ask.'

'If I was in your position and I looked at pictures like that, I wouldn't be able to stand the pain. I think I'd go insane.'

'But you're not in my position, Mr Lomax. And you're not the least bit like me.'

'And you're more cut up about this than you're admitting. You shouldn't even think about looking at pictures like that.'

'I might be cut up, but my feelings are completely under control.' She shook the keys again. 'Don't get mad, get even. Help me get even, Mr Lomax.'

Reaching out, I took the keys, consoling myself with the thought that business wasn't so good that I could afford to turn the work down.

'What's the address of your husband's office?' I asked.

'It's on Parkways, that new commercial

development just outside town. Telford Place. First right as you go in. His name's on a plate by the door, and Pearson Design is etched into the glass.'

'Photos could be difficult, Mrs Pearson. Would a video be acceptable?'

'Better,' she said. 'But it would have to be crystal clear.'

I laughed wryly. 'If they draw the blinds and turn the lights out, there's no way we're going to get crystal clear. When will the office be empty? I've got to install equipment. I'll need an hour, maybe two. And then I've got to retrieve it again.'

'You'd have the place to yourself tonight. He's attending some Civic Trust dinner; they're handing out architectural awards. I'm going with him.'

'And you'll let me know when there's to be an assignation?'

'Assume it's Friday night. He usually comes home for dinner, then goes back to the office about seven. If anything happens to change that, I'll try and let you know.'

'Where's your husband's personal office located?'

'First floor. Go to the top of the stairs and you'll find yourself in a corridor. His office is at the far end. You reach it through his secretary's office.'

85

'I've got to warn you again,' I said. 'If the light level's low, we'll not get a clear picture.'

She rose to her feet. 'I don't think Andrew will fornicate in the dark, Mr Lomax. Not with his young lover.'

Pushing my chair back, I began to rise.

'Don't leave with me,' she said hastily. 'Please don't be offended, but I'd rather not be seen with you. Give me five minutes, OK?'

Nodding, I relaxed back. Seconds later, I heard her call my name and turned to see her right behind me again.

'I almost forgot. There's an alarm. The keypad's by the entrance door. You've got twenty seconds to punch in four, eight, three, two.'

I gave her a blank look.

'Eight timestable,' she said, like a schoolmarm coaching a truculent child. 'Four eights are thirty-two. Surely you can remember that.'

*   *   *

The meeting with Mrs Pearson had left me feeling low. I wanted the surveillance job like I wanted a broken leg, and the way she was handling things made me suspect she was setting me up. She'd never visited my offices; I'd never called her, she'd called me; and I was pretty sure she'd always used a public phone. She'd left no trace of her involvement with me.

I was heading home to have a meal and gather the surveillance equipment together. After stopping and starting for a while in the evening commuter convoy, I turned into a road of drab little bungalows. They were just as drab when Susan and I brought Kathy here, fourteen years ago, but they didn't look drab to me then; one of them was home, and we were too busy playing happy families.

Heaving the sticking front door open, I stepped into old familiar odours, picked up the mail and flicked through it while I moved down the narrow hall and into the sitting room. The place was pretty much as Susan had left it. I wasn't preserving a shrine, so it was no longer tidy, no longer spotlessly clean and new-looking. The furniture was tired, the carpets worn, the curtains faded. When you live alone, you tend to let things go; you stop noticing.

I dropped bills behind the clock on the mantelpiece, circulars in the kitchen waste bin; then found a curry and tossed it in the microwave. Legacy of empire: frozen vindaloo.

A meal, a shower, a change into jeans and a clean shirt later, I was turning into Parkways, the new commercial estate on the fringes of town. I made a right into Telford Place and began to cruise past office buildings sur-rounded by lawns and islands of low shrubs. Pearson Design was etched into impressive glass entrance doors, a stainless-steel plate announced his name and qualifications.

I parked the Jaguar in the nearest bay, got the box of equipment out of the boot and headed for the entrance. It was 7.30 and the place looked deserted. I unlocked the door, keyed in the code that killed the alarm, then headed up the stairs. Pushing at some double doors, I found myself looking across a big drawing office. There were a few drafting machines, but it was mostly computer screens. When I moved on down the corridor and stepped into the secretary's office, I saw a brown-leather door in the far wall. Everything was as Mrs Pearson had described it.

I slid the second key into the lock, pressed the handle and entered Pearson's inner sanctum. The desk, a plan chest, a conference table and chairs, were all in some dark streaky wood. A drafting table stood end-on to the window. It was covered by a green canvas sheet. At the other end of the room, a long brown leather sofa and a couple of matching armchairs were arranged around a low table. Arty magazines were stacked in neat piles on its glass top. I stood there for a few moments, straining to hear the faintest sounds. The silence was complete. I was as sure as I could be that I had the place to myself.

There was a another door behind the sofa. Padding over oatmeal-coloured carpet, I opened it and peered into darkness. I felt for a switch and clicked on the light. Walls and floor were covered in green marble tiles, the hand basin and toilet were big chunks of white porcelain, expensive looking bottles were lined up on a shelf beneath a mirror, and there was a chrome and black leather chair. Pearson could have held the firm's Christmas party in his personal washroom.

Stepping back into the office, I began to think about siting the camera. It was too big an area to cover, so the surveillance would have to be confined to the desk and conference table, the carpet in front of the desk and, above all, the long sofa. A bookcase, made from the same dark streaky wood, faced the desk, and binders containing sanitary-ware catalogues were lined up across its top. Dragging one of the conference chairs over, I climbed up and examined the dust. It was going to be the best I could do.

The camera was smaller than a matchbox. After wedging it between *Baths and Bidets* and *Urinals and Water Closets*, I connected up the battery pack and transmitter, hid them behind the binders, then stretched the aerial along the top of the bookcase.

Climbing down, I switched on a hand-held monitor. Heat from my body was activating the sensor in the camera and switching the system on. I walked around. Coverage with the wide-angle lens was good: from the edge of the drafting table to the washroom door behind the sofa. When I moved out of range, the system shut down to conserve the batteries and the screen went blank. Everything had checked out OK, and the tiny camera, lost amongst the fancy lettering on the spines of the binders, wouldn't be noticed.

Back at the main entrance, I looked out across the parking area: no cars, no people, just golden evening sunlight and lengthening shadows. I stepped outside and locked the fancy glass doors.

There was no more I could do until tomorrow night, so I drove home, put a sandwich together and opened a bottle of Scotch. I was trying to forget that I'd have been married sixteen years if some joyriding teenage arsehole hadn't stolen a car and hit Susan and Kathy head-on.

6

My, my, aren't we looking smart today?'
Melody was breezing in with the morning
coffee. 'I don't suppose you've had breakfast?'

'I've forgotten what it is.'

'Sonia brought you a Danish back from the
deli. It's still warm.' Melody nodded at my
dark-blue double-breasted with the restrained
pinstripe. 'What's with the suit?'

'I'm in court this morning. Some of the last
batch of benefit cheats are pleading not
guilty. I'm giving evidence.'

'Your tie's a mess.' She balanced the tray
on the papers and came round the desk.
'Push your chair back for me.'

I rolled it back on the castors.

'Chin up.' Melody stepped between my legs
and began to tease the knot this way and that.
She was wearing a rather tight red skirt and a
red silk blouse with long sleeves. The blouse
fastened up to the neck with tiny red
silk-covered buttons, and the collar was high
and oriental. Up close her fragrance was
tantalizing: subtle yet provocative. What am I
saying? Everything about the woman was
tantalizing and provocative.

'And which old school does this thing belong to?'

'Dunno,' I murmured absently. I was studying the golden hair falling around her face, the blue eyes, the soft mouth that had been painted to match the blouse. 'The same old school the chairman of the bench went to, I hope.'

She flicked her eyes up from the tie and said, 'Please don't look at me like that, Paul.'

'How am I supposed to look at you?'

'Not like that.'

I began to laugh.

'And keep still. How do you expect me to . . . there, that's better.' She gave the tie one last tweak, then said, 'Just look at your handkerchief. You can't crumple it into your pocket like that. You may as well not bother.' She tugged out the square of red silk. 'Heavens, what on earth are these?'

I glanced down. She'd pulled the big horn-rimmed glasses out with the handkerchief. 'My specs,' I said.

'You need glasses now?' ·

'Plain glass. I wear them in court when I'm reading notes and giving evidence. Lends a certain gravitas.'

She started laughing. It was a husky, heart-melting sound. She unfolded the heavy sides and slid them on to my face. 'Mmm, they certainly do something for you, but I'm not sure what.'

'And they're handy when you're watching people,' I went on. 'You slide them down your nose and look over the top while you're pretending to read.'

Melody was sitting on the desk, her legs between mine, practising origami on the square of red silk. I began to roll the chair towards her, stealthy and slow. 'You were out all day yesterday. You should try and warn me when you're going to do that. Ruth got you a pizza from the Italian. It just got wasted.'

'I had to visit Miss Hartman.'

'Hartman?'

'The artist.'

'Oh, that Miss Hartman. Dirty mac and embrocation.' She'd folded the silk now. She leaned forward, tucked it into my breast pocket and began to tease it this way and that.

'The very same. She wanted me to pose as Adam.'

Big blue eyes flicked up and gazed into mine. Scarlet lips were curving into a smile. 'Adam as in Adam and Eve?'

I nodded.

She was giggling now. 'With or without fig leaf?'

'Without.'

'And you agreed?'

'I said I'd do Adam if I could bring you along to do Eve.'

'You and me?' Melody pointed with her finger. 'Do Adam and Eve?'

When I nodded the laughter erupted. I'd wheeled the chair very close now. Reaching forward, I slid my arm around her waist and pulled her down on to my knee. Her weight surprised me. It had been a long time since a woman had sat on my knee.

She put her arm around my neck to steady herself, and her baby-blues were giving me a naughty-naughty look. 'I didn't say you could do that,' she gasped. Her husky voice sounded a little shocked.

'I didn't ask.' Her face was very close to mine. I could feel her breath on my cheek; see the tiny flecks of green and gold in her eyes. 'Marry me, Melody. Say you'll marry me.'

'You're serious, aren't you?' She began to giggle.

'Sure I'm serious.'

'I'm sorry, Paul,' she said. 'But I just can't help laughing when you get serious,' and then she threw her head back and the giggling escalated into helpless laughter.

After a while, she got it under control, and said, 'Now look what you've done. My mascara's all smudged.'

'What I've done? You were doing the laughing. And is that any way to behave when a guy plights his troth?'

She looked at me. She was struggling to keep her face straight. 'You were plighting your troth?' she said, then burst out laughing again. 'So,' she gasped presently. 'Tell me why you want to marry me?'

She'd asked me that a couple of days ago. I was sure now that she was testing me in some way; playing silly mind games. Deciding to cut to the chase, I tightened my hold on her waist, and said, 'Because you're utterly gorgeous and I fancy you like mad.'

She stood up and sent the swivel chair with me in it crashing back against the wall. 'So, it's just sex, is it, Paul?' Moving around the desk to put herself out of reach, she grabbed the coffee pot, poured a cup and added milk and sugar.

'Of course it's not just sex, it's companionship and . . . '

'We did companionship the other day, Paul.' She reached over and put the coffee and Danish on the blotter. I rolled the chair back to the desk. 'And sex is no basis for a lasting relationship. In fact, things always begin to fall apart when the sex starts.'

I grinned across the desk at her. 'I thought things came together when the sex starts.'

She blushed and flung the napkin at me. 'You're a throwback,' she fumed. 'You're just a hairy Neanderthal.'

I watched her spin round and strut towards the door. Have I told you about her posterior sway? With Melody in a tight skirt, it's electrifying; that barely perceptible lean of her hips to the left; the liquid melting of movement into movement. She never knew what it did to me.

Her heels thudded across the waiting room, then began to tap-tap over the linoleum on the landing. I heard her pause, then come back, and her face appeared around the door. 'You look older in the specs,' she said. 'Less menacing and scary: almost harmless.'

'Menacing and scary?'

She giggled. 'Sexually menacing and scary.'

★ ★ ★

There was a surprise waiting for me at the magistrates court.

The chairman of the bench was Mrs Pearson. Her silvery-blonde hair had been drawn back and tied with a big black ribbon. Maybe she felt a more severe look befitted her status as an upholder of the law. The ribbon matched a black suit that had tight sleeves and padded shoulders. She'd been generous with the eyeshadow, but had toned her lipstick down to a brownish pink that was just a little lighter than her tan. She made the other members of the bench look drab. One was a bald-headed, beady-eyed little guy in a brown suit; the other taller, with big florid features and a lot of white hair.

Emma Pearson rapped on the rail in front of the bench and the Clerk to the Court jerked around. He was responding to training. She was turning him into a success. 'Mr Tipton, we must make a start if we're to have any chance of getting through this amount of business. Are they all benefit fraud cases?' Her voice carried across the court-room.

'All but one, ma'am.' His tone was deferential.

Mrs Pearson began to preside over affairs with a haughty efficiency, and by 10.30 I was in the witness box answering questions. It was a ponderous business, one foot placed carefully in front of the other as we trod slowly over the facts.

'Mr Tipton.' Emma Pearson sounded exasperated as she leafed through a pile of papers. 'We have four . . . Mmm . . . No, five cases to hear this morning. Can't we progress things a little more quickly? Mr . . . ' She

97

glanced down at her papers, pretending not to know me. 'Mr Lomax has already told us he saw the defendant, without his wheelchair, dancing in the Kit Kat Club.'

'The Pussy Cat Club, ma'am.'

Mrs Pearson's glare was venomous. 'Kit Kat, Pussy Cat. It was some place where people dance to music, wasn't it?' She glanced at me. 'Was it ballroom dancing, Mr Lomax?'

'Much more energetic than that, ma'am. It was what's known as a rave.'

'A rave? Really!' She sniffed loud enough for everyone to hear, then glared at the clerk, a tall, handsome young guy with oiled black hair who was challenging her in the deep-tan contest. 'I take it the defendant denies being at this rave?'

'Strenuously, ma'am.'

She treated the prosecuting solicitor to an impatient look. 'You intend to submit photographic evidence?'

'Indeed I do, ma'am, but there are . . . '

'Then present it,' she snapped.

He looked down at his papers, tossed two or three sheets aside, then glanced back at me. 'You were able to take photographs of the accused during the early-morning hours of the twenty-third?'

'I was.'

'And which images are they, Mr Lomax?'

I checked my notes. 'The photographs numbered nine, ten and eleven.'

The lawyer held up the three enlarged shots. 'Are these the photographs, Mr Lomax?'

I pushed the horn-rims up to the bridge of my nose and looked. 'They are.'

He turned to the bench. 'I'd like to show these to the defendant, ma'am.'

'You can show them to me first,' she snapped, then glanced at the clerk and inclined her head.

Tipton gathered up the glossy photos and scampered over to the bench. I guessed he was well into the Pearson training pro-gramme; probably halfway through the course.

Mrs Pearson took the photographs, then leaned back in her high chair so her wingers could look at them with her. Cool grey eyes glanced up and studied the scowling defen-dant, then she handed them down to the clerk. 'The photographs are very clear, Mr Tipton. As far as I can see, there can be no doubt about who is prancing around on the dance floor and who is swinging from the door frame in the toilets.' She glanced at me. 'Is the young lady in the photograph naked, Mr Lomax?'

'I recall she was wearing very tight flesh-coloured hot pants, ma'am, and a spangled top that was cut down to the waist at the back. From the rear, she does appear to be naked.'

She rolled her eyes upwards, then rapped on the rail with her pen. Tipton jumped. 'Show them to the defendant,' she barked.

The photographs were handed to a sullen-looking guy in a wheelchair. After a few whispered words, his solicitor rose and told the bench his client had decided to change his plea to guilty. There was a gleam in Mrs Pearson's eye, and a smug little smile was tugging at her lips. She was knocking this bunch of silly time-wasters into shape. Things were moving now.

* * *

I got back to the office in the early afternoon. It suited me: the Benefits Agency paid me a fixed fee for every fraudster convicted, plus a fee for a court attendance. The lawyers on an hourly rate wouldn't be overjoyed about it, though.

Thoughts about Velma Hartman still troubled me. I couldn't get it out of my mind that what I'd done could have put her in more danger. Reaching for the phone, I found the spot on the blotter where I'd scribbled her number and keyed it in. I had to wait a long time before she answered.

'Sorry,' said a breathless little voice. 'I could hear the phone cheeping, but I couldn't find it. Who is — '

'It's Paul, Velma. Just thought I'd phone and check you're OK.'

'Everything's fine, thank God. You can't imagine what a relief it is to be rid of those men. I . . . I'm sorry I was rude when you were at the farm. I was getting a migraine and . . . '

'I don't remember you being rude, Velma. How's the painting coming along?'

'Stuck. I need an Adam. I don't suppose you'd reconsider?'

'No, Velma. Other commitments and things.'

'And things,' she said, and laughed. 'You shouldn't be shy, Paul. And I could work the sessions around your free time.'

'I work unpredictable hours.'

'I paint through the night.'

There was no answer to that, so I said, 'Try not to mislay your mobile, Velma. Keep it with you always.'

She promised she would, then said, 'A man called yesterday. I thought it was you driving into the yard: he had a fast-looking car a bit like yours. He said he was trying to find a farm for a client who'd just come back from Australia. He asked me if I wanted to sell. He said he'd been up to see Murray at Top Farm, and Murray had told him he rented the land from me. The agent said his client wouldn't haggle over the price.'

'Did he say where he was from?'

'He left me his card, told me to call him back if I was interested. Just a second.' The phone clattered down, then scraped up again. 'Charles Allot, of Allot and Jones. He was very charming.'

'Maybe he could model for Adam.'

I heard a peal of laughter. 'Not unless Adam had short legs, a paunch and combed his hair over a bald patch.'

The conversation was somehow making me even more worried about her, even more guilty about giving into my stupid pride. I said, 'Can I give you some advice?'

'Of course.'

'Give the guy a ring; tomorrow maybe. Don't wait too long. Tell him you're thinking about his offer, but it's a big, life-changing decision and you'll need a lot of time to consider it.'

'But I really don't want to sell, Paul. I'd be wasting his client's time, I'd be — '

'Phone him, Velma. String him along. Let

him think you might be interested.'

'If you say so,' she muttered doubtfully. Then said, 'When are you going to send me your bill?'

'I'm working on it. Probably by the end of the month. You'll phone me if you have any more problems?'

She said she would, I caught a breathy little goodbye, and the line went dead.

Footsteps crossed the waiting room, the half-glazed door opened and Melody was coming towards the desk. Her red skirt was uncreased, and the red blouse looked as crisp and fresh as it had that morning. 'How did court go?' she asked.

'OK. All convicted. Don't know why they pleaded not guilty. Probably wanted their day in court; they all got legal aid.'

She was stacking that morning's coffee things on a tray. 'You didn't eat your Danish. I don't know why I bother.'

'Had to dash.' I took the big horn-rims out of my top pocket and perched them on the end of my nose. When she glanced up, she giggled.

I relaxed back in the swivel chair and eyed her steadily. 'That estate agent, Charles Allot: the guy who wined and dined you. What did he look like?'

'I told you what he looked like.' She tossed

her hair back from her face and gave me a coy little smile.

'I've forgotten. Tell me again.'

'Tall. About as tall as you. Quite slim: he'd not let himself go. Greying hair, nice teeth, very distinguished. Perfect manners and very charming.'

Pushing myself out of the chair, I sauntered around the desk. 'Tall and handsome?' I said.

'Tall, handsome and distinguished,' Melody insisted, then picked up the tray and made to head out. I took it from her, laid it down, then put my hands around her waist, lifted her and sat her on the desk.

'Paul! These old papers are filthy. They'll dirty my . . . '

I propped myself up on the desk, my arms on either side of her, trapping her there. My face was very close to hers. I was looking at her over the spectacles. She was giggling and her colour was high, but she wasn't trying to escape.

'Perfect manners?' I went on. 'Cultivated and charming?'

She was looking embarrassed now. The giggles were turning into peals of laughter. 'All of those things,' she insisted.

Frowning at her over the horn-rims, I said, 'He's just visited a client of mine.'

'Really?' Laughter erupted again. She was

still happy to be sitting on the desk.

'My client said he was short, paunchy, and combed his hair over a bald patch.'

'Then she's not met *my* Charles Allot,' Melody protested.

'You know what happens to women who try to wind guys up and make them jealous?'

'Made you jealous, did it?' Her tone was triumphant.

'You *tried* to make me jealous. You didn't succeed.'

'Rubbish!' She was laughing helplessly now. 'And what happens to women who . . . '

I kissed her, and took some time over it.

'I didn't say you could . . . '

'I didn't ask.'

She let me kiss her again.

Taking my lips from hers, I murmured, 'Don't tell porkies to a private eye, Melody. You'll always get caught out.'

She pushed me away and slid off the desk. 'Private foureyes now.' Giggles suddenly turned to moans of dismay. She reached up and touched her mouth. 'My lipstick! What have you done to my lipstick? I can't go downstairs like this.'

I nodded towards the landing and the toilet designed for a dwarf. 'There's a mirror through there.'

'I'm not going into that awful place.'

Sliding my arm around her waist, I said, 'Stay up here for the rest of the afternoon. Wait until the girls have gone.'

'You're stupid,' she snapped. 'You're just an overgrown child. And it's all your fault. God, I'm so embarrassed.' She jerked free, snatched the napkin from the tray and stormed out on to the landing. I heard the toilet door slam.

Quite a while later, she stormed back into the office. The trademark scarlet lipstick had gone, and her freshly-washed cheeks were pink with embarrassment.

Smiling, I said, 'You can still tell.'

She snatched up the tray. 'Well, unless you've got a lipstick there's nothing I can do about it.'

'Your girls are going to know.'

'And it's all your stupid fault. I don't know what's got into you this week.'

'You'll have to marry me now.'

'And why on earth will I have to marry you now?'

'When all your girls see we've been kissing.'

Anger chased embarrassment from her features. 'You're not just a Neanderthal throwback, Paul Lomax. You're a mentally retarded throwback; an emotional illiterate. You've no idea how to have a tender, sensitive conversation. It's just stupid remarks and pathetic jokes all the time. I'm sick and tired of it.' She strutted to the door, then stopped and spun round. 'And the Charles Allot who took me out to dinner was tall and handsome and knew how to treat a woman.'

★   ★   ★

The DVD recorder was in the passenger footwell; the small portable monitor unfolded on the seat. In it I could see Andrew Pearson sitting behind his desk, leafing through correspondence. He'd got the main office lights on and the image was crystal clear.

A car whispered up the connector road. Glancing across the grass, between the islands of shrubs, I saw a black BMW pulling into the parking bay next to Andrew Pearson's silver Mercedes. The door swung open and a heavily-built guy stepped out: close-cropped blond hair, grey slacks, the collar of his check shirt folded over the neck of an expensive-looking sweater. He locked the car, sauntered over to the entrance to Pearson's offices and gave the glass a pounding. Glancing down at the monitor, I saw Pearson push his chair back. When he left the office, the screen went blank.

Less than a minute later, the screen blinked back into life and I reached down and switched on the DVD recorder. Andrew Pearson was gesturing towards the conference table. I turned up the sound.

'Have a seat, Alan. I'll get the drawings, then I'll pour you a drink. What do you fancy?' He strode past the front of the desk, then disappeared from view. I guessed he'd gone to the plan chest, or maybe the drafting table by the window.

The man he'd called Alan, said, 'Tonic. Slimline.' Then pulled out a chair and sat down.

'Nothing stronger?' came a voice.

'I'm driving,' the seated man said. 'Got to be careful with your wife on the bench.' He laughed softly. 'How is Emma, by the way?'

'Fine. She's absolutely fine, Alan.' He came back into view, laid a pile of drawings on the table, then disappeared again. I heard a door open and clinking sounds, then he reappeared carrying a small bottle and a glass. He put the glass by the man's elbow, half filled it with tonic, then sat down.

Andrew Pearson pointed at the topmost drawing. 'This is the elevation facing the church; the one you were most concerned about.'

The man sipped at his glass. 'Gallery Saint John. Not bad. Sounds classy.'

'Just a suggestion,' Andrew Pearson said.

'The Strathmore Centre sounds good, too.' I sensed he was trying to ingratiate himself.

'Best to stay in the background,' the man said. 'The less people know about your business the better. We'll run with Gallery Saint John until we come up with something better.'

'I've made the church-facing elevation rather like the sweeping Georgian terrace that's already there. It's a conservation area and we don't want trouble from the Civic Trust.'

'Looks OK,' the blond-haired man said. 'Classy.' He didn't seem very interested. 'How many retail units?'

Andrew Pearson selected another drawing from the pile and pointed at features. 'We access the back-land through a big archway. A covered arcade links the twenty units at the front with another thirty at the back; the shops at the back are smaller.' He glanced across at his companion. 'You'd have to acquire the properties in Church Walk and Furnival Street to do the full scheme. How's that side of things going?'

'I'm working on it. Charles is chatting up the tenants, and the Church Commissioners are keen to sell the freehold.' He laughed. 'Pensions for the clergy. A dozen tenants are willing to clear out. When the others see the place emptying, they'll get nervous. We give 'em twenty-eight days to consider a reasonable offer, and they accept. It always works that way.'

'But what if one or two of them don't?'

'They will, Andrew.' The heavily-built man laughed softly. 'Trust me, they will.'

'I've got more than sixty staff, Alan. They take some keeping busy. If we could be more open; apply for planning permission . . . '

'I'll sort it, Andrew. I just need another couple of months. Until then we keep everything under wraps. If what we're doing gets out, the tenants will get greedy.' He slid the drawings back to Andrew Pearson, then said, 'How's the housing scheme coming along?'

'Same position, really. I need access. Until we go public, there's not much more I can do. I've split the development into phases; about a hundred units a phase. Do you want to see the drawings?'

The man called Alan shook his head. 'If you've kept it more or less the same as the Headlands site, it'll be OK. They've not been expensive to build and they've all sold well.'

'We need to talk about the mix,' Pearson said. 'Demand for flats seems to be buoyant.'

'We make more on the town houses.'

'How's land purchase going?' Pearson asked.

'Been working on that for a while, too. Had a little setback, but I'm dealing with it. Charles made a first approach yesterday. Didn't get an outright no, but he could tell the owner wasn't interested. Like I said, I'm working on it.'

'The land's deep in the green belt,' Andrew Pearson muttered. 'Is Bradley sure he can pull it off? And even if he does, there's going to be a big problem with drainage.'

The blond guy laughed. 'You worry too much, Andrew. Trust me, he'll get it through the planning committee.'

'But what about the officials? There was a furore over the Headlands site, and that was within the village envelope and there was a foul sewer we could connect into.'

'Don't worry, Andrew. Leave it to Bradley. And the foul drainage is being taken care of.' He tapped the side of his nose. 'The outfall from the eastern region sewerage scheme's going to be relocated in the valley. The surface water can go into the beck. But for God's sake, keep the drawings under lock and key. The site's got to be bought as agricultural land, and if word gets out . . . ' He rose to his feet, moved towards the bookcase, and stared up at the camera. For a few seconds I thought he'd seen it. His face was filling the screen: broad flat features, cold eyes that were dead and still, a thin-lipped mouth. He suddenly yawned and stretched out his arms. A lot of cosmetic dental work had left him with large teeth that looked too white and too even. 'God, I'm bushed,' he muttered. 'I've got to have an early night.' He turned back to the conference table. 'Barbara asked me to invite you and Emma over for dinner. Next Friday. Is that OK?'

Andrew Pearson nodded. 'Fine, Alan. I'll look forward to it.'

'Been a while now. You've not been over for months.'

The two men wandered towards the door and the screen went blank. I switched off the gear and gazed across the grass. A few seconds later, they appeared behind the entrance doors. The blond-haired guy stepped out, waved then sauntered over to his black BMW. A starter whined, and he accelerated away down the connector road.

Five minutes later, Andrew Pearson was running over the forecourt and climbing into his car. When he drove off, I followed. He led me across town to a network of narrow streets lined with terrace houses and located behind some old railway workshops. Mostly student lets, they were emptying at the end of the summer term, and there was plenty of parking.

He pulled up outside a house that looked cleaner than the rest and crossed the pavement. I parked on the opposite side of the street and watched. The door opened as he was reaching for the bell. I hardly recognized her. The faded denim skirt was short and her long legs were bare. The man's shirt she was wearing was unbuttoned.

Andrew Pearson stepped inside and the red front door closed. Mrs Pearson had got the night right, the time a little wrong, and she was way out on the place. I noted the address, then found my way out of the network of narrow streets and headed home.

*   *   *

Eggs, bacon and four fingers of scotch had put me to sleep in the glow of the gas fire. I hardly heard the mobile bleeping. Reaching for my jacket, I groped for it. After muttering my name, I listened to silence for a few seconds, then the line clicked and an ultra-refined voice said, 'How did it go, Mr Lomax?'

'It didn't, Mrs Pearson. It was a business meeting, with a man called Alan.'

'Norris,' she muttered. 'It would be Alan Norris.'

'They talked about some plans for a while, then Norris left. A few minutes later, your husband drove to Albert Street, to one of those old terrace houses behind the railway workshops. The young lady let him in.'

'I might have known,' she muttered. 'Student accommodation. Her father owns most of it. She must have got the key to one of the houses. What time did my husband arrive there?'

'8.30, maybe 9 o'clock.'

'Hmm . . . He hadn't come home when I slipped out to phone you, and it's almost midnight now. Could you get pictures in this house?'

'Can you get me a key?'

'I could try. I imagine Andrew would have a set. But he carries so many keys. How would I know which one it is? Can't you be resourceful?'

'Breaking and entering, Mrs Pearson?'

'So? You'll just have to be careful.'

'I've got to recover the gear from your husband's offices before I can do anything. When would it be safe?'

'According to his diary, tomorrow night. He's supposed to be wining and dining a client in Leeds, but he'll probably be bedding his girlfriend.' Anger and bitterness mingled in a sigh. 'When do you think you could have

114

something for me?'

'The young lady still lives at home? She's not living at the house in Albert Street?'

'Young lady?' I could hear the sneer in her voice. 'That's not quite the title I'd give her, Mr Lomax. But, as far as I know, she's still living at home.'

'When I've retrieved the gear, I'll go round to the house in Albert Street. If I can get inside, I'll install it. Could you tip me off when you think they might be meeting?'

'Will there be any need to tip you off, Mr Lomax? I expect they're meeting on a daily basis.'

7

They were standing right in front of me. I reached out to touch them, but they were just beyond my grasp. When I tried to move closer, I realized I was buried in warm wet sand.

'Susan . . . Kathy.' I began to moan their names, over and over.

Kathy had grown. She was almost as tall as her mother now. She looked different. All the lost years. But I could tell it was my girl: the dark hair, the soft brown eyes. They were holding hands and a stiff breeze was tugging at the skirts of their gingham dresses, pressing the fabric against their legs. We were on a beach somewhere. I could hear waves pounding against rocks.

Grief and loss surged through me like an electric current. I felt a sudden desolation. The sand was pressing against my chest and I could hardly breathe. Stretching out my arms, I yelled, 'Susan! Kathy!' They didn't answer; just gazed at me while waves pounded and spray hissed into the bright air.

Then they smiled at me and, looking at each other, reached some wordless agreement. Susan blew me a kiss, Kathy waved, and they turned and walked away along a narrow crescent of sand that bordered a rocky headland. I was screaming their names, struggling against the hold of the sand. They were distant now. They turned and waved again, the breeze still tugging at their skirts. And then they were gone. All that was left was the endless sea pounding against black rocks. Pounding . . . pounding.

I jerked upright, sobbing like a baby, sweat-soaked sheets tangled around my legs and body. Tense voices were muttering things I couldn't hear and a fist was pounding on the front door. Kicking the sheets aside, I swung my legs to the floor. I was still sobbing; still living in the mystery of the dream.

A voice yelled, 'Police. Open up. It's the police.' The pounding started again.

Staggering out into the hall, I grabbed a robe from a hook behind the bathroom door and pulled it on. I managed to call, 'Coming; I'm coming.'

'Get the ram,' barked a voice. Booted feet began to scrape in the shallow porch.

'Coming, I'm coming,' I yelled again. Then metal crashed on wood, the frame splintered and the door swung open, yielding at the first blow. 'I was coming,' I snarled at the sea of angry staring faces.

A man in a suit squeezed past men in

uniforms. 'Lomax? Paul Lomax?' He took out a blue wallet and let it drop open so I could see his badge and ID.

'Yeah,' I muttered. 'I'm Lomax. And you didn't have to wreck the place. I was coming.'

He gestured down the tiny hallway. 'Could we come inside, sir?'

Nodding, I padded along the hall and went into the sitting room. Through French windows, I could see more cops grouped around the back door. They were all wearing yellow visibility jackets; making sure the neighbours knew they were paying me a call.

'That's far enough, sir.' The plain-clothes cop stopped me on the hearth rug. 'I'm arresting you for the rape of Miss Velma Hartman. You do not have to say anything, but it may harm your defence if you do not mention . . .'

'Spare me the spiel. You're crazy. Absolutely crazy.'

He ignored me; just went on reciting the caution. He wasn't going to let a flawed procedure get in the way of a conviction. Three or four uniformed men had crowded into the tiny sitting room with us. They were glancing around at things with cold, curious eyes, no doubt trying to keep the contempt from their faces.

'Where were you last night, between eight and midnight?'

'Out and about.'

'Don't mess with me, Lomax. Where were you?'

'I just told you; out and about. Driving home.' I suddenly recognized the young cop who'd visited me at the office with the incredibly ugly cop. He wasn't wearing the wraparound shades now, and he wasn't smiling. 'DI Hogan,' I said. 'You paid me a call. A few days ago with . . . ' I snapped my fingers, trying to remember. 'With the guy called Foster.'

'We've not come to make small talk, Lomax. Where are the clothes you were wearing last night?'

'Jeans and a sweater, over the back of the chair in the bedroom. Shirt, vest and socks are in a basket in the bathroom. I'm still wearing the boxers.'

He turned towards one of the uniformed men. 'Tell Lewis she can come through.'

The man headed back down the hall. I heard him calling, 'Debbie . . . Debbie. Come through now.'

'I'm going to ask you again, Lomax,' Hogan snapped. 'Where were you between the hours of eight and midnight?'

'Heading home. Got here about nine. Had a meal, fell asleep on the couch, went to bed.'

'Heading home from where?'

'From town. I didn't leave town. I wasn't anywhere near Branwell Farm.'

'Who said she was raped at Branwell Farm?'

A brown-haired young woman in a white plastic suit, her hands sheathed in surgical gloves, pushed her way into the room. Rounding on her, Hogan snapped, 'Get the underpants he's wearing; and get the jeans and sweater in the bedroom, and the stuff in the laundry basket in the bathroom.'

A poker-faced Debbie Lewis fixed me in an icy stare and shook one of the bags she was holding. I turned my back on her and stepped out of the boxer shorts. Holding the bathrobe around me, I turned to face her again and dropped them in the bag. She plucked a pen from her top pocket and made a note on a white panel in the transparent plastic. 'Where's the bedroom?' The girl's voice was as frosty as her stare. Rapists are lower down the evolutionary chain than reptiles.

'Second door down the hall. First's the bathroom.' I looked at Hogan. 'Can I get dressed?'

'Keep the robe on, Lomax. We might come back for the rest of your gear.' He glanced at the girl. 'Find him a clean pair of underpants.'

She glowered at me. Her revulsion was

almost tangible. 'Where?' she demanded.

'Airing cupboard. In the bathroom.'

'Keys,' Hogan snapped. 'Where are your house and car keys?'

'Bedside table.'

'Lewis!'

'Sir?' The young woman's voice came faintly from the bathroom.

'Get his keys, they're on the bedside table. When you've got the clothes, do the car. Bag everything.'

★   ★   ★

A drunk had spent the night in the cell, and the smell of vomit was overpowering. I sat on a concrete bench, leaned against the chill of a glazed-brick wall and closed my eyes.

The dream still haunted me. Vividly real, I was living in it: the blown kiss, the wave from a child who was almost a woman. They were saying goodbye. After seven years, they were moving on. I had to let go now.

And I felt sick with guilt about Velma Hartman. If I'd insisted she go back to the police. If I'd not tried to act the man. If I'd just left it alone . . . Keys rattled against the door. When it swung open, two cops were standing in the opening. They were big and bored looking; overweight from spending too much time cruising around in cars. One of them jerked his head and grated, 'You're wanted, Lomax.'

Rising, I joined them in a brightly lit passageway, heard the cell door crash shut behind me, then they led me, one on either side, up a short flight of concrete steps that ended in a corridor. I gathered the bathrobe around me. Without socks, my feet were uncomfortable in leather shoes as we walked the fifty yards to the interview room. They pushed me inside.

Hogan was sitting with his back to the door. The harsh fluorescent light was making his spiky hair seem blacker, his skin even more pallid. He didn't turn round. He just nodded towards a chair facing his across a dark-blue Formica-topped table, and said, 'Take a pew, Lomax. Have they given you breakfast?'

I sat down and shook my head.

He turned towards the cops by the door. 'Cuppa and a bacon roll, Jock.' He glanced at me. 'Sugar?'

'Two.'

'And you can go with him, Stan. I'll start the interview when you get back. Tell Agnes to do a fresh fry and make the bacon really crisp, OK?'

After the door closed, Hogan stared at me

in silence for quite a while, with eyes that glittered like tiny fragments of black glass. He'd done the night shift, but he still looked cunning and sly. He needed a shave. His jowls and chin were black with stubble. Presently, he sighed out his tiredness, and his voice was calm and matter of fact when he asked, 'Did you fancy her, Lomax?'

I nodded towards the recording equipment mounted on the wall above the desk. 'Are we taping this?'

'Off the record, Lomax. We need another officer, and you might want a lawyer, before we start taping.'

We eyed each other through another long silence. Then he said, 'You fancied her, didn't you, Lomax?'

'Fancied who?'

'Don't play games. Velma Hartman.'

'She's very attractive.'

'You had a meal with her at the farm. She cooked you dinner.'

'How do you know that?'

'You told me. You told DCI Foster and me when we paid you a visit.'

We did some more eye-wrestling, then he made his voice chummy as he said, 'She probably fancied you, Lomax.' He gave me the once-over. 'I mean, you look the kind of bloke who doesn't have to try very hard. You probably get tired of the pestering.'

I grinned at him. I hadn't been pestered so much I'd noticed, and the only woman that mattered found my advances hilarious.

'How long have you been a widower, Lomax?'

'How do you know I'm . . . '

He grinned. Some of his teeth were badly decayed. 'I know a lot about you, Lomax,' he said. And then his tone became mocking as he added, 'The Barfield Bounty Hunter; that's what we call you at the station.'

I grinned back.

'Courts are so crammed with benefit cheats, the bench can't find time for serious villains. You must be making a packet.'

'I do OK.'

'And you've been a widower six years?'

'Something like that.'

'Living alone, no partner, no female company?'

'I live alone.'

'Do you often dine with female clients?'

'Almost never.'

'Long time, six years. Attractive woman. Let's forget the age thing, she's a very attractive woman, in a farmhouse on the edge of nowhere. Maybe she wanted to find out if a man would still find her attractive, got flirty, and when you responded — '

There was a tapping and a woman PC poked her head around the door. 'Could I have a quick word, sir?'

'Not now, Perry. Later.'

'But sir, I think you'd — '

'I said, not *now*, Perry,' Hogan snarled.

The head disappeared, and the door slammed. He leaned back in the plastic chair and rested the palms of his hands on the table. His shirt collar was unfastened, the knot of his tie loosened. His grey suit was crumpled. He was tired. He needed a sleep, a shower and a shave, and he was struggling to recover the thread of what he'd been saying.

His voice became more driven. He was no longer the chummy father confessor. He was living it. 'Six years, Lomax. Six weeks would be a long time for some guys. So you made a move on her, she seemed to like it, started laughing and giggling, like they do. And you'd no idea whether she was being serious or whether she was playing silly games. How could you know? Maybe she'd let her skirt ride up, so you could see the goods. Maybe you . . . '

There was a defiant knock and the door opened. The same woman PC, scrubbed and smart in her white shirt and black tie, strode in and came up to the desk.

'What is it now, Perry? I told you . . . '

She didn't speak, just blushed and slid a sheet of paper on to the desk, then turned and scampered out.

Hogan glanced down at it. 'Shit!' he breathed. 'The stupid bitch. This is all I bloody well need.' He put his head in his hands and massaged his eyes. After a few deep breaths, he glanced up and said, 'You're free to go, Lomax.'

'I can go?'

'We got it wrong. She was semi-conscious when they took her into hospital. She kept moaning Lomax, Paul Lomax.' He turned the corners of his mouth down and shrugged. 'What were we expected to make of that? She came to half an hour ago. She was asking for you, Lomax, not accusing you. Seems it was two guys wearing woollen masks. She's no idea who they were.'

'What did they do to her?'

He gestured towards the note on the table. 'Seems it wasn't that serious. They yelled at her, pushed her around a little, removed some clothing, inappropriate touching. She hit her head falling down the stairs.'

'What do you call serious, Hogan? Some guys in masks stripped her, groped her, then gave her a good shoving around. Isn't that serious?'

'Hey, lighten up, Lomax! You should get

involved in some of the stuff we deal with. On a scale of one to ten, Miss Hartman's a two.' He nodded at my bathrobe and picked up a phone. 'I'll have your clothes brought down.' He punched in some numbers. 'Bring Lomax's things down, Jock. Clothes, keys, everything.'

We were looking at each other across the table. Tiredness and embarrassment were fuelling his anger. Making conversation until my things arrived, I said, 'Where's Foster, your partner; the guy with the scar?'

'You mean The Prince.'

'The Prince?' I raised an eyebrow.

'Bonny Prince Charlie.' He laughed. They had a robust sense of humour in the force.

'How did he ... ?' I didn't finish the question.

'Bloke with a meat cleaver went berserk in a supermarket. Foster was off duty, doing a shop with the wife. He saw him deck one of the staff, then went in. Bloke managed two good swipes before Foster got him down. Took three years to make him pretty again. Got the George Cross. They tell me his wife left him. Couldn't bear to look at him.'

'Barfield's finest,' I said.

'Birmingham's finest. He's on secondment. He's not my partner. I was just driving him around; acquainting him with the Borough.'

'Seconded for what?'

He smiled at me. Without the shades he no longer looked sinister, but the glittering black eyes were quick and watchful. 'That's for me to know and you to guess, Lomax.'

The door swung open without anybody bothering to knock, and one of the overweight cops wandered in holding a bundle of plastic bags. He dropped them on the desk. 'What about the breakfast?'

'Forget it,' Hogan said. 'He's leaving. He can get his own. But he'll need transport. Ask McKenzie if he's going — '

'Someone's already come for him.' The overweight cop was leering now. 'Woman called Melody Brown. Half the force has walked through reception to take a look.'

Hogan grinned up at him, then grinned at me. 'She your squeeze, Lomax?'

'I'm working on it.'

He laughed and held out a hand. 'No hard feelings?'

'No hard feelings.'

★ ★ ★

Tight black skirt, black sweater, tiny crimson jacket, crimson and black shoes: Melody looked sensational. And she'd pinned her hair up. Along with the tiny black ear studs and vibrant red lipstick, it was increasing the allure. I could understand the guys at the station wandering through reception to take a peep. I relaxed back in the office chair and enjoyed the view.

'Heavens, the police have made a mess,' she said huskily. She was stepping over the old files and papers the police had tossed on to the floor. 'They were ransacking the place when I arrived. One of them told me you'd been arrested. Then he got a call on his radio telling him to stop the search because you were being released without charge. You'd have thought they'd have tidied things up a bit before they left.' Big blue eyes swept over the mess, then blazed at me. 'It's the artist, isn't it? The Hartman woman. She's landed you in trouble. Whenever you're hired by a woman, you end up in trouble.'

'I caused the trouble for Velma Hartman,' I muttered.

She nodded towards the open drawers of the filing cabinet. 'Did they find anything?'

'Nothing to find. I don't keep records. It's stuff left by the accountants when they let me have the place.'

But the cops had found something in the car. They'd found the DVD of the meeting in Andrew Pearson's office. I'd shoved it in the glove compartment after the surveillance.

When I checked before I drove to the office, I discovered it had gone. If Pearson had any pull with the Bill, I could have big problems.

'Lunch,' she said. 'Do you want something brought in?'

'That would be good.'

'What?'

'Anything.'

She picked up a bundle of papers from the floor, crossed over and dropped them on the desk.

Gazing at her, I said softly, 'Marry me, Melody.'

She let out an exasperated little sigh. 'Not *that* again.'

'I can ask.'

'You're as house trained as a ferret.'

'Some ferrets are very house trained.' I swung gently in the office chair and grinned up at her. She was trying hard not to smile. 'It's the bungalow, isn't it?' I asked.

'I was surprised, Paul. No, I was shocked.'

I shrugged. 'It's the way my wife left it.'

'It's not the way your wife left it. I'm sure she left it clean and neat and tidy.'

Shame and embarrassment about my home were mingling with the guilty feelings I had about Velma Hartman. I'd had to invite Melody in after she'd driven me home, and I'd cringed when she'd said yes. I needed a

130

skip for the rubbish and a month for cleaners and decorators before I could let her see the place. Not knowing what to say, I went on smiling.

'Anyway,' she sighed. 'Tell me again why you want to marry me.'

'Because you're always there for me,' I said softly.

'Always there for you. Is that all?'

I was being tested again. Trying to be smart, I said, 'When I look up, you'll be there; and when you look up, I'll be there.'

Her nose wrinkled. 'You really are serious, aren't you?' She was trying hard not to laugh, but giggles kept erupting.

'Sure I'm serious.'

She turned and headed for the door. 'I don't know what it is, Paul, but I can't help laughing when you get serious. Especially when you start quoting Thomas Hardy.'

'Who's Thomas Hardy?' I called after her.

Husky laughter rustled around the landing and then she disappeared down the stairs. A few moments after the sounds had faded into silence, the desk phone began to ring. 'You've got a visitor, Paul.'

'Do we know his name?'

'It's a her: a Miss Jane Garner.'

'I don't know a Miss Jane Garner.'

'She seems to know you. Very pretty, dark

hair, big brown eyes, short skirt.'

'You'd better send her up.'

I heard more husky laughter. 'Thought that would get you interested,' she said, then the line went dead.

Uncertain footsteps thudded on carpet, then scraped on linoleum. There was a nervous tapping on the outer door. It squeaked open and a slight figure crossed the waiting room and stepped into the office.

'Mr Lomax?'

'That's me. And you're Miss Garner?' I nodded towards the visitor's chair. 'Have a seat.'

She picked her way between the files and papers the cops had tipped on the floor and sat down. Her grey pleated skirt reached halfway down her thighs. White socks came up to her knees. The badge on her red blazer said, Sycamore Street Comprehensive School. She looked about fourteen. Dark wavy hair and big brown eyes; when she gave me a nervous little smile I was suddenly back in the dream and my heart was breaking all over again.

'Mummy sent me.'

'Mummy?'

Her eyes brightened and she smiled, suddenly understanding my confusion. 'You probably know her as Miss Hartman? Velma?'

'Velma!'

'She uses her maiden name all the time now. She used to be Mrs Garner when she was married to Daddy.'

'How is she?'

'Very shaken, but she's OK. She banged her head when she fell down the stairs and the concussion's making her woozy.'

'And how can I help you?'

'She needs clothes and some other things from the farmhouse. She said you'd take me there, then take me to the hospital.'

I pushed myself out of the chair. 'Sure,' I said, relieved at the prospect of doing something to atone for my stupidity. 'I'd be glad to.'

Smiling at her, I waited while she rose and headed for the door, then followed. 'Have you had breakfast?'

'No. When the hospital phoned, I dashed out, caught the bus and went straight there.'

'We'll have breakfast,' I said. 'Then we'll head out to the farm.'

8

The police had gone. They'd left behind yellow tape fluttering across the farmhouse door, and some cloudy patches of fingerprint powder on its boards and frame. Velma's daughter knew her way around the place. She spent less than ten minutes in the bedroom and bathroom, packing things into an old leather suitcase. While she was doing that, I wandered around, checking the windows. There was no sign of a forced entry.

'Did you go and live with your father when he left your mother?' I asked her. We were motoring across country, heading back towards Barfield and the hospital.

'I stayed with Mummy for more than two years. Then I went to Daddy. Getting to school was difficult. I used to cycle into Moxton and catch a bus from there. And there were other problems.'

'Did you mind? Them splitting up, I mean?'

'What do *you* think? It was awful. And it was such a shock. They hadn't been rowing or anything. I didn't realize there was anything wrong. Daddy's married again now. She's called Charlotte. And I've got a baby brother. He's called Joseph.'

'You get along with your stepmother?'

'You ask a lot of questions.'

'It's what I do for a living.'

Jane laughed. 'She's OK. She's the opposite of my mother. Tidy house, meals at set times. And the baby's nice.' She gave me a sideways look. 'Are you my mother's boyfriend?'

'No,' I said. 'I'm not your mother's boyfriend. She hired me because she was being pestered by hoodlums.'

'You didn't do a very good job.'

I winced. She had the simple directness of the young.

We were on the inner ring road now, circling the town, moving with the flow of lunchtime traffic, and closing on the hospital.

'Is your mother going to stay on at the farm?'

'So she says. I'm going to stay with her for a while. It's almost the start of the summer holidays, so I won't have a travelling problem.'

'What does your father think about it?'

'He doesn't know yet. I suppose he'll worry.'

I let it go at that. Turning into the hospital car park, I found a vacant slot, then carried the case while we took the lift up to the ward.

They'd given Velma a private room so she could be watched and questioned by the police. Jane crossed a small waiting area near the ward reception desk, tapped on the door to her mother's room and stepped inside. I took a chair and waited, still remorseful at the way I'd let her mother down, still haunted by teenage girls with dark wavy hair and soft brown eyes.

Double doors at the end of the ward swung open and a tall slim youth, dressed in a white linen suit, hurried to the desk. He was beautiful, like some women are beautiful: big dark eyes, long lashes, plenty of curly black hair, an expressive mouth. Broad shoulders and a two-day growth of black stubble defined his sex. He reminded me of the youths who scamper around Greek vases.

The duty nurse looked up and they began to talk. Something he said seemed to surprise her. Gesturing for him to stay where he was, she rose, went over to Velma's room and pushed her head around the door. When she returned to the desk, they spoke briefly. He went on standing there, looking agitated, until Jane emerged, then he headed for the room. When he passed Jane they barely acknowledged each other. She flounced down in the chair next to mine.

'Tarquin,' she hissed angrily. 'I might have guessed he was on his way.'

Looking at her, I raised an eyebrow. Her high colour was probably caused as much by embarrassment as anger. 'Might have guessed?'

'When Mummy asked for her best summer dress and shoes, and her make-up, I thought she was smartening herself up for you, but it was Tarquin. God, I hoped I'd never see him again.'

'Who's Tarquin?' I remembered Velma talking to her model about a guy called Tarquin.

'You'd better ask *Mummy* who Tarquin is,' she snapped, then pressed her fists into her lap and scowled across the reception area at a print of Van Gogh's *Sunflowers*.

We sat there, her scowling and me brooding about the way I'd let her mother down. Eventually, the door to Velma's room opened and I could see her and the youth standing there. She was wearing the white muslin dress and vermilion shoes she'd worn when she entertained me to dinner. Tarquin reached up, gently brushed wayward curls of red hair from her cheeks, then gently cupped her face in his hands and kissed her. It was a tender, lingering kiss.

'For God's sake!' Jane hissed viciously. Blushing, she looked away, unable to watch the spectacle.

When I glanced back into the room, Tarquin was holding Velma's hands in his and gazing down at her. He suddenly let them go, spun around and came towards us. His face was wet with tears and his lips were trembling. As he passed us, he choked out, 'See you, Jane,' then shoved at the double doors and disappeared. Jane didn't speak. She just went on scowling, her pretty mouth reduced to a hard line.

The doors swung open again almost immediately and a nurse carrying a white paper bag headed for the reception area. The ward sister went over to Velma's room and I heard her saying, 'You can go now, Miss Hartman. Your medicines have been brought up from the pharmacy.'

Velma Hartman emerged holding the battered leather suitcase. I strode over and took it from her. She slid her hand around my arm and clung to me. 'Thanks for taking Jane to the farm, Paul.'

'It was no trouble. How are you feeling?'

'Dizzy after the fall. Bit shaken up and scared, but the headache's gone.'

'We need to talk,' I said.

'Must we?'

'We must. And in private. I'll take you home.'

★ ★ ★

'How many were there?'

'Only two. One huge, one not so big.'

Velma was reclining against cushions on the settee. I was sitting in an old armchair facing her. We were in the parlour, and Jane was across the passageway, washing dishes in the kitchen.

'What persuaded you to let them in?' I asked.

'When I asked who it was, one of them said, 'It's Paul. Paul Lomax.' ' Velma's voice was slow, her speech a little slurred. The medication they'd given her was having its effect.

'Did you tell anyone you'd engaged me?'

She shook her head. 'No one. I don't see anyone to tell.'

'What about the models who come here? What about the one who was leaving when I called the other day?'

'I didn't tell Molly who you were. She was in a hurry. She wanted to get away.'

The cops, Foster and Hogan, knew she'd hired me. Apart from Melody, no one else had been told.

We listened to the clatter of crockery and pans in the kitchen across the passage. Presently, I said, 'Was it very bad, Velma?'

She laid a hand over the exposed swell of her freckled breasts and closed her eyes. 'Nightmarish. I couldn't see their faces; they were wearing black balaclava things with eye and mouth holes. And they kept yelling, 'What's a woman like you doing living alone in this isolated place? You're asking for it.' And all the time they were tugging at me and shoving me around, and saying things.'

'Saying things?'

'Sexual things. They took me up to the bedroom and the big one pushed me on to the bed. Then the smaller one started slapping me and spitting at me, and yelling and screaming. After they'd gone, I phoned the police, then went to lock the door. I was shaking so much I fell down the stairs. When I came round, I was in hospital.'

'Do you think they were the men who were here before?'

She shook her head. 'These men weren't foreign. One was Scottish, and I think the other had a Birmingham accent.'

'Are you going to stay here?'

'What else can I do? My studio's here. This is where I work. It would take me ages to set up again somewhere else.'

'You think you could live here alone?' I asked.

She shivered. 'Jane said she'd stay with me for a few days, and then Tarquin's coming. I hardly dare tell Jane. She loathes Tarquin.'

'I think it's time you told me about Tarquin,' I said softly. 'You've been holding things back.'

'A woman can have her secrets.'

'Not when she's being harassed and assaulted and threatened with worse. If you want me to sort it, you've got to give me something to work on.'

'Tarquin isn't relevant. If he was, I'd have told you.'

'The situation might be relevant, Velma. Tell me about it.'

She leaned forward as if to rise, then winced.

'You OK?' I asked.

'Just a twinge. I must have hurt my hip as well as my head. I need a drink if I'm going to tell you about Tarquin.' Gesturing towards an old oak sideboard, she said, 'There's a bottle of Scotch and some glasses in there. Could you . . . ?'

'Sure, but should you? I mean, all the tablets and pills and things.'

'I'm not going to operate any machinery, Paul. And I can't get through telling you about Tarquin unless I have a drink.'

After I'd poured a generous measure and handed her the glass, she asked me to close the door.

'It was when I was lecturing at the college,' she began. 'Tarquin came two afternoons a week to my fashion design sessions. At first I thought it was a bit of a cheek, allowing him to join the course mid-term, and then I realized how talented he was. And he was keen to the point of obsession.' She gazed past me, through the window, towards the sunlit trees that enclosed the farm and its sheds and outbuildings. She was alone with her memories.

'Talent,' I prompted. 'Tarquin had talent.'

She turned her vivid green eyes on me. 'I'm sorry?' she said absently and took another sip at her drink. 'Yes. And obsession. When talent and obsession combine . . . He was the best pupil I ever had. Did you see him at the hospital?'

I said I had.

'Then you'll have seen how utterly beautiful he is. He began to model for me, here at the farm.' She gazed towards the trees again and her voice was little more than a whisper as she said, 'We became lovers. Somehow his mother found out. Perhaps she'd noticed some change in him and started probing. Anyway, she went crazy. She's a leading light in some Pentecostal church group, and that probably made it even more shocking for her.

'Tarquin didn't show up at the college for a couple of weeks, so I got his address from admin and phoned his home.' Velma turned and looked at me, then held out her glass. 'Pour me another, Paul, and don't go on at me about the tablets. I need it.'

I rose, stepped over to the sideboard, poured her another three fingers and handed it to her. While this was going on, she continued to talk.

'And don't tell me how stupid I was. I've been doing that myself, ever since. His mother came to the phone, started screaming at me about having seduced her son; saying that I'd corrupted him, stolen his innocence. A couple of days later, the dean called me to his office. She was there, with her husband, Daniel Dalton. He's the MP for Barfield North. The long and short of it is, Tarquin wasn't quite sixteen when the affair started.' She took a big sip at her drink. 'How was I to know? He was tall and mature looking. We didn't talk about ages. I didn't even think about it. I just assumed he was at least eighteen. And the dean hadn't told me he'd arranged with Tarquin's art tutor at his private school for him to attend my classes. I thought he'd been properly enrolled, and that would have made him at least eighteen.

'Amanda, that's his mother, started ranting about sexual abuse and demanding the police be called in. The dean was gloating; Faulkner and I had never hit it off. Tarquin's father was more reasonable. He wanted to keep it out of the papers. The elections were coming up and he was worried about his majority.'

Footsteps sounded in the passage, the door opened and Jane peered in. 'I've tidied the kitchen up a bit. Just going to take a walk down to the orchard. It's been a long time.'

'Of course, darling.' Velma turned back to me when the outer door had slammed. 'They said they wouldn't call the police in if I resigned with immediate effect and agreed not to see Tarquin again. If I didn't, I'd be suspended pending the outcome of a police enquiry, and I'd end up being put on the sex-offenders register.' She laughed bitterly. 'Sex-offenders register! His mother thought I'd seduced him, but it wasn't like that at all, and I wasn't the first. I should have seen it coming though.' She gazed out of the window again. The whisky had brought a flush to her cheeks.

'Seen it coming?' I murmured.

'He was so sweet and gentle. He didn't

144

have that aggressive know-it-all insensitivity that most men seem to have. He hadn't been hurt. Nothing had happened to him to make him hard and cynical.' She drained her glass. Drink and the painkillers had blurred the edges. She seemed to have lost the thread of what she was trying to say.

'You said you ought to have seen it coming,' I reminded her.

'It was one afternoon. It was hot and thundery, rather like today. He'd been posing for me. I was cleaning the pallet and he came up behind me and put his arms around me. When I turned, he was still naked. He kept saying, 'Please let me touch you: I must, I must.' I just laughed, told him not to be crazy, and tried to push his hands away. And then he kissed me.' She turned her green eyes on me and sighed. 'That was it. That's when it started. He was four days short of being sixteen. I had sex with an underage boy.'

'And his mother took it badly?'

'Took it badly!' Velma let out a bitter laugh. 'She was homicidal. I thought she'd calm down after they'd made me resign, but when I bumped into her at the supermarket one day she started screaming at me; called me a smelly old tart, loud enough for everyone in the store to hear. I suppose that's why I've hidden myself here. What woman wants to be called a smelly old tart at a Tesco checkout?'

'Don't you think Tarquin's mother could be behind all this trouble you're having?' I said. 'It seems she hates you enough.'

She shook her head. 'Too respectable, too religious; and she and her husband have too much to lose.'

I gave her a searching look. She hadn't listened to a word I'd said the other night. 'What happened to Tarquin?' I asked.

'They arranged for him to go to London. A fashion house. He's done very well. He writes to me and phones me, but we don't see each other. His mother has quite a hold on him; he promised her . . . ' She let the words hang in the air.

'He came to see you in hospital,' I said softly. 'Who told him you'd been hurt?'

'The police must have. I was distressed and confused when I came to and I kept asking for him. I remember giving someone his number. And I must have been calling out your name, because I heard the police talking about you.'

They'd done more than talk. Smiling wryly, I asked, 'How do you feel about him?'

She looked down at her glass for a while, then said, 'He's tender, attentive, gentle; and he communicates with me. It's all so very flattering. But I'm old enough to be his

146

mother. What can he possibly see in me? It's crazy.'

'I don't think it's crazy, Velma.'

She laughed. 'You're very sweet, Paul. But he scares me a little. He's so intense.'

'You don't feel quite the same way about him?'

'I'm older,' she said earnestly. 'When you're thirty-six you don't feel as intensely as you did when you were sixteen. But I do love him. I suppose I've been too scared to let go and flow with the current of things.'

The outer door opened. Seconds later, Jane stepped into the room, looking distraught. 'I've just phoned Daddy. He went ballistic when I told him where I was. He said I can't stay. He says it's not safe and I've got to go home.'

Whisky and pills couldn't deaden the impact of that. Velma looked shocked. 'Just a few days,' she begged. 'Someone's coming to stay at the end of the week.'

'Daddy said it's too dangerous for a woman to live in such an isolated place. He said you should leave.'

'And go where? Can't you just stay tonight, Jane? I'll be alright after tonight.'

'He says I've — '

'I'll stay with you tonight, Velma,' I said. 'I'll take Jane home, then I'll come back.'

'You'll come straight back?'

'I've just got to make one call.' I had to recover the gear from Pearson's office.

'But you'll be back before dark?'

'I'll be back before dark.'

★ ★ ★

Thunder had been grumbling for most of the afternoon, and the downpour started when I was driving through the estate of bay-windowed semis, closing on Jane's home.

'Dad's going to go crazy.'

I took a quick look at her. She was chewing her lip and looking worried. 'Your mother was in hospital,' I said. 'Anyone would dash to see their mother.'

'But I didn't tell anyone. I was pretty sure he'd stop me going, so I just ran out when the hospital phoned. Charlotte was feeding Joseph, so she didn't see me leave. They'll have thought I was at school.'

'Why would they stop you going to see your mother?'

'Did Mummy tell you about Tarquin?'

I said she had.

'When it all blew up, his mother made sure Daddy knew. She even phoned Social Services and told them. Everyone started saying Mummy wasn't a fit person, and

Daddy got custody. God, I felt like a parcel. Mummy still has access, but I hardly ever go to the farm. She meets me in town.' She pointed to a house. 'We're here. It's that one; the one with the blue Volvo on the drive. Daddy's home.'

'Would it help if I came in?' I asked.

'Don't think so, but thanks, anyway. He'll just rant for a while and then Charlotte will calm him down.'

I pulled up in front of the house and gave her a business card. 'Show your father that,' I said. 'Tell him your mother arranged for you to be driven around, and that you weren't on your own. And keep it. If you need me, if you hear anything that might help me find the people who've hurt your mother, give me a ring. OK?'

Jane opened the door, hunched her shoulders, then launched herself into the downpour and disappeared around the back of the house. I waited a couple of minutes, then headed back into town.

It was too early to visit Andrew Pearson's architectural practice to recover the surveillance gear, so I eased the car up the pedestrianized area and parked close to the office steps. Melody and her girls had gone. I headed up the stairs, unlocked the office and got behind the desk. The storm was making the place dark, and rain was drumming on the slates and gurgling along the gutters, just beneath the windows.

I switched on the desk lamp and finished sifting through the mail: a couple of cheques, another list of suspected benefit fraudsters, and instructions regarding an insurance scam. Pocketing the cheques, I dropped the correspondence on that week's pile and found the phone book amongst the old files and papers the police had thrown on the floor. Tarquin's mother had good reason to be distressed, but did she have to tell Velma's husband and Social Services? Hadn't getting Velma dismissed been enough? Her feelings seemed to have escalated from outrage to hatred.

There was half a page of Daltons listed, but only one Daniel Dalton, MP. The number was for his constituency offices. I dialled it on the off chance and a female voice answered. She told me he was holding his monthly surgery during the afternoon and evening of the next day. I booked myself in for an evening chat.

Thunder was growling, lightning flickering, and the rain was pelting down. The noise of it all had masked the tread of his feet on the stairs and across the waiting room. When I cradled the phone and glanced up, I saw him, framed in the office doorway, water running from his grey trilby hat and saturated raincoat.

'You're working late, Lomax.' His voice was like the growl of a big animal, and there was a hint of breathlessness in it after the climb up the stairs.

I nodded towards the visitor's chair. 'Step inside and sit down.'

Detective Chief Inspector Foster moved into the office, looking even bigger and bulkier in the soaking coat. After flopping down in the chair, he removed the hat and dropped it on the floor. The pool of light from the desk lamp reached halfway up his chest and his misaligned eyes were glittering at me out of the shadows. I could hear the water dripping from his coat.

'They tell me Hogan pulled you in for the Hartman assault.'

I nodded. 'I used to be the Barfield Bounty Hunter. Now I'm the Barfield Ripper.'

His mouth curved into the smile that made his face almost human. 'He's young and keen. It makes him impetuous.' Displaced eyes gazed at me in a disturbing way while thunder crackled above the slates. When the rumbling had faded, he said, 'Learned anything that might interest me, Lomax?'

I grinned at him. 'Are we trading info, or is

this just me telling you secrets?'

'You help me, Lomax, and I might keep you out of trouble.'

I gazed at the tiny points of light reflected in his eyes and listened to the rain swirling along the gutters. 'I'm used to trouble.'

'Strathmore Developments,' he said. 'What do you know about Strathmore Developments?'

'You asked me that the last time you called. The answer's still the same. I don't know a thing about Strathmore Developments. Miss Hartman's my only private client. I normally work for insurance companies and the Benefits Agency. I try to avoid private clients.' I didn't mention Mrs Pearson. It was the last thing she'd have wanted.

'Then why take on Miss Hartman?'

'I've been asking myself that. A woman in trouble; you somehow get drawn in.'

'Yeah, she is quite a looker.' He was smiling at me.

'If you like the mature type.'

'Let's not get hung up on mature, Lomax. I've seen her spilling out of the frock. She's a stunner. Why do you think she's having all this trouble?'

'Not sure. I'm working on it.'

His smile widened. 'And you're giving her protection?'

'As far as I can. There are limits. Anyway, protecting the public's your business. What's that motto you paint on all the squad cars? Vigilance with courage?'

He laughed. 'She probably needs us with you on the job. You've made a bit of a balls of it so far.'

I winced. First the daughter, now the Old Bill. And what made them think I needed reminding? 'You're on secondment,' I said, trying to jump the conversation on to fresh tracks.

'Who told you that?'

'Hogan. Something serious must be stirring in Barfield.'

Ignoring me, he growled, 'What about Andrew Pearson, Alan Norris, Ben Bradley, Dennis Osborne? They ring any bells?'

I gave him a shrug and tried to keep the surprise at hearing Pearson and Norris's names from my face. And the way he kept banging on about Strathmore Developments should have been telling me something. I smiled across at him and said, 'Don't mean a thing.'

He let out a tired sigh. 'You're either very smart or incredibly stupid, Lomax.'

When he reached down and groped for his hat on the floor, his face moved into the pool of light. The scar, the displacement of bone, suddenly cast a diagonal shadow from forehead to cheek. The disfigurement was appalling; the misaligned eyes seemed to belong to different men. He pressed the hat down on his head and heaved himself out of the chair.

'Smart or stupid, Lomax, you do careless things.' He reached into his raincoat pocket and took out a DVD. 'Like leaving this in your car.' He tossed it down on the desk. The cops had stuck a label on the case and written my name and a date on it. As he ambled towards the door, he called over his shoulder, 'Don't tread on my toes, Lomax, or I'll cut your feet off. And stay close to the Hartman woman. Sleep with her if you have to.' He faded into the shadows in the waiting room.

Thunder was still grumbling overhead; rain still pelting down on the slates and gurgling along the gutters. Taking an old envelope from one of the piles on the desk, I noted down Strathmore Developments and the four other names he'd mentioned.

The surveillance gear had to be recovered from Pearson's offices, and Velma would be scared and desperate for company. Switching off the desk lamp, I locked the inner door, then moved down through the storm-darkened building and made a dash for the car.

9

Strong morning sunlight was doing nothing to redeem Albert Street's tired drabness. It was 9.30, and the love nest in the grimy terrace behind the railway works looked deserted. Andrew Pearson should have left for the office by now, even if they'd stayed the night, but there was a chance the girl was still in there.

I checked my wallet. The fake British Gas ID card was nestling next to my locksmith's friend: a piece of thin springy plastic a little smaller than a postcard. Gathering up the bag that held the tools and the surveillance gear I'd recovered from Pearson's office the previous evening, I crossed the street, rapped on the door, then glanced around. There were no twitching curtains. This was student bedsit territory. If the tenants hadn't already left at the end of the summer term, they'd be sleeping off the excesses of the night before.

The house was silent. I knocked on the door again, waited another minute, then pressed my knee against it. A narrow gap appeared between door and frame. I forced the piece of plastic into it above the Yale and dragged it down. When I turned the old iron knob and pushed, the door opened.

A quick walk around revealed two bedsits and a kitchen on the ground floor; two bedsits and a bathroom upstairs. Dust and discarded papers on cheap ill-fitting carpets; wire coat hangers rattling in flimsy wardrobes. The accommodation was basic and the occupants hadn't been diligent with the domestic chores. In three of the rooms, the beds had been stripped and the wardrobes and drawers were empty. The students had taken their washing home to mother.

Someone was still using the first-floor bedroom at the back of the house. Lamps with pink shades and deep fringes stood on bedside tables. A couple of white rugs covered the cheap carpet. The single bed was untidy, but the linen was clean and the pillows large and lace-trimmed. Pink curtains that matched the lampshades were drawn across the window. I strode over and pulled them aside, looked down on small rear yards that ended in outside toilets. A narrow alleyway separated the yards from the high and windowless brick wall of the old railway workshops.

An empty bottle, two champagne flutes, and a black and gold chocolate box stood on the bedside table nearest the window. The chocolates had been eaten: pleated paper wrappers and a red-ribbon were scattered over the floor beside the bed. Three or four cigarette butts nestled in a cheap metal ashtray on the other table. There was an old wooden kitchen chair, but no cupboards or wardrobe, no dressing table, no bookshelves; nowhere to locate the tiny camera. A gas fire had been fixed in the fireplace, but it was low down and the camera had to be elevated to secure a clear view of the bed. I realized I'd have to locate the transmitter and battery pack in an another room; drill a hole through the wall, close to the ceiling, and hold the camera in place with its connecting cable.

A bathroom, and the bedsit at the front of the house, adjoined the hideaway. I checked the bathroom. Someone had been keeping it clean. It was tiled, floor to ceiling, and there were no cupboards on the shared wall where I could have hidden the gear.

When I wandered into the bedsit, I found a wardrobe in a recess next to the fireplace. Batteries and transmitter could be hidden inside, and a hole through the wall above it would put the camera in a perfect position for viewing the lovers' bed.

It took no more than a couple of minutes to drill the tiny hole and clean up the brick and plaster dust that fell on the love-nest side. After connecting camera to cable, I stood on the chair, threaded the cable into the hole, then returned to the bedsit and gently pulled it through until I could feel the camera pressing against the plaster on the other side of the wall. Back in the lovers' room again, I glanced up. The camera, too small to be noticed, was nestling just below the ceiling. I climbed on to the chair, reached up, and set it square and level.

Minutes later, I'd connected up the batteries and transmitter, dangled the aerial down the back of the wardrobe, and was reaching into the holdall for the monitor to make sure the installation was working.

Keys rattled, the front door opened and closed, then feet thudded up the stairs. I froze. A soft female voice began to hum a popular tune, then high heels clicked on the tiled bathroom floor, a door slammed and the toilet seat clattered down.

Shoving the monitor back in the holdall, I glanced around the room; took in a dressing table that had been used as a desk, a new-looking upright vacuum cleaner, and a single bed pushed against the wall. The wardrobe I'd concealed the transmitter in was small and flimsy. There was no hiding place. Deciding to make a dash down the stairs, I moved towards the door. The toilet flushed. I paused, mid-stride. If I suddenly appeared on the landing, I'd scare her rigid, and she'd scream the house down. Sliding the holdall into the wardrobe, I dragged the bed with its bare mattress a few inches into the room, then squeezed down behind it. I was lying prone on the floor, my back against the wall, my face close to a forgotten sock and a pair of stained Y-fronts.

The bathroom door opened, footsteps crossed the landing and moved into the room. I heard the squeak of tiny wheels. Seconds later, the hoover began to drone to-and-fro. She was sprucing up the love nest.

I hid there for at least half an hour, listening to the tread of her feet and the sound of running water in the bathroom. Then tiny wheels squeaked again as the hoover was trundled back. I tensed. What the hell would I say if she came over and peered into my hiding place next to the wall?

When the bedroom door slammed, I let out a breath that stirred the balls of fluff under the bed. Minutes later, feet descended the stairs and the front door opened and closed. Struggling up, I stepped over to the window and tweaked the curtains aside. She was crossing the street, long legs sheathed in tight jeans, her brown hair drawn back and secured with a rubber band. She tossed a shopping

159

bag into the back of a new-looking silver Vauxhall Astra, then slid behind the wheel and drove off.

I got the monitor out of the holdall and went into the back bedroom. The chocolate wrappings and cigarette butts, the champagne bottle and glasses, had been cleared away. The bed had been carefully made and the room was fragrant. The sensor in the camera picked up my body heat, and a picture flickered on to the screen. With the bedside lamps on, the image of the bed and the area around it was crystal clear.

It was a relief to step out into the street. The job was demeaning. I thought it had ended when I'd handed Mrs Pearson her photos, but I was still acting the voyeur. Wanting to forget it, to distance myself from it for a while, I decided to spend the rest of the day doing some groundwork on the insurance scam. When I was inside the car, I checked the Barfield A to Z, got my bearings on the street where the food storage place was located, then drove off.

* * *

Daniel Dalton held his surgery in a hired room above a travel agent's in the main shopping street. He was using an old dining table for a desk, and he was sitting behind it on a high-backed dining chair. A couple of chairs from the same suite faced it. I dragged one over and sat down. His long face was heavily jowled, his complexion rather florid, and grey hairs were beginning to show amongst the brown. The smile he was giving me looked as sincere as his election manifesto. Pressing his fingertips together, he said, 'How can I help you, Mr Lomax?'

I didn't speak, just eyed him steadily while I tried to work out how to question him about Velma's problems. There was no round-about way, so I opened with, 'I believe you know Miss Velma Hartman?'

The smile froze on his lips, and his eyes became wary. 'I know Miss Hartman. What of it?'

'A couple of years ago she was involved with your son. I understand the affair upset you and your wife pretty badly.'

'I rather think that's my personal business, Mr Lomax. My constituency secretary booked you in because you told her *you* had a problem you wanted me to help you with.'

I smiled at him. 'I'm representing Miss Hartman. Her problems are my problems. She's been pestered for weeks by hoodlums who go to her farm most nights and scare her half to death. A couple of nights ago, some guys tricked their way into the house and subjected her to a serious sexual assault.'

He gave me a blank stare. I stared back. After a while, he turned his hands palm up, and said, 'I still don't understand what this has to do with me.'

'You and your wife were outraged by the affair. You did all you could at the time to make sure she paid for it. Maybe that wasn't enough. Maybe you and your wife still bear a grudge.'

'This is absolutely outrageous. I've never been spoken to like this in my . . . ' He suddenly paused, then said, 'If you're suggesting what I think you're suggesting, I must insist that you leave. Why, you're not even a member of the police. How dare you.'

'It would still make a good story for the press,' I said. 'Maybe I should have a word with Owen Thomas on the *Barfield Echo*. 'Attractive artist suffers serious sexual assault.' Been living an isolated celibate life since an affair with the local MP's son. Local MP's a rising star at Westminster. Son's in the fashion industry, and he and Velma would photograph well. Owen could probably sell the article on to the national dailies.'

'You don't know what you're talking about,' Dalton snarled. 'I felt sorry for the woman. I managed to prevent her being prosecuted and ending up on the sex-offenders register. And this is all the thanks I get!'

I grinned at him. 'Tarquin's not the blue-eyed boy your wife thinks he is, Dalton. He made the first move. He couldn't keep his hands off her in the studio. And he was a big boy; looked a lot older than sixteen, and you'd done some deal with the dean to get him into the fashion lectures at the college. All the kids at the college are at least eighteen. How was Velma Hartman to know he was different?'

'He was fifteen when she started having sex with him.'

'Four days short of sixteen. A technicality. If she'd got herself a decent lawyer instead of wallowing in remorse, she could have walked away unscathed. You and your wife used your position to inflict a lot of retribution.'

'Rubbish!' he snapped. 'I saved her from prosecution. I probably saved her from jail.'

'She lost her job, her reputation, her child.'

'Child?'

'Your wife informed Velma's ex-husband and Social Services. They decided Velma was an unfit parent. He got custody.'

Dalton looked surprised. I guessed his wife hadn't told him that. He swallowed hard, then ran his tongue around his lips. He wasn't enjoying this. His mind was working overtime, trying to decide how to handle it. He dragged in a breath and his voice was shaky as he said, 'I'm telling you the truth, Mr Lomax. I felt no particular animosity to the woman. Between ourselves, I was grateful to her. Tarquin always had a highly developed feminine side. Women's clothing fascinated him, still does, he's in the fashion industry. And he was always very close to his mother. I thought . . . Well, let's put it this way, I was relieved to discover his appetites were normal, and if Miss Hartman had anything to do with him discovering his true sexual nature, I'm grateful to her.'

'I don't think your wife would be quite so pragmatic.'

He gave me a resigned smile. 'Is any girl good enough for a mother's son, Mr Lomax? And when it's not a girl, when it's a woman who's almost as old as you are, feelings run high. Add to that the unusual closeness between Tarquin and his mother, and you can begin to understand how distressed my wife was.'

'Distressed enough for the hurt to fester until she had to inflict more pain on the woman who'd inflicted so much pain on her?'

'That's utterly fanciful. My wife's a deeply religious woman. She was counselled by the pastor at her church for more than a year: turn the other cheek, forgive and forget, all that sort of thing. You really are barking up the wrong tree.'

'Where's Tarquin now?' I asked.

'Is that any of your business?'

'Just asking.'

'London. He took a job in a fashion house after his affair with the Hartman woman. I managed to pull some strings for him. Must say, he's done very well.'

'I mean, where is he today? Is he at home with his mother?'

'If you dare to pester my wife with this . . . ' His voice was angry.

I said nothing, just stared at him across the old dining table he was using for a desk. There was an A4 pad with some scribbled notes, an open diary and a blue ballpoint pen by his elbow. I wouldn't get to see him again. He'd tell his minders to keep me away from him. All the interview had done was confirm the hatred his wife felt for Velma. I was pretty sure there was nothing else he could tell me. Perhaps if I waylaid his wife at church, exposed a few raw nerves, I might learn more.

Rising to my feet, not bothering to extend a hand, I said, 'Thanks for seeing me, Mr Dalton.'

'My wife's still in a very fragile state because of this. I won't have you rekindling . . . ' He shouted the words after me as I strode over to the door. I tugged it open, walked on past a couple of party-faithful folding leaflets in the outer room, then headed down some dingy stairs to the street. There was a café in the next building that did pretty decent all-day breakfasts. I decided to get one before I began my evening stint outside the house in Albert Street.

★   ★   ★

Wanting to be sure of a good signal, I parked as close as I could to Pearson's love nest. The DVD recorder was in the passenger footwell, the receiver and monitor were on the front seat, and everything was connected up. When I switched on the monitor, its screen was blank: there was no one in the bedroom to trigger the camera.

Hopefully, Pearson and the girl wouldn't leave it too late. He had to go home some time, and the longer they spent wining and dining the less time they'd have here.

I pushed the driver's seat as far back as it would go and settled into the leather for the long wait. I began to run my mind over the Hartman business; pondering on one or two things that had been troubling me. Velma had let the guys into the house because one of them had said it was me calling, but the cops were the only people who knew she'd hired me. Maybe the farmhouse was being watched. The guys I'd chased off could have seen me arriving at the place. How else would one of them be able to cat-call about a boy, a pretty boy, being in the bedroom with Velma? And then the penny dropped. They'd been talking about Tarquin, not me. Pretty boy was an accurate description of the youth I'd seen at the hospital. But how would a couple of foreign guys know about Velma's past? Had they heard it from Tarquin's mother? Or had Velma been lying when she'd said she'd not seen Tarquin since their affair was rumbled? Maybe they'd spent the occasional night together, down on the farm.

The hoodlums who'd visited most nights and made a nuisance of themselves had always avoided going when the police were there. Someone on the force was probably tipping off whoever was organizing the mayhem. Maybe that's how the villains who'd assaulted Velma knew they only had to call out my name to gain entry. And when they'd got inside, they'd said nothing about the assault being a revenge thing for the battering I'd given the two guys with the van.

Tussling with it was tiresome. On top of a fat-saturated all-day breakfast, it was sleep inducing, and I had to stay awake. Straightening myself up in the seat, I wound the window down a couple of inches to let in some fresh air, then began to ponder on the dream of Susan and Kathy that still seemed vividly real; then on Melody and me, and then just on Melody; on her face and fragrance, on the fabulous shapes that . . .

Andrew Pearson's silver Mercedes turned into the street and headed towards me. I slid down behind the wheel, heard him brake hard, then manoeuvre into a vacant space in front of the house. Doors slammed.

She was wearing the black and white designer dress with the striking zigzag pattern, and a faint evening breeze was tugging at her dark hair. She swirled across the pavement and unlocked the door. He followed and the door slammed shut behind them.

I began to watch the monitor. Its screen remained blank. After five, maybe ten minutes, I began to suspect the gear wasn't working; that I'd wasted my time that morning. And then it blinked into life.

She was switching on one of the bedside lamps. He moved into view and switched on the other. Then she joined him on his side of the bed, reached up and slid her arms around his neck. I heard her speak for the first time then. The electronic paraphernalia was stripping out the lowest tones, but her voice was very clear. It sounded young and refined. 'I've been thinking about this all day, Andrew. I've been simply longing for it. God, you're like a drug.'

He kissed her hard. She pulled away and gasped, 'Don't make my mouth all puffy. They'll start asking questions.'

'Sorry. I keep forgetting. I can't help it. I want to eat you.' His head bent forward and he kissed her again, more tenderly this time.

She began to fumble with the knot on his tie. When she had it unfastened, she got to work on his shirt buttons, then peeled the light-grey jacket of his suit over his shoulders. He shook it off and left it lying on the floor. As if working to a familiar routine, she turned her back to him, and he reached for her zip and drew it down. He slid the fabric from her shoulders and began to kiss her back while she wriggled the dress past her hips and stepped out of it.

Stockings and suspenders and white silk underwear: she was trying hard to please. Kicking off her shoes, she knelt on the bed and let him caress her buttocks and thighs for a while, then she rolled on to her back and gazed up at him.

The picture was sharp and vividly clear, the microphone so sensitive I could hear his breathing. Soft light from the bedside lamps was casting shadows that defined every curve and swell and hollow of her body. She raised her hands above her head, tangled her fingers in the mass of dark hair on the pillow, then her refined young voice was saying, 'Don't just stand there looking, Andrew. Do something about it. I've been simply longing for you all day. I want . . .'

I switched off the monitor. I'd seen and heard enough to know that Mrs Pearson was going to get what she wanted. I'd seen and heard more than was good for me.

It was almost eleven when they stepped out of the house, and I was bored and tired after being cooped up in the car. She climbed into her Vauxhall Astra, he got behind the wheel of his silver Mercedes, and they went their separate ways.

I toyed with the idea of going in and retrieving the equipment, but it was already dark and Velma would be on hot bricks. When the Jaguar rumbled into life, I let out the clutch, cleared the network of narrow streets, then motored across town, heading south for Moxton and Branwell Farm. The surveillance gear could wait until tomorrow.

10

Would you like me to do you bacon and eggs?' Velma's voice was coming from the bedroom.

I was in the ancient bathroom, trying to shave with the pathetic little razor she'd given me. I called across, 'Toast and coffee would be fine.'

'I don't mind. It wouldn't be any trouble.' She sounded happier. I'd been with her for two uneventful nights, and last night she'd worked in the studio into the early hours. Things were returning to normal.

'Just toast and coffee,' I mumbled, and began to scrape away at the other cheek.

He must have crept up the stairs like a cat. The bathroom door suddenly crashed against the wall and he was standing in the opening, eyes horror-stricken, his mouth twisted into an ugly shape. 'You . . . ' He suddenly recognized me. 'You're the bloke I saw with Jane at the hospital. What the hell are you . . . ?' He spun round and kicked at the bedroom door. Velma was sitting on the edge of the bed, looking shocked, the hem of her nightdress around her thighs, her tights halfway up her calves.

'How could you, Velma?' His outraged voice was tearful. 'You know how much you mean to me, and you've been sleeping . . . ' Suddenly, something snapped. Turning to face me, he screamed, 'You bastard,' and swung a punch.

When I dodged the blow, I brushed against a soap rack and heard it clatter down into the bath. He drew his fist back again and swung another. I grabbed his wrist and squeezed it until the bones crunched.

'Christ,' he screamed. 'Don't . . . Let me go. Don't. Please don't.'

I relaxed my grip, he tugged his wrist free, and then Velma had her arms around him and she was saying, 'It's not what you think, darling. He's . . . '

'Get away from me.' He pushed at her. 'You know how much I love you. Christ, all my letters. How many more ways are there for me to say it? And you've been sleeping with this great hairy oaf.' He glared at me for a few heavy breaths, rage and jealousy distorting perfect features. Then he threw another haymaker.

Ducking, I grabbed both wrists this time. It was like manhandling a tall girl. 'Velma's telling the truth, Tarquin. She hired me because of the trouble she's been having.

When her daughter said she couldn't stay, I spent the night here.'

'Liar. You're a couple of liars.' He turned his head so he could glare at Velma. 'And I loved you. God, how I loved you.'

I gave him a shaking and snarled, 'She knows that, Tarquin.' Then pushed him across the landing and forced him down the stairs. He was hanging his head and sobbing, and through the sobs he kept moaning, 'I loved you, Velma. I loved you so much.'

The door into the parlour was open. I shoved him through and dragged him over to the big settee. There were pillows, a crumpled sheet, and a duvet on it. My shirt and jacket and tie were hanging over the back of one of the dining chairs.

'This is where I've been sleeping, Tarquin.'

He didn't look, just went on sobbing and mumbling about loving Velma.

I gave him another good shaking, then put my mouth close to his ear, and said, 'Take a look, Tarquin. I've been downstairs; Miss Hartman's been upstairs. She's a client. That's all she is to me, Tarquin, a client.'

Velma came into the room, her white cotton nightdress swirling around her ankles, her red hair all over her shoulders, her freckled face pale with shock. She stepped between us. I let go of Tarquin and she led him over to one of the dining chairs and made him sit down. Standing beside him, she put her arms around his neck and drew his face between her breasts. The sobbing was muffled now. Without making a sound, she mouthed at me, 'Go. Please go.'

Stepping past them, I snatched my shirt, jacket and tie from the back of another chair, my keys and mobile phone from the table, and crept out. While I finished dressing in the porch, I could hear her whispering soothing words to him, his surprisingly deep voice murmuring things I couldn't catch, and then the talking stopped and the kissing and groaning started.

I closed the big door as gently as I could, got the Jaguar out of the tractor shed, and began the drive back to town. I understood then what Velma had meant when she'd said the intensity of it all scared her.

*   *   *

There was nothing to delight me in that morning's mail. Just a letter from the accountants who sublet the office to me, putting me on warning that my lease might not be extended. I laid it on that week's pile and tossed the circulars into the bin.

Melody was late coming up that morning.

When I heard her footsteps it was as if a dark cloud was lifting and sunlight was about to flood the room. I couldn't remember when I'd last had that feeling. It was the dream. I was moving on.

'You look pleased with yourself this morning.' Melody lowered the tray on to the papers. 'And you were in early for once.'

'Came straight in from Branwell Farm. Slept there last night.' I watched her face when I said that.

'With Miss Hartman?' A smile was tugging at her lips as she began to pour the coffee. 'Boots, trousers, dirty mac, headscarf and rubbing oils Hartman?'

'The very same.'

Melody gave me a reproachful look. 'You know, Paul, sometimes I just can't believe how immature and pathetic you are.'

'What's immature about sleeping on the farm?'

'If you're trying to make me jealous; if you're trying to get your own back for my night out with gorgeous Charles Allot, you'll have to try harder than that.' She sighed. 'Miss Hartman, indeed.' She lowered a plate on to the blotter. 'I did you some toast. Or has Miss Hartman already given you something more satisfying?'

I smiled up at her. 'Toast is fine.'

175

'Do you want the girls to bring you something back for lunch? You were out again yesterday. Another meal wasted.'

'A sandwich would be great.'

She gave me another reproachful little smile and did some tut-tutting as she headed for the door.

'Have you given my proposal any more thought?' I called after her.

'What proposal?'

'My troth-plighting proposal.'

She just laughed. She didn't even bother to play her little whys and wherefores game.

The desk phone rang. I swallowed a mouthful of toast and recited my name into the receiver, then had to wait a few seconds before the distinctively high-class voice came through.

'Have you resolved that matter for me, Mr Lomax?'

'It's all dealt with, Mrs Pearson. Would you like to call in, or would you like me to deliver it?'

'You know I wouldn't,' she said tetchily. 'Have you looked at it?'

I said I hadn't.

'Then how do you know it's what I want?'

'I watched the first few seconds, Mrs Pearson. Unless they switched off the lights or something went wrong with the camera, it's what you want.'

'If I wait in that supermarket car park, the one on Gladstone Road, could you bring it to me there?'

I said I could, then asked, 'What car do you drive?'

'A yellow Mini Cooper.' She was telling me what I already knew. 'I'll try and park near that bottle bank thing. Shall we say in about fifteen minutes?'

'Make it thirty,' I said, and the line went dead.

She was still going to some lengths to conceal her association with me. When I tugged open the bottom drawer of the desk and took out the disk in its plastic case, I got to wondering, all over again, if she was trying to set me up in some way. Lifting the office bottle from the knee hole of the desk, I soaked my handkerchief with the spirit, wiped the disk and its case, then dropped them into an envelope and headed out.

★ ★ ★

The sweltering heat was making the air shimmer over the supermarket car park. After driving aimlessly between rows of cars for a while, I saw the bottle bank, tucked away down the side of the building. Mrs Pearson's yellow Mini Cooper was parked under some sycamore trees close by. I pulled up alongside, climbed out and opened her passenger door. I slid in beside her.

She was wearing a black trouser suit with a broad red pinstripe. A red handkerchief was spilling from her breast pocket, and her silvery blonde hair was drawn tightly back and tied with a red ribbon. When she reached for the envelope, I held on to it. Cool grey eyes locked on mine.

'Do you really want to look at this, Mrs Pearson?'

'Your concern's misplaced, Mr Lomax. Please give me the disk.'

'You may see things that'll haunt you for the rest of your life. If it was my wife, I think I'd go crazy watching it.'

'And I've already told you, Mr Lomax. I don't allow my emotions to rule me. I'm paying you for the disk. Please give it to me.'

I let the envelope slide from my fingers.

'I'd like to settle up with you now.'

'Hadn't you better check it first?' I asked.

'I thought you said it was what I wanted?'

'I'm pretty sure it is, Mrs Pearson, but I only viewed the first thirty seconds or so to make sure the quality was OK.'

She gave me a long steady look. 'Your old client, Alan Palmer, said you'd more scruples than his maiden aunt. I thought men liked watching these things?'

'They weren't performing for the public, Mrs Pearson. And I feel degraded enough having got the thing for you. I'd feel even more soiled if I'd viewed it.'

She glanced at her watch. 'Can I meet you somewhere in three hours time, say about 2.30? If the disk is satisfactory, I want to pay you. I don't want to leave any loose ends.'

'How about the place we used before?' I suggested. 'The Travellers' Friend snack bar. Parking's usually easy outside the railway station.'

'That would be satisfactory, Mr Lomax.' She forced her lips into a bleak little smile and I climbed out of her car.

★ ★ ★

Three hours to fill. I began to drive across town, heading for the house in Albert Street, intending to recover the surveillance gear, then decided it was best left until Mrs Pearson had given the recording the OK. Changing direction, I headed back to the office.

Behind the desk, I began to leaf through papers on the insurance scam, but my mind was still on the Hartman business, pondering on recollections of the meeting I'd watched in Pearson's office, and things the disfigured cop had said. The phone began to shrill. It was Melody. In a terse, chilly voice, she said, 'You've got a visitor.'

I tossed the papers down. 'What's his name?'

'It's a her. Most of your callers are women, Paul.' Melody's tone was cutting. 'The only male callers are the police, coming to arrest you or ransack your office. It's Velma Hartman.'

'Boots and dirty mac?'

'No, Paul, no boots and dirty mac.' Her voice had dropped below freezing. 'You've been keeping secrets. I'll send her up.'

There was hardly time for me to take pleasure at Melody's displeasure before I heard the tapping on the office door. When Velma stepped through, my smile widened. Melody must have been stunned. The grey dress, with bands of black silk around the hem, fitted a little too well, and it was short enough to show plenty of the opaque black stockings that went with the black patent leather shoes.

Velma waved her black satin clutch bag at the desk and smiled. 'Bit of a mess,' she said. 'Makes me feel quite at home.' She sat on the visitor's chair and crossed her legs. She looked radiant. Her green eyes were sparkling, her hair was neatly gathered back.

'How's Tarquin?' I asked.

'He's sleeping now. I borrowed his car and drove into town. I wanted to say sorry about this morning.'

'It was understandable,' I said. 'Forget about it. And tell Tarquin to forget about it, too.'

We eyed each other across the cluttered desk while traffic sounds wafted in through the high window. The neckline of her dress was a deep V bordered by a band of black silk. She looked relaxed; sated almost. There was a glow about her.

'Tarquin's rather ... ' I groped for inoffensive words. 'Highly strung.'

She nodded. 'It's the creative temperament.' She uncrossed her legs and settled the little black bag on her lap. 'I had a letter from the Leeds valuers, making me an offer on the farm. I've been thinking seriously about it.'

'You said you didn't want to sell.'

She sighed. 'Those men scared me. Since they got in, the place doesn't seem the same any more.'

'It's early days,' I said. 'And you shouldn't accept the first offer they make.'

'I took it to some valuers in Barfield. They said it was more than the figure they'd have

181

suggested for an asking price. They said if I wanted to sell, I should think seriously about it.'

'Don't do anything hasty, Velma.'

Laughing, she said, 'I'll try not to.' Then rose to her feet. 'I was passing, so I thought I'd call in and say sorry about this morning. And I'm still waiting for your bill.'

'End of the month,' I said, then frowned at her. 'Do you feel safe on the farm with only Tarquin there?'

'He's sensitive and gentle, Paul. He's a lover, not a fighter. But he'd die for me.'

'You can't ask more than that,' I said softly.

She smiled, then turned and headed out. The sway of her hips didn't set the hem of her dress swinging: the movement wasn't as classy or as electrifyingly eye-catching as Melody's, but it was one of the best sights I'd seen all day. Just in case you're wondering, I ought to tell you, right now, that I consider myself to be a leading authority on posterior sway in the human female. It's something I've made a long and careful study of.

★   ★   ★

I arrived at the Travellers' Friend snack bar ahead of Mrs Pearson, so I got a couple of coffees and found a corner table. She kept me waiting almost twenty minutes. When she walked towards me across the almost empty eating place, her face was composed and her posture erect. She was immaculate in the black pinstripe suit. The creases in the tight-fitting trousers were razor sharp and her black shoes were trimmed with a red that perfectly matched the stripe in the suit.

I rose and pulled a chair out for her. She sat down without thanking me. 'I got you a coffee,' I said. 'But it's probably cold now.'

She dismissed the small talk with a nod, then levelled those cool grey eyes on me. For a moment, I thought she was going to complain that the disk was useless, and then she said, 'It wasn't a quick shag, Mr Lomax.' Her refined voice made the words more shocking. 'And the girl's a slut. Uninhibited is one thing, but allowing herself to be used in that way; doing some of the things she did . . . ' The corners of her mouth turned down and she shuddered. 'Ugh!'

'The picture was clear?'

'Fellini would have been proud of it. You've missed your vocation, Mr Lomax. It could get you a gold at Cannes.' She laughed. 'You're blushing. I've shocked you again.'

'I'm just a little surprised you're able to take it so calmly. I couldn't have watched it.'

'I've had some time to adjust to the

situation. And I've already told you, I'm not ruled by my emotions.'

Her fingers were laced together on top of her handbag. They were quite still. I'm sure she was being truthful, but I was amazed she could stay that calm after spending more than two hours watching her husband make love to another woman. The tender sex — when it suits them, they can have iron-hard hearts.

'How much do I owe you, Mr Lomax?'

I'd begun to feel angry at the way I'd allowed myself to be pressured into doing the job, at the high-handed way she'd made her demands. On a sudden impulse, I doubled the figure I'd worked out during the drive over.

She didn't even blink, just clicked open her handbag and flicked through the contents. Folding the notes, she laid them on the table, covered them with her hand and slid them over. When I took them, my fingers touched hers. They were icy cold, despite the warmth of the day.

'We've never met, have we, Mr Lomax?'

'Only in court,' I said. 'When you were presiding over the bench.'

She smiled. 'Of course. Only in court. And you've no copies of the disk, no notes, no records?'

I shook my head.

'I'm very grateful to you, Mr Lomax. You've been most efficient. Would you give me five minutes to get away before you leave?'

She rose and walked off. Her high heels were rock steady, and so was her rather scrawny posterior.

I gave her the five minutes' start, then drove over to the love nest in Albert Street and retrieved the surveillance gear. There were no empty bottles, no chocolate wrappers; but the tangled sheets were still permeated by the fragrance of the girl's perfume, and the more acrid odour of Andrew Pearson's sweat.

11

The Admiral Nelson is the only pub in Barfield that's escaped the modernizers' restless hands. Brass and mahogany, cut glass and stained glass; it's a gloomy Edwardian building that specializes in real ale. Hidden away behind an archway off the market square, it's the place I head for when I want to talk to Stanley Willis, a guy who knows the Barfield building scene. It was 11.30, it wasn't a market day, and we had the place to ourselves.

Sliding from the stool, I moved round the table, sat next to him on the bench seat and unfolded my latest list of benefit cheats. 'Recognize any of these names, Stanley?'

He pointed with a nicotine-stained finger. 'These two are plastering on a flat conversion job. Big house down Boswell Road.'

I scribbled a note on the sheet.

'These guys are working for Spender, the landscaping sub on the Headlands site at Connington. And these,' he picked out three or four names, 'are working for O'Gradys, the road surfacing firm. They're on the Headlands site, too. Don't know the rest, but it's a pound to a penny they'll be somewhere on the Headlands development. Norris wants it finished. Sacked the site foreman last week and brought another man in to drive it along faster.'

'Norris . . . Norris . . . ' I remembered my conversation with Foster, the ugly cop, and something Mrs Pearson had said when I located her husband's love-nest. 'Would that be Alan Norris?'

Stanley drank deeply at the glass of Old Nathan. 'That's right.' He belched. 'Alan Norris. Strathmore Developments.'

'Fair hair, cut short, heavily built, flat face, lot of expensive dental work?' I said.

'That's Norris. Had to have his teeth fixed after a subcontractor gave him a beating a few years ago. Sub hadn't been paid. Norris said the work wasn't up to scratch, but Terry never did a bad job. They had a row on site. Terry lost it, grabbed a putlog and laid into him.'

'Putlog?'

'Length of steel scaffolding tube. Month later, Terry, his wife, two kids: all dead.'

'And you think Norris . . . ?'

'Certain of it. Terry had this big caravan at Mablethorpe. There was a gas leak while they were sleeping; explosion tore the place apart.' He hoisted up the glass of Old Nathan and sipped noisily. 'Norris is a ruthless bastard.

I've always thought he's a bit crazy. If he walks past you when you're working on one of his sites and he doesn't like the look of you, he'll have you kicked off the job.'

'Let me get you another,' I said. He was starting to talk. I didn't want his throat to get dry. I wandered over to the bar and asked a woman in a wraparound pinafore for the same again. Curtains of wrinkled flesh drooped from her arm when she pulled the pint. Maybe she'd been Lady Hamilton's maid.

Returning to the table, I put the glass beside the three he'd already emptied, then hunched down on the stool, facing him again. 'Did you ever work for Norris, Stanley?'

'Almost everybody's worked for Strathmore Developments. Last time was just before I lost the leg. Foreman picked three of us to go up to his house. His wife wanted a fancy patio laying and some garden walls building. We were told it had to be perfect or we'd never work in Barfield again. Wife's called Barbara. Dark-haired piece. Absobloody-lutely gorgeous. She was scared of him; you could tell that. She'd bring tea out and chat to us when he wasn't there. When he was around, she kept herself scarce. Got a daughter called Sophie. Tall, dark hair, attractive, but she's not got her mother's looks. Used to play tennis with another girl most days; there's a tennis court and a big pool at the house.' He drained his glass then reached for the pint I'd just brought over.

'Where is the Norris spread?' I asked.

'Skelton: little village north of town, on the Wakefield road. House is called Skelton Grange. It's in about ten acres of ground. Big stone place, covered in ivy; set well back at the end of a drive with high walls and a shrubbery all around it. Got three or four guard dogs. Let's 'em loose in the grounds at night and when they're out. Savage-looking things. Big as donkeys.'

I watched him take a few swallows from the glass. I was struggling to make some sense of the video of the meeting in Pearson's office, things Mrs Pearson had said, the gossip I'd just heard. It was like trying to arrange the big pieces of a nursery jigsaw. I knew it was simple, but I couldn't quite get them to fit together and make a picture. 'Does Norris own any of the terrace houses behind the old railway workshops?' I asked.

Stanley wiped a line of froth from his upper lip with the back of his hand. 'Just about owns the lot. Student accommodation in Albert Street and Gladstone Road. I've worked on 'em, got 'em ready for letting. He doesn't do much; just enough to satisfy the housing officer at the college.'

Remembering Fatos and Roman, the two guys I'd put in hospital, I said, 'What about Steelyard Street and the other streets of terrace houses that run down the hill beyond Ashford Park? Does Norris own property there?'

'Quite a bit. He does even less to those. Lets them to migrant workers employed on his sites. A few are let to immigrants.' Stanley raised his glass and drank deeply. The surgeons must have removed his intestines when they amputated his leg. The one and only time I'd drunk a pint of Old Nathan, I'd had to ride the porcelain horse for a couple of days.

I rose and went over to the bar. Lady Hamilton's maid smiled at me, let me see gold glittering amongst translucent teeth. Her sparse hair had been frizzed out and given a blue rinse, and she'd put a lot of powder and lipstick on without bothering with a mirror.

I asked her for another pint of Old Nathan, a large pork pie and sixty Players. She found a tray and a jar of mustard, put the pie on a plate and cut it into portions, then pulled the pint and got the cigarettes. I carried everything over to the table.

'Got to go now, Stanley, but thanks for the chat.'

He eyed me steadily: no small achievement after four pints of Old Nathan. 'You're not messing with Norris, are you?' he said, then belched.

'Not after talking to you.'

'Don't, Paul. He's a hard bastard. Upset Norris, and you're maimed or dead. And the law won't be interested. I'm told he's bunging the Bill, and some of the officers are pretty senior.'

I stepped through the archway and strode off across the market square, relieved to be out of the gloom of the pub and breathing the Barfield air. I'd got a lead on half the benefit cheats on the latest list, and a light was glimmering over the Pearson-Norris business. When I'd told Mrs Pearson her husband had met the girl at a house in Albert Street, she'd said that followed because the girl's father owned most of them. Andrew Pearson was having an affair with Alan Norris's daughter. Short of having an affair with Norris's wife, there was nothing more recklessly stupid he could do.

If I'd kept my thoughts on the business in hand and off Melody Brown, I might have made the connection sooner.

* * *

After you've watched them leaving their homes, you can recognize their faces. When you know where they're employed, it's not difficult to get compromising photographs. By mid-afternoon, I had a dozen images of the two plasterers who were working on the Boswell Road flats. I scribbled names and time-and-place details on an envelope, then dropped the camera's memory chip inside. My mobile phone began to bleep. When I patted my pockets, I couldn't feel it and had to follow the sound until I found it between the seats.

'Paul . . . Is that you, Paul?'

I ran my tongue over the flap of the envelope and stuck it down. 'I'm here, Velma.'

'Thank God. Can you come to the farm? I need you to come now.'

'What's the problem?'

'Tarquin thinks he's killed someone.'

'Thinks?'

'Don't ask questions, Paul. Just come. Come now.'

I took a last look across the debris strewn garden of the big old house. A guy who was supposed to have spinal injuries and needed crutches to walk was shovelling the plaster he'd just mixed into a wheelbarrow. Through an open window, I could hear his 'disabled' friend's radio blaring while he skimmed ceilings. I started the engine, let out the clutch and headed for Branwell Farm, curious to know what fine little mess Tarquin had got himself into.

⋆ ⋆ ⋆

We were in the parlour. Velma and Tarquin were sitting on the huge settee. She was wearing the faded cotton frock and scuffed shoes she worked in. Tarquin's business suit was dark and double-breasted with high lapels, tight in the sleeves and trousers. His head was in his hands. Velma's arm was around his shoulders. Distress was making him incoherent.

'My mother sent them,' he moaned. 'I know she did. God, you can't begin to imagine what her friends are like.'

'Her friends?'

'The New Pentecostals. I've been harangued, prayed over, exorcised. And now they're threatening me.'

'And why would your mother send men to threaten you?'

'Because I'm with Velma. She's found out I've left London and come here. They'll be from the congregation; the men they send to hound people who've dared to leave the church or who aren't paying their tithes. They

193

kept saying, 'Stay away from the farm; stay away from Velma Hartman'. When I told them to piss off, they got angry. I thought they were going to hit me, so I ran away from the lift and went through to the stairs.'

'Lift . . . Stairs?'

'In the multi-storey car park,' he explained irritably. 'Next to the shopping precinct. When I got to the stairs, I went up and waited round the landing. They ran down. When they'd gone, I dashed back to the car. By the time I'd got inside and pulled out, they were running up the ramp from the lower level. I was scared and fed up with it, so I just drove at them. One got out of the way, but I hit the other; threw him against the concrete wall that runs alongside the ramp. He fell and I felt the wheels going over him. When I looked in the mirror, he was just lying there.'

'How did you know they were from your mother's church?' I asked. 'Maybe they're involved with the people who've been tormenting Velma.'

'These men weren't thugs. They wore dark suits and ties. The elders at the church go around like that. Hey!' he protested. 'I know these people. I've had them up to here.' He touched his throat with the side of his hand. 'You should see how they torment the poor buggers who've dared to apostatize, or the people who don't pay their tithes.'

'And you think you've killed one?'

'I know I've killed one. I felt the car bouncing over him.' Tarquin began to rock to and fro, moaning, 'Christ, oh Christ.' Velma wrapped her other arm around him and drew his cheek down on to her breasts.

'I'll have to go to the police,' he wailed. 'It's hit and run. They'll crucify me.'

'Not if you were going to be assaulted. Is your car that blue soft-top?'

When he nodded, I went out into the yard and looked it over. There were no dents or marks on the bodywork. I got down on my back and checked the projecting parts underneath. There were no signs of blood or hair; no disturbance to the film of dirt. Puzzled by it all, I headed back to the parlour. Fundamentalists of all persuasions can get carried away sometimes, but sending half the congregation to rough up a wayward son seemed too crazy to be true.

'Can't see any marks on the car.'

'I hit him,' Tarquin insisted. 'I felt the bump, saw him fall against the wall, felt the wheels . . . '

'Yeah,' I said. I was running out of patience now. 'You've told us that, Tarquin. But there are no marks on the car, and I can't believe your mother would send a couple of guys to hurt you.'

'You don't understand. You've got to live with it to know what it's like. I can't remember how many times she's told me she'd rather see me dead than fornicating, and she means it. I know they were from the church, and I've killed one. Christ, I've killed — '

'What time did this happen?'

'Twelve, twelve-fifteen.'

I flicked open my mobile, dialled a directory enquiries number, asked for Barfield General, then asked to be put through to accident and emergency. When I heard the female voice, I said, 'I'm calling from the car park next to the shopping centre. I've been waiting to meet a colleague, and I've just been told there was an accident here about a couple of hours ago. I'm beginning to wonder if it was the guy I'm supposed to meet.'

'What was his name?'

'Don't know. We're both British Telecom engineers. I was supposed to identify him from the logo on the van.'

'If I don't have a name, I can't — '

'Just tell me if someone was brought in from the shopping centre car park about a couple of hours ago.'

A sigh came down the line. 'One moment.' I heard fingers tapping on keys, then she said, '12.55 — ambulance crew brought in someone from the Princegate multi-storey, level four.'

'Is he — '

'Suspected broken leg,' she interrupted. 'Says here he was hit by a car.'

'Thanks,' I said. 'I'll contact the office and let them know.'

I switched off the phone, looked across at Velma and Tarquin, huddled together on the settee, and said, 'Guy taken in with a suspected broken leg.'

The tension seemed to ebb from Tarquin's body and he managed to lift his cheek from Velma's cleavage. 'I've not killed anyone? It's only a broken leg?'

'Suspected broken leg.'

'Should I contact the police? Tell them I — '

'Forget it, Tarquin. If they were from the New Pentecostals, they might think twice about hounding heathens in future. And if they were from the gang who tormented Velma, they both deserve broken legs.' I made for the door. When I'd reached the gloom of the passageway, I glanced back. 'If I were you, I'd throw a few things into the car and vanish for a while. Enjoy what's left of the summer. Put yourselves out of reach of everyone.'

'We will,' Velma said. She unwrapped her arms from Tarquin's shoulders, rose from the settee and walked me to the outer door. Her hair and her dress were in disarray. She tugged open the heavy door. 'Next week,' she said. 'We'll go somewhere next week.'

'Why not tonight?'

'The Martin Walton commission: *Adam and Eve.* I need another few hours with Tarquin and then a session with Molly and Tarquin posing together. Then I can let it go.'

'Tonight,' I insisted. 'Take my advice, Velma, and leave tonight.'

During the drive home I stopped off, grabbed a burger and fries and had my first meal of the day. I couldn't buy that business about Tarquin's mother having sent her Pentecostal chums to molest him. The gang who'd been tormenting Velma were the more likely culprits.

Things that had been said at the meeting between Pearson and Norris, things that old Stanley Willis had mentioned, kept churning around in my mind. And the visit Velma had had from the valuer called Allot was probably more than a coincidence. I got to thinking a look at the plans locked in Pearson's office might be revealing. Gaining entry wouldn't be a problem: I'd not handed the keys back to Mrs Pearson. Maybe I should go in again and take a more careful look around.

The sun was setting beyond the Barfield skyline, gilding a mackerel sky and silhouetting the spire of the parish church and some high-rise flats. I turned into the car park of the building next to Pearson's offices. I was wearing jeans and a dark sweater. The tools I might need to open locked drawers and filing cabinets were in a holdall in the passenger footwell.

I studied the darkness beyond the windows and glass doors: there were no signs of architects toiling on into the night. Tugging on a pair of thin leather gloves, I grabbed the holdall and strode out across the grass, heading between the islands of shrubs that separated the buildings. When I slid the key into the lock, the glass doors moved. When I pushed, they swung open. Maybe someone was working late after all. The reception desk and a pair of doors leading to rooms beyond were in deep shadow. Everything was steeped in silence. I stood there for a few moments, listening to the sound of my own breathing, then turned and looked back across the parking area. There were no cars other than my own.

The stairs were an arrangement of concrete slabs surfaced with terrazzo. Moving slowly and silently, I climbed to the top, then crossed the landing and looked into the drawing office. The last of the evening sun was gleaming on the bright metal fittings of some drafting machines. It was deserted. I crept along the corridor, entered the secretary's office and padded over carpet to the door in the far wall. Opening it slowly, I peered round the edge. Pearson's office was full of shadows. He wasn't sitting in the swivel chair behind the desk; he wasn't working at the drafting table. I stepped inside. It was all neat and tidy and pretty much as it had been the last time I'd been there.

When Pearson had gone to get the drawings, he'd walked towards the window and moved out of range of the camera. The only thing he could have headed for was the big plan chest. I crossed over and examined it. The shallow drawers didn't have individual locks, but a steel bar that rose up the front could be secured by a padlock under the projecting top. The bar had been swung aside and the padlock was lying on the chest.

I slid open the topmost drawer and looked down on narrow rolls of tracing paper, sketch pads and pencils. Working my way down, I discovered the others were almost empty: just a few faded drawings of schemes that had been designed years ago; nothing for the shopping complex he'd called Gallery Saint John, or the big housing project they'd been talking about.

Moving over to the drafting machine, I rolled back the green canvas cover and saw a half-finished drawing of an ornamental gateway. It looked grubby and smudged, as if it had been there for some time. I replaced the cover, then went over to the desk where some papers were arranged in two neat piles. I flicked through them; they were staff time sheets.

Keys still dangled from a lock beside the knee-hole. Sliding open a deep bottom drawer, I saw files of correspondence with clients, spreadsheets displaying fee income, the sort of stuff a guy running a firm would keep around him, but nothing that mentioned a shopping development near the parish church, or a housing scheme. The other desk drawers held stationery and the usual office stuff. In one I saw neck ties and boxed cufflinks, handkerchiefs and an expensive fountain pen, still in its case. Maybe they were presents from his young lover, things he daren't wear or use in case he was rumbled by his wife.

Rounding the desk, I stepped over to the cupboard that formed the base of the bookcase. It held a meagre stock of bottles, a carton of cigars and a few packets of cigarettes.

The glass-topped table was still stacked with arty magazines. Treading softly over thick carpet, I walked past it, then went behind the long sofa and pushed at the door of Pearson's personal washroom. The light was on. I let go of the handle and the door went on swinging open until it bumped into the wall.

I didn't recognize him at first. He wasn't wearing a jacket, his shirt was open to the waist and the knot in his blue necktie was somewhere over his shoulder. He'd peed his pants: the dark stain was all around his crotch and down his thighs. His eyes were no more than narrow slits in puffy swollen flesh, and he'd lost his front teeth. Without them, his gaping mouth seemed no more than a dark hole.

I was going to step over and feel for a pulse when I noticed blood on the floor and up the walls. I stayed where I was. His flesh had that grey pallor you only get to see on the bodies of dead men. He was beyond help.

Leaning forward through the opening, I glanced around. The glass shelf and expensive bottles were smashed on the floor, and there was a big star-shaped crack in the mirror. Blood, smeared across the white porcelain basin was still a vivid red. I looked closer. Hair and flesh were sticking to the handles of one of the taps, and some pearly fragments in the blood near the basin outlet were his teeth. He'd been dragged in here and beaten to death. As I closed the washroom door, I noticed feet had left dark stains on the oatmeal-coloured office carpet. They faded away beyond the sofa.

This wasn't a good place to be. Picking up the holdall, I headed for the landing, closing doors behind me. At the bottom of the stairs, I stood in the shadows behind the glass entrance and gazed out over grass and shrubs and tarmac. It was growing dark, and street lamps were flickering on along the winding estate road. The place was still deserted.

Minutes later, I was driving across town, heading for home and what was left of a bottle of Scotch.

12

It was a handsome detached house with steep gables and bay windows. Small red tiles covered the roof and its red brick walls and stone trimmings had been mellowed by time and the polluted Barfield air. I'd had some difficulty finding it. Daniel Dalton, Member of Parliament for Barfield North, kept his home address secret. Maybe he didn't want his family pestered by whining voters. Maybe he was afraid the restrained grandeur of the place could lose him a few.

Gravel crunched under my best black brogues when I stepped out of the car and crossed over to the porch. A hoover was droning away deep inside the house, so I held my thumb on the bell push until the noise stopped. Seconds later, the door was opened by a slim fair-haired woman in a green smock.

'I'm trying to locate Mr Dalton,' I said. 'Mr Tarquin Dalton, the dress designer. Is he here?'

'London,' the woman said. 'Mr Dalton in London, doing the government.'

I smiled. Most of the electorate would like

to go to London and do the government. The woman was Polish. Her command of English was limited. I let my smile widen. 'I mean, Mr *Tarquin* Dalton, Mr Daniel Dalton's son. He designs dresses and women's clothes?'

'Dresses?' She gestured at her smock.

I nodded. 'Dresses.'

She turned the corners of her mouth down and shrugged. 'All I know is, he does government. I don't know about dresses.'

'Is Mrs Dalton in?'

'Church,' she said. 'Madam at church.'

'Where is the church?'

She stepped out beneath the porch and pointed down the tree-lined road. 'Two hundred metres. You go that way two hundred metres. Then,' she turned and pointed to the right, 'down lane. Church at end of lane.'

'Thanks,' I said, and smiled. 'You've been very helpful.'

She beamed at me, then blew a raspberry and said, 'Dresses!' before stepping back into the house and slamming the door.

I'd confused her. She was probably thinking the master who did the government indulged in a little cross-dressing. Maybe they didn't go in for that sort of thing in Poland. Either way, she'd see him in a whole new light.

There was room for about twenty cars down the side of the simple brick chapel. Only one car was there; a white Renault Clio. I parked the Jaguar in the adjoining space, then headed round to the entrance. As an afterthought, I plucked the heavy horn-rims from my top pocket and slipped them on. A modicum of gravitas might go down well with the New Pentecostals.

I turned the handle and entered a lobby area. Hymn books were stacked in a tiny bookcase, a wall rack held pamphlets and a blue baize-covered notice board carried a sprinkling of neatly typed announcements. Pressing my nose against a stained glass partition, I peered into a space big enough to garage a couple of buses. Thirty or forty uncomfortable-looking wooden chairs were arranged in rows in front of a refectory-style table and a lectern. Across the back wall, blue and gold gothic letters spelt out: The New Pentecostal Church of God and His Prophets. A baby grand piano, its lid up, stood beside a half-open door in a side wall.

I stepped inside, headed down a central aisle, then crossed over to the open door. The woman standing at a table in the room beyond had dark hair, refined features, huge dark eyes and an expressive mouth. It was Mrs Dalton. The likeness between mother and son was striking.

She was trimming the stems of white lilies and arranging them in a couple of vases. Engrossed, she hadn't heard me approach over the carpet tiles. When I tapped on the open door, she glanced up, startled, then looked me over. The blue pinstripe suit, crisp white shirt and old school tie seemed to reassure her. I smiled, and said, 'Mrs Dalton?'

She gave me an apprehensive look. 'That's right. And you are?'

Moving into the room, I took a visiting card from behind the handkerchief in my top pocket and handed it to her. 'Mark Merrill,' I announced. 'We manufacture women's clothing. We're looking for someone to breathe new life into our range. A buyer who visits us has given me your son's name. She said he was Barfield based. I'm trying to track him down.'

She glanced down at the card. 'He works in London, Mr Merrill; for a fashion house. I doubt very much that he'll be able to freelance for you.'

'He was warmly recommended.'

She smiled proudly. 'He's very talented.'

'Will he be home this week, or at the weekend? We're based in Leeds. I could easily — '

'He's not at home, and he won't be home

this weekend. He's so busy he hardly ever comes up. My husband dines with him once or twice a week, and I go down and see him sometimes.'

'Perhaps I could contact him at the fashion house?'

She frowned, looked uncertain for a moment, then said, 'It's called Sula Zorema.' She gave me a Mayfair address. 'I don't remember the phone number. You'll be discreet, won't you? He's doing so well and they might get upset if they think he's being approached by outsiders.'

Nodding, I noted down the details. 'And there's no chance of him coming home over the next few weeks? I could drive over — '

'No chance, Mr Merrill. But I'm hoping to travel down to see him early next week. Would you like me to give him your card?'

'Would you? I'd be grateful.' I pocketed the pen and notebook and smiled across at her. She responded with a nervous movement of her lips. There was no grey in her hair, no make-up on her tanned face and the pattern on her pale-green summer dress was so understated it hadn't been worth the bother. I could see her shins beneath the work table. They were deeply tanned and her bare feet were tucked into brown leather sandals. I nodded at the flowers. 'You're obviously busy,

Mrs Dalton. I'll let you get on, but thanks for talking to me.'

Back in the car, I realized she hadn't mentioned her husband was in politics when she'd said he dined with their son in London. Most small-town politician's wives would have. Maybe it didn't amount to much as far as she was concerned. Only her boy mattered and, one way or another, she'd lost him.

I keyed the ignition, moved out of the car park, then drove off down leafy lanes, heading for the outer ring road. Her husband hadn't been exaggerating. You only had to the see the haunted look in her eyes, the tension in the muscles of her face, to realize her state of mind was still fragile. I'd managed to find out what I wanted to know without distressing her. As far as she was concerned, Tarquin was safely in London. She hadn't arranged for him to be hassled by men in suits. She'd no idea he was back in Barfield, lying in the arms of Velma Hartman at Branwell Farm.

It was mid-morning, traffic was light and the air was shimmering over sun-baked tarmac as I circled the town. I decided to head out to Skelton and give Alan Norris's place the once-over.

* * *

I slowed to walking pace as I drove past the ornamental gates. Skelton Grange couldn't be seen; its driveway curved into a dense shrubbery that hid the house from the road. A bright steel intercom box had been fixed to one of the massive pillars. It looked out of place beside all the carved stone and black and gold ironwork.

Picking up speed, I motored on. After a hundred yards or so, the high stone wall that enclosed the place turned away from the road and disappeared into a copse of tangled bushes and trees. I eased the car on to the verge, found a gap in the hedge, then made my way back, through the bushes, to the wall, and began to walk beside it.

Up ahead, the trunk of a rotten tree had fallen close to the stonework. I found a foothold amongst exposed roots, clambered on to it, then walked gingerly along moss-covered bark until the top of the wall was at waist level. Skelton Grange was visible now, across a couple of acres of well-tended lawn. Ivy covered its stone walls and whispered against a dozen windows. Ornate chimneys rose out of blue slates that were just visible above the parapets.

Leaves rustled and a dog bounded out of the shrubbery. It leapt up at the wall, snarling, teeth bared, in a frenzy because it couldn't reach me. It was joined by another, then by two more. They were evil-looking, cross-bred things, with black eyes and black bodies and huge slobbering mouths. The barking could probably be heard back in Skelton village. If old Stan Willis had got it right, the Norris's weren't at home and the hounds had been set loose to roam the grounds. They made the place impregnable.

Turning, I retraced my steps down the sloping trunk of the tree, then struggled back through the copse to the road. The dogs were still barking and howling when I tugged open the car door and climbed inside.

Empty drawers in Pearson's office, the disk of him making love to Norris's daughter, his battered body in the washroom . . . the pieces of the jigsaw were clicking into place, and I was pretty sure Velma's problems were all part of the same puzzle. I keyed her number into my mobile, listened to the bleeping, then got the usual announcement about voicemail. Messages were a no-no. I'd have to call again later.

★ ★ ★

Melody waved at me through her reception window as I was climbing the stairs. I came back down and crossed over. She slid the glass aside and whispered, 'The police; they're waiting for you.' I'd been expecting a visit. 'It's the unspeakably disfigured one and the black-haired man who wears gangster sunglasses.'

'Been waiting long?'

'Ten, fifteen minutes.'

'Thanks,' I said, 'I'd better go up.'

She gave me a worried look. 'You're in big trouble this time, aren't you?'

I grinned at her.

'I don't think it's funny, Paul. It's that Hartman woman. When the clients look like that, you always end up hurt or in trouble.' She slid the glass shut and strutted off between the desks.

They were waiting in the outer office. I could hear them talking in low tones as I climbed the carpeted stairs. They fell silent when I began to thud up the old brown linoleum.

'Chief Inspector Foster and Inspector Hogan,' I said brightly. They just looked at me. They didn't say a word. I unlocked the inner door and they followed me into the office. Foster took the only visitor's chair. The black-haired cop with the wraparound shades took up his usual position against the filing cabinet, folded his arms across his chest and grinned at me.

Foster looked around and sniffed. 'Does this place ever get tidied, Lomax?'

'No point. Your boys keep breaking in and throwing stuff around.' I flopped down in the swivel chair, grinned at them across the desk and jacked up an eyebrow.

'Pearson,' Foster growled. 'We've reason to believe you know a party called Andrew Pearson.'

I kept my expression blank.

'He's an architect. Has offices in Telford Place on that new commercial estate called Parkways.'

'Name doesn't mean a thing.' I met Foster's gaze. He knew it was a brazen lie. He must have viewed my DVD of the meeting in Pearson's office before he handed it back. He was watching and waiting; trying to find out if I knew more than he did.

Foster cleared his throat. Hogan stopped grinning.

'You're holding out on us, Lomax. You're refusing to disclose information. I could book you for refusing to disclose information.'

I kept up the blank look. When the silence was becoming unbearable, I was rescued by the tap of heels on linoleum, the rattle of crockery on a tray, then Melody breezed in and swept up to the desk.

'Coffee?' She beamed at Foster. She was

making up for the little scream she'd let out when she'd first seen him.

'Thanks. I'd appreciate a cup.' He smiled back, and his fractured face morphed into something almost human. He could give me lessons in ogling. His misaligned eyes were feasting greedily on the vision in the yellow summer dress. Hogan was grinning again.

Melody began to pour. 'It's the over-sixties line-dancing classes, isn't it, inspector? He's been making a nuisance of himself again.' She smiled at Foster: 'Milk and sugar?'

'No milk,' Foster growled. 'Just three sugars.'

Melody ladled in the spoonfuls, handed him the cup, then went through the ritual with Hogan. When she put my cup on the blotter, she frowned at me, and said, 'I told you the old ladies would complain.'

Foster and Hogan were too busy looking to listen. She gave Foster another dazzling smile, then headed for the door. They turned and gazed after her until she'd moved out on to the landing.

The atmosphere had lightened. Foster watched me while he sipped noisily at the coffee, then he said, 'You're about as much use as a ballet dancer with a wooden leg, Lomax.'

I grinned at him across the cluttered desk and said nothing.

'Mrs Pearson,' he went on. 'Do you know Mrs Emma Pearson?'

I laced my fingers over my chest and looked thoughtful, then let my face brighten. 'Magistrate,' I said. 'I've been in court when a Mrs Pearson's been presiding. Would that be the woman?'

Foster glowered at me. Hogan swirled coffee around his mouth like a wine taster, swallowed, then started grinning again.

'Yesterday evening,' Foster growled. 'Where were you yesterday evening, between seven and eleven?'

'Drove home from Branwell Farm. Had a meal. Pottered around. Went to bed.'

'You drive a dark-green Jaguar, FD51 UH0?'

I nodded. He'd had the records trawled.

'We've got a team going through traffic and surveillance videos. Tedious job. Sure you didn't motor through that commercial estate where Pearson has his offices?'

'Home,' I insisted. 'Like I said, I ate something, pottered around for a while, hit the sack.'

He let out a resigned sigh. 'Norris,' he growled. 'You know anyone called Alan Norris? Owns a big construction firm called

Summerfield Developments. Lives out at Skelton.'

I shook my head. He was repeating the same old question. The grin was freezing on my face.

Foster's voice softened. 'How's Velma?'

'Coping,' I said.

'She's getting over it?'

'She's coping with it,' I snarled. 'She'll never get over it.'

He smiled. It was like two men staring out at me above the one mouth. 'Yeah,' he said, 'I think she's gorgeous, too. You still giving her protection?'

'Her partner's staying with her, so I'm bowing out. He came up from London. Dress designer.'

'You mean the politician's son? Tarquin Dalton?'

'The same,' I said, surprised he was so well informed. Dalton had taken pains to keep his son's amorous adventure from the police. Maybe the details had been fed back when his wife told Social Services.

'Does his mother know?' Foster asked.

'She thinks he's in London,' I said. 'It's best for her, best for him, best for Velma, if it's left that way.'

Foster's smile widened. 'It's still a love thing, then?'

'Passionate,' I said, still wondering how he knew so much.

Foster looked at Hogan. 'Better set up a second team to trawl through those traffic and surveillance videos.' He heaved his great bulk out of the chair. The movement was slow and probably painful. 'That business with Velma Hartman — the hoodlums and the assault — what do you make of it, Lomax?'

I shrugged. 'Bunch of sick bastards pestering a woman living alone.'

He started to laugh. 'You're a plausible sod, Lomax. Either that or you're the kind of guy who adds two and two and gets three.'

Hogan's grin widened. He pushed his shoulder off the filing cabinet and followed Foster out.

When their footsteps faded, I picked up the phone and dialled Velma's number. After a dozen bleeps, I got voicemail again, so I rang off. Velma was too preoccupied with one thing or the other, probably the other, to concern herself with mundane things like telephones. If I wanted to talk with her, I'd have to drive out to Branwell Farm.

★　★　★

Tarquin's blue soft-top was parked next to the little red Fiat owned by the model called

Molly. The farmyard was getting pretty crowded, so I lurched on over the rutted ground and docked the Jaguar next to some old chicken coops. Walking back to the house, I began to understand why Velma had wanted to hold on to the place. Tall trees were sheltering the house and its outbuildings from the worst of the sun's glare, and the muted sounds of birds singing and insects droning were defining the peace and quiet of the place.

The iron-bound door was locked. Velma and Tarquin were remembering to take some precautions. I gave the boards a pounding, then pulled in a couple of lungsful of fresh air and listened to country sounds while I waited. After what seemed like quite a while, a faint voice called, 'Who is it? Who's there?'

'It's Paul, Velma. I need to talk with you.'

Feet clattered down the stairs, then tapped along the flagged passageway. A key turned, and the heavy door swung open. 'Come on in.' She stood aside. I entered the windowless porch and waited beside the old bike while she closed the door.

When I followed her into the passage, I said, 'Tried to reach you on the phone. I just got voicemail, and I didn't want to leave messages.'

She laughed. 'I'm not sure where the

mobile is. And I keep forgetting to charge the batteries.'

'That's not sensible, Velma; not after all the trouble you've had.'

She laughed. 'Don't scold me, Paul.' She still had that glow about her. She was wearing the faded cotton dress, the scuffed down-at-heel shoes that she worked in. Her red hair was drawn back and restrained with a broad green ribbon.

'We need to talk, in private; you, me and Tarquin. Can we?'

'Just give me ten minutes,' she begged. 'Molly's here; modelling with Tarquin. I'm putting the finishing touches to the painting. She'll be gone in ten minutes.' She pushed at the parlour door, gestured for me to go inside, then dashed back up the stairs and clattered into the studio.

I wandered into the parlour, sank into the big settee and closed my eyes. Images began to flicker through my mind: the body in the washroom, slavering dogs beyond a high wall, the cop with the fractured face and his grinning sidekick with the wraparound shades. Mrs Pearson was clever and shrewd. She'd hired me, but she'd managed to distance herself from me. I'd supplied two disks. The cops had found one, and Foster had handed it back. Why, when it was

219

evidence of illegal entry; evidence that I knew Pearson? Maybe he didn't want it held in police files for bent coppers to find. And why the porno flick? Why had Mrs Pearson asked for that? The stills of her husband and the girl, at the gallery and in the lift at the Radisson Hotel, were all she needed to prove infidelity. I was pretty sure I knew where I could find the disk, if it hadn't been destroyed.

Time. Things needed time to work themselves out. And I needed time so I could help them along a little. If Foster hadn't been winding me up about the team trawling through traffic footage, time might be something I didn't have too much of. If the cops came for me, I'd have to start bleating about client confidentiality. There was no chance Mrs Pearson would stand up and be counted. She'd deny ever having seen me outside the court she presided over. Two videos of a murdered man, and they'd both been recorded by me: I made a mental note to dump the video camera and disk recorder. The cops were sure to have an expert who could prove the disks had been made on my equipment.

Women's laughter floated down the stairs, then feet began to clatter on bare boards. I peered through the half-open doorway into the gloomy passage. The dark-haired woman called Molly trotted past, followed by Velma. The outer door opened. Molly said something I couldn't hear, then the two women shrieked with laughter. Goodbyes were exchanged, the door slammed and a still-smiling Velma came into the parlour. 'Sorry I kept you waiting, Paul. Tarquin's in the studio. Shall we go up?'

'Will I be safe?'

She laughed. 'He's got over that silly misunderstanding.'

I followed her up the stairs and into the studio. Tarquin was lounging on the empire style couch in a red silk dressing gown embroidered in the oriental manner. When I stepped into the room, he gave me a sulky glance, then drew its folds over his thighs and the darkness around his groin.

'The picture's more or less finished,' Velma said. 'Come and take a look.' She linked her arm in mine and led me over to the far wall, then we turned and looked back at the canvas clamped in the huge easel. 'Just a few tiny changes here and there, then I'll have to stop tinkering and let it go.'

Light was flooding through the glazed half of the roof, illuminating forms and colours, the hard bright edges and soft shadows. The figures were life size. It was vividly real. I could see now why she'd wanted the models to pose together. The woman's body, the hand holding the gleaming red apple, cast shadows over the man. Tarquin's broad slender form contrasted with Molly's voluptuous softness. Velma hadn't painted in their public hair. The omission somehow intensified their nakedness, made them seem more sexual, more elemental.

'Breathtaking,' I murmured, and meant it.

A sneer curled Tarquin's lip. I guess he was thinking it was the no-account opinion of a hairy oaf. Velma squeezed my arm. She'd taken pleasure from the comment.

'It should be in the Tate,' I said. 'Not hanging over some bidet-importer's dining table.'

Velma laughed. 'Pictures become a part of you, but you've got to let them go.'

She still had her arm linked in mine. I walked her back to the elegant little couch. Tarquin edged along and she sat down beside him. When he wrapped his arm around her, his robe fell open. He didn't seem to care. Why should he? His naked image was exposed for all to see on the canvas.

I sat down on the old wooden chair that had lost its back, and said, 'Your mother didn't send those men to hassle you, Tarquin.

She's no idea you're in Barfield.'

He sat up straighter and took his arm from around Velma's shoulders. 'How do you know?'

'I went to see her.'

He looked outraged. 'You went to see my mother!'

'It's OK,' I said soothingly. 'She didn't know who I was. I told her I was a clothing manufacturer looking for a designer; that you'd been recommended and I was trying to locate you. She said you were in London. She said she was seeing you next week and that she'd give you my card. She even gave me the name of the fashion house, Sula Zorema, and told me to be discreet when I phoned.'

He calmed down, settled back into the couch and drew Velma close to him again. She laid her hand on his thigh. I got to thinking it would soon be time I left.

'The men in suits must have been part of the team that's been pestering Velma,' I said. 'I think you should ship the painting out, then take that holiday. Disappear for the rest of the summer.' I looked at Velma. 'And don't even think about selling the farm if you don't want to.'

'But I already have,' she said. 'At least, I've said I will. The Allot man, the land agent looking for a place for a client, called again yesterday. The valuers in Barfield said the offer was more than fair, and after all that's happened, I thought I'd be better off selling.'

'Promising's a long way from signing,' I said. 'String him along.' I rose and made for the landing. Velma joined me, and followed me down the stairs.

When we were standing in the porch with the door open, she said, 'You still haven't let me have your bill.'

'End of the month,' I repeated.

'It was the end of the month yesterday.'

I smiled. 'So it was.' I was about to head for the car when I paused and said, 'The agent that came to see you, the guy called Allot; was it Charles Allot?'

'Yes, Charles. He gave me a card. I'm almost certain it says Charles.'

'Tall guy, handsome, distinguished-looking, cultured, very charming?'

She laughed. 'You've asked me this before, Paul. The Charles Allot who came to see me was middle-aged, short, plump and combed his hair over his bald patch. But he was very pleasant in a fussy kind of way.'

'Thanks,' I said. 'It's just that a valuer called Allot's been described to me as being tall and handsome.'

'Perhaps the firm's run by father and son,' she said.

'Maybe.' I stepped out into the yard and smiled back at her. 'Don't sign anything, Velma. Just keep stringing them along.'

13

Barfield Borough Council's Planning Department is on the tenth floor of a grimy concrete office block located close to the railway station. The view from the reception area takes in the north- and south-bound tracks, the marshalling yards and the streets of terrace houses that back on to the old railway workshops. While I waited for a planner to see me, I passed the time locating Albert Street and working out which roof belonged to the house where Andrew Pearson had met his young lover. I wondered if she knew he'd been murdered. The news hadn't broken in the press.

'Mr Merrill . . . Mr Merrill . . . '

Suddenly remembering Merrill was the name I'd given, I turned and beamed at the receptionist.

'Miss Holland will see you now.' She gestured towards a door. 'Take a seat in interview room three. She'll be with you shortly.'

'Miss Holland; is she . . . ?'

'She's the assistant planner who deals with Moxton and the other villages to the east of the Borough.'

'Thanks.' I flashed the cute little blonde another smile, then went into the windowless interview room, pulled a chair from under the long table and sat down. I didn't have to wait long. Seconds later, a plump woman of about thirty, with short mousy hair, stepped through another door. For the few seconds it was open, I had a glimpse of sunlight flooding a big general office. Working hard at being the gentleman, I rose when she entered and smiled across at her.

'Mr Merrill?'

I nodded, held out a hand, and said, 'And you're Miss Holland.'

She unfolded a map and turned it so it would be easy for me to read. After we'd sat down, I fumbled in my top pocket, plucked out the heavy horn-rimmed spectacles and slid them on.

'Reception told me you're looking for sites in Moxton that have been cleared for development.' She sounded tired and not very interested; she was giving information because it was what she was paid to do.

'That's right,' I said. 'We're involved in identifying land for housing, but it's a site to the east of Moxton I'm interested in.'

Glancing down at the map, I found Moxton, then ran my finger along the meandering country road. Hawthorne Lane and Branwell Farm were at the edge of the sheet. I pointed at the farm, peered at her over the horn-rims and said, 'Around here. I understand there's more than a hundred acres up for sale.'

She was interested now. Her body had stiffened and her brown eyes were suddenly alert. She gave me a worried little smile. 'I thought you wanted to discuss sites within the Moxton village envelope.' She laughed. 'Branwell Farm's well into the green belt. There's absolutely no possibility — '

'Pocket handkerchief plots in Moxton wouldn't interest the people I represent, Miss Holland. And I've been reliably informed that consideration's being given to releasing a swathe of land to the east of the village for housing development.'

She let out another nervous little laugh. 'Reliably informed?'

I looked at her and beamed. 'Very reliably informed, Miss Holland.'

She gazed back at me, her expression puzzled and concerned. Her plump face was greasy, her mouth turned down. The short-sleeved blouse she was wearing had a high scooped neck. Its green and brown leaf pattern made it look drab. There was a ring, made from some black material, on her wedding finger, and a narrow black leather bracelet around her wrist. She chewed her lip, then said, 'Services; the land's distant from all services.'

'I understand provision's currently being made for foul drainage, and surface water can be discharged into the beck.' I spoke with conviction. Having viewed the video of the meeting in Pearson's office several times, I could almost recite the conversation he'd had with Norris, word for word.

Worried brown eyes flickered over my face. 'I . . . I'm not aware of any arrangements of that kind, Mr Merrill.'

Ignoring her, I went on, 'I need to establish when drainage will become available, and what type of development would best satisfy the planning authority.'

'I really do think you've been misled about this, Mr Merrill. The land's outside the village envelope, deep within the green belt, and I'm unaware of any proposals for drainage.'

Softening my voice, making it persuasive, I said, 'My information's completely reliable, Miss Holland. Could it be that you've not been kept informed of things that are being arranged?'

She swallowed hard. 'I . . . I think I'd like to invite my section head to join us, Mr Merrill. He might know something about this, but I very much doubt . . . ' The words tailed off in a nervous little laugh and she rose to her feet. When she dashed back through the door into the big general office, I noticed she was wearing brown culottes.

I leaned back in the uncomfortable chair and did some more waiting. Talking about developing land around Branwell Farm had made little Miss Holland very uneasy. Pearson and Norris had said nothing to indicate where the housing land was, but I was becoming more certain by the minute that it all belonged to Velma Hartman.

The door swung open and a tallish guy in a neatly pressed dark suit followed Miss Holland into the room. Rising to my feet, I held out a hand. 'Mr . . . ?'

'This is Mr Sheldon, Mr Merrill.' Miss Holland sat down while we were shaking hands. 'He's the senior planning officer responsible for development in the rural areas of the borough.'

Sheldon sat next to Miss Holland, found Branwell Farm on the map and rested his finger on it. When he looked up at me he was smiling. I guessed it was with amusement; he wasn't trying to be friendly. 'Miss Holland tells me you've been informed that land belonging to Branwell Farm is going to be cleared for housing development.'

Returning his smile, I said, 'Reliably informed.'

'May I ask by whom?' His smile widened.

'I'm in the business of searching out building land for clients, Mr Sheldon. I'm given a lot of confidential information and I'd rather not reveal my sources.'

'How many hectares?'

I frowned at him over the horn-rims. His smile had become knowing. I sensed he was trying to check me out. Velma had said she owned more than a hundred acres, but I'd no idea how many hectares that made. Pursing my lips, I shrugged and said nonchalantly, 'About 150 acres.'

Miss Holland's eyebrows shot up.

'And you've learned that arrangements are being made for the drainage?' Sheldon asked.

'The eastern region sewerage scheme. The sewers beyond Moxton are to be re-routed along the low side of the land.'

Sheldon sucked in his cheeks to hide a satisfied smile and looked at his colleague. 'Mr Merrill may have information we're not privy to, Mary. I think he needs to discuss this with Mr Osborne.'

'Mr Osborne?' I remembered the name.

'The borough's chief planning officer,' Sheldon said.

'Could I see him now?'

'Meetings,' Sheldon said. 'He's in meetings all day.' He reached for an internal phone and keyed in a number. After a few seconds, he said, 'Could you have a word with Mr Osborne, Wyn? I'm in a meeting with a Mr Merrill and he's raised proposals that really ought to be discussed with the chief.'

I heard a high-pitched twittering.

'I know his diary's full, Wyn, but this is something he'd want to be involved in. Can you slip a note into him at the meeting? Tell him Mr Merrill wants to discuss a large housing development to the east of Moxton.'

There was more twittering, then Sheldon leaned back in his chair, phone against his ear, and stared up at the ceiling. Miss Holland looked down at her hands. A few seconds later, the door to the general office opened, beady eyes peered at me around the edge, then it closed again.

Miss Holland glanced at Sheldon and whispered, 'Who was that?'

'Langham,' Sheldon muttered tersely.

Miss Holland mouthed a silent, 'Oh.'

Faint sounds came from the phone. Sheldon looked at me and said, '2.15 today. Would that be convenient?'

'Fine,' I said.

'Mr Merrill says that's fine.' More faint sounds drifted over and Sheldon glanced up at me. 'Could you tell us the name of the firm you represent, Mr Merrill?'

'This afternoon,' I said. 'I'll put Mr Osborne in the picture this afternoon.'

Sheldon passed the message to the woman called Wyn, cradled the phone, then asked, 'What type of development do your clients have in mind, Mr Merrill?'

'Mixed,' I said. 'But high quality.' I struggled to remember Pearson's conversation with Norris. 'Town houses; they're popular. Apartments for singles, but mostly decent detached housing.'

'What about density?' he asked. 'What figure would you be aiming for?' I guessed he was checking me out again.

Beaming at him across the table, trying to win time to think, I said 'Density?'

'Dwellings per hectare, or per acre if you prefer.'

'That's something the architects engaged by my client would discuss with you, Mr Sheldon.' He was smiling broadly now. I whipped off the horn-rims and slid them behind the handkerchief in my top pocket. '2.15 then,' I said, and shook hands with them both. 'I'll ask at reception for Mr Osborne.'

I crossed the green-carpeted lobby, punched the button for the lift and watched the illuminated floor numbers change. Out of the corner of my eye, I saw someone tall, in a dark suit, push at the doors to the stairwell and pass through. When I stepped out on to the street, Sheldon was waiting for me.

'Forgive me for asking this, but you're not a planning consultant, are you, Mr Merrill?'

'I'm checking out land for housing around Moxton, Mr Sheldon.'

He was frowning at me now. 'But you're not interested in acquiring it, are you? If you tell me who you are, I might be able to help you.'

I eyed him steadily; said nothing.

'You're from the police, aren't you?'

'I'm carrying out an investigation,' I said evasively.

He gave me a knowing look. 'So, you've finally moved in. It's not before time.'

I just smiled and met his gaze while I listened to the traffic rumbling by on the busy road. He was frowning at me in a thoughtful kind of way. A lorry with a heavy load roared past, then he seemed to reach a decision.

'I'd like to talk to you,' he said. 'I feel I've got to talk to someone before I go.'

I nodded towards a pub on the far side of the road. 'Fancy a drink?'

'Too early for me. And it's too near the office. How about that little snack bar in the market square?'

'Fine,' I said. 'Now?'

'Fifteen minutes. I'll let them know on reception I've been called away, then I'll join you.'

★ ★ ★

'It's instant,' I said, sliding the cup across. 'They've not heard of cappuccino.'

Sheldon grinned at me and reached for the sugar dispenser. We looked out of place in the grubby snack bar; him in his neatly pressed dark-grey suit, me in my courtroom pinstripe with the old school tie and pocket handker-chief.

'You said you wanted to talk to someone before you went away. You're going on holiday?'

'Emigrating.' He sipped at the coffee. 'Canada. I've got a post with the Montreal City Planning Department. Wife's a pharma-cist: she's got a job at the hospital. We want somewhere decent for the kids to grow up. The problems at the council gave me the push I needed.'

'Problems?'

Ignoring the question, he went on, 'My leaving do's on Friday. We fly out next Wednesday. You've got to keep what I tell you to yourself until after we've gone. And I don't want dragging back to give evidence. I just want to tell you things I know before I leave. OK?'

'That's fine,' I said. 'There's just you and me here. No witnesses. What you tell me might fill in some gaps; confirm things we're not sure about.'

'It's been going on for more than three years. Mary's worried sick. So are most of the other professional staff.'

'Mary?'

'Mary Holland: the planner you met today. They allow her to work part-time, ten until four. She's a single mother so the job's important to her. She's scared to do or say anything that might get her the push.' He was feeding me information I didn't need; trying to explain why they'd kept quiet. Maybe he was feeling guilty.

'Why would she be scared?' I asked, then sipped at the coffee. It tasted like roasted rabbit droppings.

'We began to sense things weren't as they should be when they approved a housing development on a site called the Headlands. About a hundred houses, just outside Tadwell. You probably know it.'

I nodded. 'Little village a few miles north of town.'

'It should never have been approved. It

more than doubled the size of the settlement, and sewers had to be extended and enlarged; but Osborne put a persuasive report to committee, Bradley lobbied the members, and it went through.'

'Bradley?'

He gave me a questioning look. Clearly, I should have known who Bradley was.

'Chairman of the planning committee,' Sheldon explained.

'*That* Bradley,' I said. 'Are you telling me they were taking back-handers?'

'Chief throws a drinks party at Christmas; just senior staff and the chairman and vice chairman of the planning committee. Bradley got a bit plastered one year. Started bragging about what he called his consultant's fee. Any application that's tricky, and that means every housing site of any size, he gets a thousand pounds a house for nursing the planning application through the system.'

'This Headlands site: you said a hundred houses, so that would make him a hundred thou'.'

Sheldon nodded.

'The Branwell Farm site,' I said. 'Hundred and fifty acres. How many houses there?'

'Depends on quality, mix and layout, but you could reckon on fifteen hundred. They'd develop the site in phases; probably spread it over five or ten years.'

'Fifteen-hundred at a thousand apiece: million and a half. Feelings could run very high over that kind of money.'

'That's just Bradley's consultant's fee,' Sheldon said. 'It's the developer who makes the serious money.'

'Alan Norris, Strathmore Developments?'

Sheldon nodded.

'Strathmore did the Headlands site,' I said. 'Any others?'

'Three sites, all smaller, one an infill they'd have got planning permission for anyway, but the other two wouldn't have been approved if Osborne hadn't massaged the committee report and Bradley hadn't worked on the members.'

We eyed each other in silence for a while, then he grinned and asked, 'How did you find out about the re-routing of the sewer to the low side of Branwell Farm? The report's not been to committee yet.'

I ignored his question, asked one of my own, 'I suppose moving the sewer will have cost implications?'

'Significant,' Sheldon said. 'Osborne's going to tell committee it's an investment for the future. Even if the land's within the green belt now, they may want to release it for development later, and they may as well make provision for the drainage. Trouble is, putting it in the valley means the sewage has to be pumped when it gets further down the system. Engineers put the extra cost at more than a million. Osborne's going to suggest it should be recovered from developers.'

'Sounds plausible,' I said. Then asked, 'This eastern region drainage scheme, when does it start?'

'It's started. They've linked up most of the outlying villages served by small sewage works and cesspools. The new sewers should be passing through Moxton in about a year's time.'

I gave him a thoughtful look. 'You're emigrating, Mary Holland's too scared to talk; I know it's the kind of sleaze no one wants to be mixed up in, but why so scared?'

'A colleague called Jackson raised concerns with the union rep about a year ago. He only told a few of us what he was doing; he didn't want it spread around that it was him pointing the finger. We haven't been able to discover much about what happened after that. We know the union rep went to the chief executive and got nowhere, so he went to the police. Three months later, Jackson left without saying a word; went lecturing at some university down south.'

'And the union rep?'

'Dead. Truck loaded with gravel crashed into his car. Crushed it flat.'

'What about the truck driver?'

'He scarpered; just left his truck on top of the car and ran. Albanian without a work permit. He'd fled the country before the police knew it was him driving the truck. Seems he didn't even have a licence to drive.'

'Do you think Osborne's getting back-handers?'

Sheldon took a deep breath and let it out slowly. 'Maybe, maybe not. But he and his wife spend a lot of time at Skelton Grange; playing tennis, drinks around the pool, partying with Norris and his wife. Osborne's a bit of a social climber, so he'd like that sort of thing, but I wouldn't say he'd be stupid enough to take a cash handout. Anyway, Bradley and the other committee members would make his life a misery if he didn't toe the line. They probably control him that way.'

'When we were in the interview room,' I said. 'Someone put his head round the door and took a good look at me. Who was it again?'

'Langham,' he said. 'Brian Langham. Acts as Osborne's deputy. He usually does the first draft of sensitive committee reports.'

'Is he in on it?' I asked.

'He must know about it: most of the senior

staff know something's going on. And he'll understand the pressures Osborne's under. He's old enough for the pension to be starting to matter, so he's probably keeping his head down and doing what he's told.' Sheldon grinned at me. '*He* doesn't get invited to Skelton Grange.'

'More than a million quid,' I said softly. 'Enough to make some guys stab their granny.'

'And grandpa too,' Sheldon said. He leaned on the table. 'Don't think there's anything more I can tell you. Thanks for the coffee.'

We rose to our feet and ambled out into the market place, leaving behind the lingering aroma of a thousand greasy meals. I said, 'Thanks, Mr Sheldon. You've been very helpful.'

He grasped my hand and shook it. 'Had to tell someone before I left the country. I realized you were getting in amongst it back there at the meeting. You've got police written all over you.'

I smiled, said nothing.

'You'll be discreet, won't you; at least until I've flown out?'

'No witnesses, no notes,' I said. 'It stays with me. And one way or another, I'll use it to nail the corrupt bastards.'

14

It was noon when I arrived at the office. Hot July was drifting into scorching August, and the heat in the attic was unbearable. I opened both dormer windows, then ambled back to the waiting room and opened the window through there. When I got behind the desk, a faint breeze was stirring papers and the temperature was dropping down to blood heat.

I slit open an official-looking envelope and pulled out another list of tax dodgers and benefit cheats. The covering letter asked for a progress report on the names they'd already sent me. It brought home the fact that I was spending too much time on Velma Hartman's business, and not enough on my own. I hadn't billed her yet, and when I did I intended to keep it modest. It was guilt. I still felt bad about having acted the way I did; about not having insisted she pressed the police to give her more of the attention she'd paid taxes for.

Dropping the letter on that week's pile, I mulled over the conversation with Sheldon. What he'd told me was interesting. It put flesh on the skeleton, confirmed what I'd suspected, but, apart from telling me I ought to warn Velma, I couldn't figure out how I could use it.

The tap of heels on old linoleum sounded through the open doors and Melody breezed in, blonde hair pinned up, diamond studs flashing on her ears, the black designer suit fitting her like a second skin.

'Been to court?' She nodded at the pinstripes, then balanced a tray on the piles of papers. 'Chilli con carne. Is that OK?'

'Borough Planning Office. And chilli con carne's fine.'

Melody peeled foil from a carton and emptied rice on to a plate. 'Jane fetched it from that new Mexican place. The manager's taken a shine to her, so it should be edible.' She took foil from a second carton and poured out the sauce.

'Smells good.' I unwrapped cutlery from a paper napkin.

Melody tut-tutted. 'You're going to get sauce all over that nice silk tie.' Taking the napkin from me, she unfolded it and tucked it in my collar, then perched her neat little posterior on the edge of the desk.

I forked up some of the rice and sauce, then drew in rapid little breaths, trying to cool the hot mouthful while I chewed. 'Tastes

'. . . as good . . . as it looks.'

She eyed me reproachfully. 'It's like feeding time at the zoo, Paul. If you ate more delicately it wouldn't burn your mouth.'

'I'm not what you'd call a delicate kind of guy.' I grinned up at her, then forked up some more.

'You're not even a guy, Paul. You're a Neanderthal. In fact, I may be insulting Neanderthals. Perhaps you're just a primate.'

'Primate?' I panted and chewed.

'As in monkeys and apes.'

I swallowed. 'Thought you meant as in archbishops.'

She rolled her eyes upwards and laughed. 'You, in a cope and mitre, giving a blessing? The mind boggles.'

'I'd give you a blessing you'd never forget.'

'Now you're being blasphemous.'

'What's blasphemous about giving a blessing?'

'Don't provoke me, Paul. You know what I mean.'

I forked up another mouthful. My eyes were browsing over the vision perched on the desk. While I chewed and sucked in cooling air, I mumbled, 'You're looking formidable again today.'

'Business meeting. Charles Allot wants to know whether or not I've decided to sell.'

'Couldn't he have asked you that over the phone?'

She gave me a coy little smile. 'He said he'd prefer to discuss things with me over dinner.'

'Charming Charles is taking you out to dinner again?'

'Do you have a problem with that?' Her smile had widened and her big blue eyes were sparkling.

I put the fork down, plucked the horn-rims from my top pocket, slid them on and frowned up at her. She started to giggle.

'Should I have a problem with that, Miss Brown?'

She managed to get the giggling under control. 'He's very handsome; very sweet and gentle. I think you *should* have a problem with that, Paul.'

'Sweet and gentle?'

'Sensitive, too. We can have serious conversations. He doesn't make jokes and silly remarks all the time, and he wouldn't dream of posing in old-fashioned horn-rimmed specs.'

'Just what a woman needs on a big night out; plenty of serious conversation.'

Beaming at me, she said brightly, 'It's called being charming and attentive, Paul.' She slid off the desk and strutted round to the visitor's side. 'By the way, the police called again. The big man said to phone him as soon as you get in. The number's on the slip of paper on the tray.' She headed for the door. 'And the Hartman woman phoned. She wants you to call her. I didn't bother asking for the number. I'm sure it's in your little black book.' When Melody reached the waiting room she paused and looked back. 'Did you catch the news on TV?'

I shook my head.

'Architect called Pearson murdered. Found him in his offices on that new commercial estate.'

The news had broken. 'Did they say how he was killed?'

'Just said he met a violent death; no details.' She turned and headed out on to the landing. Heels began to tap on linoleum, then on stairs, as she descended to the coolness of the lower floors.

Who to call first: Velma or the police? If the police had found something on the traffic monitoring videos, they'd have been waiting for me. They probably just wanted to hassle me on the off-chance I'd let something slip. It had to be Velma. Reaching for the phone, I keyed in her number, listened until the voicemail girl started her spiel, then put it down. Velma had mislaid her mobile again.

Meal eaten, I was tugging the napkin from my collar when I recalled something Velma had said when I'd asked her to describe Charles Allot; about the possibility of the firm being run by father and son. Niggling little doubts began to scurry like spiders. What if Melody hadn't been winding me up about Allot? What if she'd been meeting his son?

Grabbing the phone, I dialled directory enquiries and asked the operator to get me the valuation firm in Leeds. After a short wait, a cheerful female voice announced, 'Allot and Jones?'

'Name's Merrill,' I said. 'I've been meeting quite a few estate agents in Leeds over the past week and I've become confused over a couple. Is Mr Charles Allot a tall distinguished-looking man; I suppose you'd call him handsome?'

A hint of suppressed laughter came down the line. 'Not really, Mr Merrill.'

'Does he have a son, perhaps? Or an associate who'd fit that description? How about Mr Jones?'

'Mr Jones died several years ago, Mr Merrill. There's no one here who'd fit that description.'

'Then he's the short rotund man,' I said, remembering Velma's words. 'Spectacles, combs his hair over his bald patch, very pleasant in a fussy kind of way?'

Laughter was tinkling in the earpiece now. 'That sounds like Mr Allot, Mr Merrill. Would you like me to put you through?'

'That's OK,' I said. 'I just wanted to make sure I'd got the names correct before I write my report. And you're sure there's no tall, handsome, distinguished-looking man at your Leeds office?'

'Unfortunately not, Mr Merrill.'

'Thanks. You've been very helpful,' I said and put the phone down.

Do you have to look at me like that? I know it was pretty sneaky, but what would you have done? What if Melody *was* being wined and dined by some handsome charmer? And Charles Allot could have had a son. A guy's got to check out the competition. Now I could go through the rest of the day free from jealous little doubts; my mind untroubled by sick pictures of a guy ogling Melody in her black designer suit with her hair pinned up in that sexy way. Let's face it, I can give her all the ogling she can handle.

★   ★   ★

There were two cars in the farmyard, a white Renault Clio and Tarquin's blue soft-top. I lurched past, bouncing over the ruts, and parked near the old chicken coops.

The iron-bound door was wide open. When I stepped into the porch I could hear raised voices, and as I moved on down the gloomy passage, I began to make out what they were saying. I paused in the shadows around the kitchen doorway, observing the confrontation.

'She's making you dissolute, Tarquin. Just look at you: it's past noon and you're still wearing that vulgar dressing gown.'

'Don't keep referring to Velma as *she*, Mother. I won't allow you to disrespect her like that.'

Velma turned her head and gave him a grateful look, then leaned into him, her back against his chest, and gathered her jade-green satin robe around her. They were standing by the chipped stoneware sink. Tarquin's mother was facing them, her back towards me, her dark hair arranged in a neat chignon, her arms looking very tanned against the whiteness of her summer dress. The big table was strewn with dirty dishes and all the things Velma had used to prepare dinner the night before.

'Disrespect her?' Mrs Dalton hissed. 'I don't just disrespect her, Tarquin. I loathe and despise her for what she's done to you; for the heartache and pain she's caused me.'

'Mother!' Tarquin protested. 'Either stop it

or get out. You might care to know it was Velma who insisted I told you. I wanted to clear off without saying anything.'

'No, I don't care to know. Because she wasn't bothered about my feelings, Tarquin. She just wanted to tell me she'd won; that she'd finally got you. She's let you have your way with her, and now it's all you can think about. She's enslaved you and you're too blind and stupid to see it.'

'It's you that can't see it, Mother. It's not like that. I love — '

'Love? You're a fool, Tarquin. It's just. You're trapped by lust. And now you're wanting to marry her.' She waved a hand at Velma. 'Marry this smelly old tart!'

Velma's eyes were huge and very bright. In a low shaky voice, she said, 'Tarquin's asked me to marry him, Mrs Dalton, but I've refused. I don't want him to be tied to me. If he changes his mind, he must be free to go. And I'm as amazed as you are by the depth of his feelings for me.'

'Depth of his feelings?' Mrs Dalton's voice was bitter and mocking. 'You seduced him. You seduced my beautiful boy. I could understand it if you were a slip of a girl.' Her voice suddenly rose to a scream. 'But you're old enough to be his mother, you filthy old tart!'

'I *didn't* seduce him. He made advances to me. And if it makes you feel any better, I can tell you I wasn't his first conquest, not by any means.'

'Conquest? How dare you talk about conquest. He was fifteen for God's sake. He was a child.'

'Four days short of sixteen,' Velma snapped. 'And he didn't look or act like he was sixteen.'

'And how old were you?' Mrs Dalton hissed. 'Old enough to know better. Old enough to send him packing. But he didn't make the first move, did he? And you *were* the first. You saw him, you wanted him and you seduced him. You stole my boy's innocence. You corrupted him.'

'No!' Velma protested. 'It wasn't like that. It wasn't like that at all.' Realizing words were useless, she folded her arms beneath her breasts and turned her head away. Anger was blazing on her cheeks and her trembling lips told me that guilt might be troubling her, too. No longer held together by her hands, the lower half of her robe had parted, exposing pale-green satin knickers and shapely legs that were very white.

Tarquin wrapped his arms around her and drew her close. 'Please don't behave like this, Mother. I'm begging you; don't be so beastly.'

His deep voice was pleading and eyes that were too soft and gentle for a man were blazing at his mother over Velma's tousled hair. 'I love Velma. We're going to buy a place in Italy and live there together. Why can't you be happy for us?'

'Buy a place? What with? You haven't got two pennies to rub together.'

'I'm buying it,' Velma said softly.

'So you can take him away from me, take him away from his mother, wreck his career when he's doing so well?'

'I've been offered a job by a fashion house in Milan,' Tarquin said. 'That's why we're going there. 'If you'd stop ranting, Mother, I could explain things.'

'You're eighteen,' Mrs Dalton yelled. 'And ten days ago you were seventeen. How dare you talk to me as though I'm an imbecile? You're still a child to me. And how dare you stand there with your arms around that half-naked whore.'

Velma turned her head and glowered at Tarquin's mother. 'I can understand your distress, Mrs Dalton; I can understand your hating me, but don't ever call me a whore or a tart again.' She'd heard enough. She was drawing a line in the sand. Her hands were on her hips now, her posture defiant, and the folds of her satin robe had fallen open, revealing impressive breasts and a plump stomach that swelled a little over the top of her skimpy knickers.

I don't know whether it was Velma's words or the careless display of so much naked flesh that was the final provocation. Mrs Dalton jerked around, her eyes flickered over the clutter on the table, then her hand darted out and grabbed the big cook's knife. When she turned and faced Velma again, her voice had become a tearful wail. 'You've ruined my life, but you're not going to ruin my son's life. You're not going to destroy my beautiful boy.'

She was gripping the knife in both hands now. I saw her sway towards them and the muscles in her arms tense. A horrified expression contorted Tarquin's features. His mother's back was straightening. She was bringing the knife up in a sweeping curve. He hurled Velma against the cooker, pots and pans crashed down, then his eyes widened and his shocked mouth went slack. When his weight sank on to the knife his mother's legs buckled and they tumbled to the floor. Velma was struggling to her knees. She grabbed at the oven door, pulled herself to her feet, then gazed, horror-stricken, at the two figures, hidden from me now by the table.

I moved into the kitchen and stood beside her. Mrs Dalton was sprawling over her son's body, trying to untangle her legs from his. The knife had entered just below his ribs, slicing upwards and inwards. Blood was everywhere: over his naked torso, his mother's arms and legs, her face, the front of her white dress. Having extricated herself, she knelt beside him, moaning, 'Speak to me, Tarquin. For God's sake, speak to me.' She began to drag in quick shallow breaths, letting them out in panicky screams. And then she grabbed the handle of the knife and tried to pull it out, and with every frantic tug screamed, 'Tarquin! Tarquin! Tarquin!'

Suddenly aware of the enormity of it, Velma gasped, 'My love, my love, what has she done to you,' and lunged forward to join them on the floor.

I wrapped my arm around her waist and held her, stopped her falling to her knees, began to drag her, kicking and screaming, around the big table and out into the passageway.

'Let go of me. Tarquin needs me. I must — '

I gripped her tighter. 'He's dead, Velma. You can't help him now.'

'Dead? How do you know he's dead? I must — '

'He's dead, Velma. It was instant. Leave him to his mother. If you go back in there you'll end up covered in blood and the police could give you a hard time.'

'I don't care. I want to go to Tarquin. I want to.'

'No, Velma. Trust me. You can't imagine the hassle you'll have if you go back in there.' Tightening my hold on her waist, I dragged her out of the house and over to the car. I bundled her into the back, slid in beside her, then reached into my jacket for my mobile phone. She was still struggling and throwing punches with her tiny fists, but the space was too confined for her to get a good swing at me.

'Please,' she moaned. 'Let me go to Tarquin. He needs me. Why won't you let me go to Tarquin?'

I turned my back towards her, let her pound it while I keyed in three nines and waited. Then I went through the endless rigmarole of who I was and where I was and what had happened, until the operator capitulated and said she'd send the police and an ambulance.

Velma was pushing at the far door. She suddenly figured out how the catch worked and it swung open. Reaching across, I wrapped my arm around her and pulled her back, then grabbed her wrists and held them.

She stopped struggling and began to sob. 'You're a callous brute. Why won't you let me go to him? I love him. He's the sweetest, gentlest — '

'He's dead, Velma. You can't help him. Leave him to his mother.'

'How dare you stop me?' she wailed.

'Trust me, Velma. There's blood everywhere. If you get it on you, it will just make things complicated. His mother might even lay blame on you.'

When I felt her body relax, I released my grip, then tried to make her more comfortable by lifting her further into the seat. The satin robe had slid from her shoulders and her legs were sprawling across mine. She was wearing the scarlet shoes with Cuban heels. They looked surreal. Maybe they were the only things she could find when the knock came on the door. Shock was hitting her now and her huge green eyes had fastened on mine, demanding sympathy.

Not many women are more beguiling without their clothes, but Velma was. I took a deep breath. I had to stop looking. Reaching over, I eased her off the leather, lifted the robe over her shoulders, and drew it across her breasts and thighs. Then, taking her hands in mine, I held them tight while the tears bucketed down.

15

He was waiting for me in the outer office. It was still stifling up there, despite the open windows and the lateness of the hour. Grinning at him, I said, 'Hope you've not been sitting there long?'

'Five minutes.' He let out a throaty laugh. 'It's taken me five minutes to get over the climb.' When he rose to his feet, the fractured face came out of the shadows. It still had the power to shock.

I unlocked the office door. He followed me in and flopped down on the visitor's chair.

'Scotch?'

'I'd kill for one.'

I hoisted the office bottle out of the knee hole, found a glass and poured him a good measure. After I'd handed it over, I splashed some in a cup for myself.

'What have you done with Velma?' He nuzzled the glass.

'Taken her to my bungalow. What else could I do? Your people are still crawling all over the farmhouse, she hasn't got anybody, and she's too close to the edge to be dumped in a hotel.'

He gave me a wicked grin. 'I wouldn't mind taking her back to my bungalow.'

'She's just watched her lover being stabbed to death,' I snapped.

Foster laughed. 'Don't get on your high horse. I only said I wouldn't mind taking her back to my place.'

'It's the way you said it,' I muttered.

'What's your blonde friend going to say about it?' He sipped at the whisky.

'Say about what?'

'About you and Velma shacking up together?'

'I'll get some flack,' I said. 'But it's only for a couple of nights. It's happened once before and I survived.'

He stopped grinning, took a long pull at his drink, then frowned at me. 'You really fancy the blonde, don't you, Lomax?'

'We've got something going,' I muttered huffily, wondering what it had got to do with him.

'Will you take some fatherly advice from an older man?'

I had to smile. He took the smile as a yes.

'Don't let your dick do all the thinking. There are some women you can never please. Nothing's ever good enough: you, your job, your pay. What starts out as the fountain of all joy becomes the source of every misery.' He drained his glass. I reached over the desk with the bottle and poured him another.

'I've seen it too many times,' he went on. 'Wives who find they don't like the nightshifts, the overtime, the pay that's never enough, the driving around in squad cars with cute female constables.' He sipped at his glass then gestured with it. 'And you're in the same line of business, Lomax. Except you don't have regular pay and a pension to look forward to; and you're not part of an organization, not part of a team. You're all on your lonesome-ownsome.'

'You'll have me crying into the Scotch,' I said.

'It's a long time since we did any crying, Lomax.' He eyed me steadily for a while, then straightened up in the chair and his gruff voice became businesslike. 'You said you wanted a talk.'

I told him about the meeting at the planning office, about the conversation I'd had afterwards with the planner called Sheldon.

'Did you keep the appointment?' he asked, when I'd finished.

'Appointment?'

'The appointment they fixed up for you with Osborne, the chief planner.'

'Gave it a miss,' I said. 'Not much point

after the conversation with Sheldon. What do you make of it all?'

He turned the corners of his mouth down. 'You've not told me anything I didn't already know. And the information's no more use to me than it is to you.'

'Get warrants; search their homes, search Norris's place.'

'For what?' Foster laughed. 'And I'd need more than accusations and suspicions to get warrants signed.'

'You don't seem to have any bother getting one to search my place,' I muttered.

'You're not numbered amongst the great and the good, Lomax. Who'd give a shit if you complained?'

'Did you know Pearson was bedding Norris's daughter?'

He froze, the glass halfway to his lips, his eyes suddenly alert and watchful. 'Does Mrs Pearson know?'

'Don't think so,' I lied. 'She eats lawyers for breakfast; she'd presume hubby wouldn't dare step out of line.'

The glass found his lips. He sipped, then said, 'Yeah, I've watched her chairing the bench.' Frowning thoughtfully, he went on, 'She's set to claim a lot of insurance. Tied in with some professional indemnity policy. More than a million, plus a pension. And there's the house and the practice.'

'That might not be worth much if Norris takes his business away,' I said.

He drained his glass. When I reached over with the bottle, he shook his head. 'You've been pouring me big ones, Lomax. It's decent whisky, but I've got to say no.' He slid his glass on to the desk. 'Mrs Pearson's been interviewed. Usual stuff: did she know of any enemies, any threats? Had he upset anyone? She just acted dumb.'

'Maybe it wasn't an act,' I said. 'She's just lost her husband. She'd be in shock. Maybe she didn't know anything. Why should she?'

He grinned at me. '*You* knew about it.'

Grinning back, I said, 'The million-dollar question is, did Norris know about it?' Then, changing the subject, asked, 'When's the funeral?'

'Soon. They've done the autopsy, taken pictures, done tests. And the widow's pressing for the release of the body.' He suddenly seemed distant. He was probably wondering if Norris knew about Pearson and his daughter.

'And Mrs Pearson's got pull,' I said.

He grinned. He was paying attention again.

'Velma's decided to sell the farm,' I said. 'She was going to live in Italy with Tarquin.'

'Maybe she'll change her mind now lover boy's dead.'

'It's not just Tarquin and Italy,' I said. 'She's scared. The hoodlums who were harassing her, the assault, Tarquin being threatened.'

Foster raised an eyebrow.

'He was threatened by some well-dressed guys in a car park. He thought his mother had sent the church elders round to stop him fornicating, but I'm sure they were laid on by Norris. He wouldn't want a man at the farm, comforting Velma, making her less inclined to sell.'

'Can you prove it?'

'Not at the moment. What about the guys who assaulted Velma?' I asked. 'Any progress there?'

He shook his head. 'Got prints and a DNA sample, but no matches in the system.'

'DNA? I thought she'd not been . . . '

'Saliva,' Foster said. 'Found it between her breasts when they got her into hospital. Someone was smart enough to collect it. When she regained consciousness, she told them one of the men had spat on her. If we find the guys, we've got the evidence to convict. When they realize they can only plead guilty, they'll start bargaining; maybe tell us who did the hiring.'

'We both know who did the hiring.'

'But we can't prove it.'

'Seems a travesty,' I said. 'A bunch of corrupt bastards scare a woman into selling land at agricultural valuation, then they wangle themselves planning permission and it's worth ten times as much.'

'Why not let her sell. You know she's been threatened; her partner was threatened; an assault's on police files. It's duress, Lomax. Duress would void any contract of sale.'

We looked at each other across the paper-strewn desk. A faint rumble of distant traffic, overlaid by the sounds of revellers out on the town, was wafting up from the street.

'She sells,' I said, 'they get planning permission, she actions to void the sale, and she gets her land back with a planning permission that makes it worth ten times as much.'

He let out a chesty laugh. 'That would be all down to luck and timing, Lomax. But if she did sell it might smoke them out. No sale, no rigged planning permission, no corruption. And we'd need proof that it was Norris who'd been intimidating Velma.'

'And if we didn't get the proof, Velma would have to go through with the sale and kiss the farm goodbye.'

'Talk to her,' he said. 'Tell her to string

them along for a while longer. I'll have a word with Daniels at the Crown Prosecution Service, see if he can recommend a solicitor she can use; someone we can bring on board; someone who'll help us nail the bastards.' He heaved himself out of the chair. 'Got to make tracks, Lomax.'

'Can I give you a lift?'

'Force rents a flat for me in one of those big Victorian houses on the other side of the church. I can walk that far.' He grinned. 'Anyway, you've got to get home and give little Velma some tender loving care.'

'She's just watched the love of her life bleed to death, for heaven's sake.'

'So? She'll need a little tenderness, Lomax. How are you on tenderness?'

★ ★ ★

'Where did you get these?' Velma was struggling with the zip of a crimson skirt that had a hem a couple of inches above her knees.

'I didn't. I persuaded a policewoman to go up to the bedroom and get you something to wear.'

'Heavens knows where she found them. I can't remember ever having worn the things.

The sweater's too tight and the skirt's at least a size too small.'

'Sorry,' I said.

Velma glanced up from her struggles with the zip. 'Don't apologize,' she said softy. 'I should be saying sorry for all the bother I've caused you. And you kept me out of trouble back at the farm; you've let me stay in your home. I'm grateful for that.'

Glancing around the drab little room with its tired decorations and threadbare furniture, I said wryly, 'It's not much of a home to invite someone to.'

'It's just fine, Paul. It's cosy and comfortable, and it's yours.' She frowned down at the zip again. 'Could you help me fasten this?'

Rising from the sofa, I went over and gripped the crimson fabric to stop it crumpling. When she pulled, the fastener glided up to her waist.

'Thanks,' she said.

Stepping back, I watched her smooth the skirt over her hips, then tug down the black sweater.

'God, I really do look like a tart now. If Mrs Dalton could see me she'd have a field day.' Velma's face suddenly crumpled. 'Oh God, what have I done? She was right. I should have slapped his face and told him to stop. It's all my fault. If he hadn't met me, he'd still be alive and she'd be happy with her family, and . . . ' Her words were smothered under the sobs.

I went down the hall, found a clean towel in the airing cupboard and brought it to her. When she'd pressed her face into its softness, I took her by the elbow and led her to one of the dining chairs that hardly ever get used. She sat down.

'It's over Velma. No going back. You didn't set out to make it happen. He was besotted with you.'

'But I wanted it,' she moaned. 'After that first time, I wanted him as much as he wanted me. And his mother was right. I was old enough to know better.'

What could I say to comfort her? Cramped and aching on the tiny sofa, I'd listened through the night while she'd sobbed her heart out in the bedroom down the hall.

'And it didn't come without a price: my job, my reputation, losing Jane.' Her voice was muffled by the towel. 'And now he's gone.' The sobbing erupted again.

Pulling out a chair, I sat facing her across the table. I'd no idea what to say or do. *How are you on tenderness, Lomax?* Abysmally poor, Foster; abysmally poor. If I'd known her better, if we'd been more intimate, if she'd been a whole lot less attractive, I could have wrapped my arms around her and held her.

The sobbing calmed into a tearful snuffling. When she lifted her face from the towel, she sighed, then threw back her head and her hair fell, like a river of burnished copper, over her shoulders and down her back.

'Take me home, Paul. Take me to Branwell.'

'You really want to go to the farm?'

'I must. It's where my studio is and I've got to work. If I don't start working again, I'll go mad.'

'You've changed your mind about selling, then?'

'I'll never sell, not now. I'll die there.' She rose to her feet, dabbed her eyes, then folded the towel and draped it over the back of the chair. 'Do you have any ribbon?'

'Ribbon?'

'So I can tie my hair.'

'Ribbon's something I don't have a need for. Would a silk handkerchief do?'

'That would be fine.'

'Red, yellow or blue?'

She patted her skirt. 'I think it's got to be red.'

I found her the handkerchief, she used it to fix her hair, then she picked up her bag and glanced at me to tell me she was ready. I nodded towards the kitchen.

'Don't you use the front door?'

'Nailed up,' I said. 'Police broke it down a week ago. They promised to have it fixed, but I'm hardly ever here.'

We walked down the narrow gap between bungalow and garage, I tugged open the side gate and we headed over the hard-standing towards the Jag.

They appeared out of nowhere; at least a dozen men, all clutching cameras. They came from behind the car, from around bushes and shrubs, from the gaps between the bungalows. Velma let out a shocked little scream and huddled into me. Shutters were clicking and bulbs were flashing, creating instants of brightness in the hard morning shadows.

'Over here, Miss Hartman: look over here.'

'Just stand clear of your friend, Miss Hartman, and look at me; just look at the camera.'

'One more, Velma. Give me one more.'

Wrapping my arm around her, I elbowed my way through the scrum of jostling press, trying to reach the door of the car.

'Miss Hartman . . . Miss Hartman . . . How did you meet the boy? Did you know he was an MP's son? Did you ever meet his father?'

'His mother, Velma, have you got a message for his mother?'

'Give her a break, boys.' I tried to sound genial. 'Miss Hartman's exhausted. She'll talk to you later.'

While I was steering Velma through the crush, I used the remote to unlock the car. When we reached it, I got hold of the nearest handle and eased the door open against the weight of bodies. It was the driver's door. Velma slid behind the wheel, then hitched up her skirt and swung her legs over the gear lever so she could scramble into the passenger seat. Lenses were pressed against the windscreen. A dozen shutters clicked.

I climbed into the car, slammed the door and turned the ignition. When we rolled forward, the crush parted, and one or two men ran alongside, greedy for the last chance of a picture. Velma turned away and covered her face with her hands.

'That was awful. How did they find me?'

'Probably followed us when I brought you home yesterday. Do you still want to go to the farm?'

'I've got to, Paul.'

'You've got to decide what you're going to do about the press.'

'What can I do? And I don't understand why they're so interested in me.'

'Because Tarquin's father's the MP for Barfield North and he's just been made Home Secretary. His son was involved with a beautiful older woman and his wife couldn't handle it. When she tried to kill the woman, she accidentally killed her own child. It's a newspaper man's dream come true: power, sex, glamour, jealousy and death.'

'I wish she had killed me, Paul. I wish to God she *had* killed me.'

'If you don't give them a story, they'll invent one you won't like. If you talk to them by yourself, they'll trick you into saying all the stuff that sells papers. You need an agent to sell your story to the highest bidder and get you some control over what's written.'

We were cruising along the outer ring road. In the rear-view mirror, I could see a couple of black leather-clad motorcyclists tailing us. There could have been more hidden amongst the traffic.

'I loved Tarquin,' she said softly. 'Selling our story would make everything seem so vulgar and cheap.'

'Not half as vulgar and cheap as they'll make it if you don't get help.'

'But where would I find an agent?'

'London,' I said. 'That guy who's always on television, dealing with the press and the media.'

'Not . . . What's he called?'

'Yeah,' I said. 'When we get to the farm, find the number and phone him. Get the best, Velma.'

And then I changed the subject; began to remind her about the situation she was in regarding her ownership of the farm, told her about my conversation with the ugly cop; tried to explain why it would be best if she agreed to sell, and the risk she ran of losing the place if the intimidation couldn't be laid at Norris's door. She was nervous about the risk. She didn't like the idea at all. I decided to let the matter rest and wait until she was more composed.

The motorcyclists roared past as we turned into Hawthorne Lane and began the descent to the farm. Shutters started clicking as soon as Velma swung her legs out of the car. They followed us across the yard, asking stupid questions, calling for poses. When I'd got Velma inside the farmhouse and slammed the iron-bound door, I said, 'You're sure you want to stay here with the press outside?'

'No one's going to come here and hurt me if the press are outside. And this is where I've spent some of the happiest hours of my life. There's nowhere else I want to be.'

I stepped into the kitchen, stared at the pans still scattered over the floor, the big table heaped with dishes. Blood had run down the front of the old brown-glazed sink and congealed on a curtain drawn across the space beneath it, but there was surprisingly little on the stone floor. It must have remained on Tarquin's body; soaked into his robe and his mother's dress.

When I turned, Velma was standing close behind me, looking desolate, and I said, 'Can you cope with all this?'

'I've got to cope. And clearing up the mess will give me something to do. Then I've got to arrange for Adam and Eve to be shipped out, make space in the studio and get down to another commission.'

'You'll be able to live here alone, after what's happened?'

'I want to be on my own, Paul.'

'Is there food in the house?'

'There's a freezer in one of the outhouses. It's full. And vegetables and salad things are growing in a garden by the old chicken coops.'

My mobile phone began to bleep. I patted my pockets, felt it and tugged it out.'

'Lomax?' It was Foster's gruff voice.

'I'm here.'

'Where's here?'

'Branwell Farm. Velma insisted on coming back.'

'That solicitor we talked about: it's sorted. Guy called Rex Russel from Russel, Maitland and Seymour, Crown Chambers, Leeds. Can you take Velma there?'

'She's not too keen on the idea,' I said. 'She's desperate to keep the farm now, and the risk of having to go through with the sale's worrying her.'

Velma was picking up pots and pans, tidying the mess on the table. She was dwelling in a distant country, completely oblivious to me and my conversation. I backed into the passageway, then stepped into the parlour.

'It's our only chance of nailing the bastards, Lomax. I was seconded here when they started talking corruption. I've spent four months in this God-forsaken hole, and I don't intend to leave empty handed.'

'And if we can't get proof of Norris's involvement, Velma loses the farm. She'll be a victim twice over.'

'She'd get the cash from the sale.'

'She doesn't want to sell,' I snarled. 'And I don't see much chance of our getting any proof.'

'Sweet talk her, Lomax. You've helped her a lot. You're close now. She trusts you.'

'You're darned right she trusts me. So why should I talk her into doing something she doesn't want to do?'

'Don't give me that crap, Lomax. You know as much about women as you do about investigating crime: sod all. Just get her to Rex Russel. The meeting's at ten-thirty tomorrow morning.'

I was tempted to switch off the phone and do what I ought to have done at the very beginning: walk away from it all. It wouldn't be long before I wished to God that I had. But, right then, I felt Velma would never be safe at the farm until Norris was dealt with. Sighing, I said, 'Why the sudden rush?'

'Things seem to be moving. Pearson's death, this trouble with the MP's son, you going into the planning offices: it's made them edgy. They want to clinch the land deal as soon as they can, then submit a report on the site to the planning committee.'

'How do you know all this?' I asked.

'I've got someone on the inside.'

'Sheldon?'

Laughter rustled in the earpiece. 'Not Sheldon; Langham. Osborne's deputy. You scared the shit out of them when you went in and told them you had a client interested in the site.'

I said nothing, just listened to his breathing while I tried to concentrate my thoughts.

Presently he went on, 'They've fixed a date for the funeral.'

'Tarquin's?'

'No,' he snorted. 'Pearson's. Next Thursday. 10.30 Ashmount Crematorium. She's having him roasted; sit-down meal at the Belmont Hotel afterwards.'

'Wouldn't have expected anything less,' I said. 'But what's all this got to do with me?'

'Norris is attending, with his wife and daughter.'

'I still don't see . . . '

'The house, Skelton Grange; it's going to be empty.'

★ ★ ★

'I thought Velma Hartman was a client,' Melody snapped, as she slid the tray on to the desk. 'It seems you're her close friend and constant companion now.'

I looked up. I'd not heard her come in. I'd spent the past two days stalking benefit cheats and I was concentrating on putting a report together. 'Friend?' I muttered, looking blank.

Melody's colour was high; her big blue eyes were flashing. I risked a quick glance at the white silk blouse and hound's-tooth pattern skirt, then met her gaze again. 'Friend?' I repeated. 'I don't follow.'

Melody took a newspaper from the tray, flicked it open and began to read one of the captions. 'Velma Hartman leaving the home of close friend and constant companion, Paul Lomax, the day after the murder. 'It was love,' she said, speaking about the son of Home Secretary, Daniel Dalton. 'Tarquin blessed me with the happiest hours of my life.' '

Melody laid the paper on the desk. 'Has her chest been sprayed black, or is she actually wearing something? And she's very proud of her legs, isn't she?'

'Legs?'

Melody flicked over the page. 'In the front seat of your car. Heaven knows what you were doing.'

'Photographers,' I said lamely. 'They were milling around. I had to bundle her into the car.'

'Bundle her! That's what you're calling it now, is it? Is she still sleeping at your place?'

'She only stayed the one night. She's back at the farm now.'

Melody sniffed. 'I've seen your bungalow. I'm not surprised.'

I gazed at the article with a stunned fascination. The agent was earning his fee. The *Sun* had serialized an exclusive and the first instalment ran to six pages. I glanced up.

Melody was pouring coffee. I was still getting coffee, so our fragile relationship was still limping along. Trying for a diversion, I said, 'How did your dinner date go?'

She banged the cup down on the blotter and gave me a frosty little smile. 'Perfect meal, and Charles was utterly charming. I invited him home afterwards; I couldn't bear the evening to end. In fact, I think he's a bit too handsome and charming for my own good. He's taking me out to dinner again, tomorrow.'

16

The steak was a succulent two-pounder, the knife razor sharp. After making a series of shallow cuts into the meat, I reached for the jar of tablets.

Acetylpomazine was the only word typed on the label: no strength, no dosage. The girl who'd sold me the pills worked for a vet who specialized in horses. I unscrewed the cap and shook a couple on to my hand. They were seriously large. How many? One? Two? Getting it wrong either way could prove very nasty.

Deciding to play it safe, I crushed two between a couple of spoons, then sprinkled the powder into the cuts in the meat. After sliding the treated steak into a polythene bag, I got to work on another and continued until four and a spare were stashed in the cool box.

Less than an hour later, I'd parked the car in a lay-by and walked the quarter-mile back to the copse of trees adjoining Skelton Grange. Forcing my way through the tangle of leaves and branches, I found the fallen tree, then crawled up its sloping trunk and peered over the wall. A dark-blue Daimler was parked near the front door of the house. I watched and listened: birds were singing, insects were buzzing, very occasionally a car murmured along the road. The dogs were silent.

Wedging the cool box and holdall between the branches, I heaved myself up on to wide copings. There was an outhouse of some kind about twenty yards further along, and its tiled roof rose almost to the top of the wall. I'd found my way in and out. All I had to do now, was wait.

They were cutting it pretty fine. It was almost ten before the door opened and a tall slim dark-haired woman, in an elegantly severe black dress, appeared. Her daughter followed. She was wearing dark glasses and a navy-blue suit. The hem of the skirt didn't quite cover her knees. They wandered over to the car. The mother climbed into the front, the daughter into the back. When they slammed the doors, a great yapping and barking started up around the back of the house.

Seconds later, Norris bustled out. His black suit somehow emphasized his barrel chest and massive shoulders; made him look like a nightclub bouncer. He busied himself locking the door, then ran a hand through close-cropped blond hair and strode around to the back of the house. The barking became frenzied. I could hear chains rattling and Norris yelling, 'Dart, Digger, Sting, Jet, here boys, come on boys.' And then he was walking back, four huge cross-bred dogs bounding after him. When he reached the car, he tossed a handful of biscuits across the lawn, then climbed inside and started the engine. The Daimler disappeared around a bend in the drive while the dogs frisked over the grass, sniffing out treats.

I opened my mouth to call them over, then had second thoughts. Making my way back to the road, I trudged the hundred yards to the huge ornamental gates and gave them a shaking. They were locked. I keyed the intercom unit. No one answered. Satisfied, I returned to the wall.

The dogs didn't need calling over. I heard rustlings in the bushes, then sleek black bodies were leaping up at the stonework, snarling and barking. Opening the cool box, I took out the steaks and tossed them down: one for each dog and one for them to fight over. I didn't matter any more. They were busy tearing at the meat, hardly chewing it before throwing back their heads and swallowing it in great chunks.

Acetylpomazine was a winner. After they'd downed the steaks, the dogs fell back on their haunches, flicked red tongues around slobbering mouths and stared up at me. A couple of minutes later, they'd all stretched out, heads against the ground, looking drowsy and bewildered.

Gathering up the holdall, I climbed on to the wall. The dogs didn't object, so I crawled along the copings until I reached the lean-to roof, then slithered down the tiles. When my feet went over the eaves, I rolled on to my chest, grabbed the gutter and swung down. Dropping the last few feet, I found myself looking into an old garden shelter. Paint was peeling off the bench at the back, and last year's autumn leaves still lay in drifts beneath it.

I pushed my way through the shrubbery, crossed the lawn and began to circle the house, peering through the ground-floor windows. Dining room, small sitting room, large sitting room, billiard room with a full-size table, a lavish kitchen, but nothing that resembled a study or office.

What had been a coach house and stable block ran the length of a paved rear yard, and one of three pairs of high doors was hooked back. Leaving the brightness of the yard, I stepped into shadows. A couple of cars were parked behind the closed doors: the daughter's Vauxhall Astra and a black BMW.

Through an archway beyond the cars, I could see the old stables. Everything was clean and tidy and well-maintained.

Narrow wooden steps led up to a tiny landing and a half-glazed door. I took them two at a time and peered in. Norris had converted the old hay lofts into an office. The glass was reinforced with wire and the door was secured by a mortice lock. Unzipping the holdall, I took out a jemmy, forced its sharpened end between door and frame, then heaved on the bar. The gap widened. When I drove the jemmy in deeper and put my weight behind it, the door splintered open.

The room ran the length of the former coach house and stables. Old oak boards had been sanded and varnished to a glassy shine; windows were small, numerous, and over-looked the yard. Sunlight was blazing through, gleaming on dust motes and casting hard shadows on the white-painted back wall. Norris wasn't a hoarder. There were no filing cabinets and no cupboards. Close by, four wine-red Dralon-covered armchairs were arranged on a Persian carpet. At the far end, a big modern desk and a matching conference table, made from some pale wood, stood in the shadows.

My rubber-soled shoes squeaked on the polished boards as I strode through shafts of sunlight. The conference table was heaped with drawings. Circling the desk, I leafed through the pile. A panel at the right-hand bottom corner of each sheet carried the legend: Pearson Design: Architects and Surveyors. Most were for the new shopping precinct that faced the Parish Church; the development that was driving Melody and me from our offices in the old Georgian town house. The rest were for a housing project east of Moxton that extended as far as Hawthorne Lane. It was on the land that Velma Hartman owned, the land that made up Branwell Farm.

I was looking at drawings taken from Pearson's office; taken because Norris had to keep the schemes under wraps. Some were marked with bloody thumbprints where they must have been picked up after Pearson had been beaten to death. Old Stan Willis had told me Norris had the police in his pocket. Even if he did, he was being careless beyond belief leaving incriminating stuff like this lying around.

Turning to the desk, I flopped down in the swivel chair and tugged at the drawers. Those on the right of the knee hole were locked. Sliding the jemmy back into the holdall, I took out a big bunch of keys, the kind that fit office furniture, and tried pushing them into a cylinder beneath the overhanging top. Of the six or so that would slide home, none would turn. I tossed them back in the holdall, took out the jemmy again, and used it to lever off the front of the top drawer. Hooking the jemmy behind a bar that dropped from the lock, I wrenched it free. When I tugged at the bottom drawer, it slid open.

A yellow duster half covered a Browning automatic pistol. I lifted it out and ejected the clip from the butt. It held six rounds. I put the gun back in the drawer, next to a carton of ammunition. A box of Havana cigars was almost empty; a bottle of Jack Daniel's, nestling close to a couple of shot glasses, half full.

The drawer was long and deep. I knelt down on the boards and gave it a hard tug, but it wouldn't open any further. When I got my head down and peered towards the back, I saw a leather photograph wallet resting on some unopened boxes of cigars. I took it out, thumbed up the clasp and flicked through glossy seven-by-fives of a beautiful dark-haired woman in advancing stages of undress. I'd only seen Norris's wife from a distance, but her face was recognizable in the photographs. The rest of her was memorable.

Dropping the wallet back on to the cigars, I slid my hand as far as the rear panel and

groped around. My fingers touched something soft. I lifted out a padded envelope.
'Personal and Private' had been typed on a
sticky label, along with Norris's name and
address. I glanced inside, then shook out a
DVD in its plastic case. Mastec: it was the
brand I'd used to record his daughter's
passionate moments with Pearson. I was
pretty sure it would be the porno flick, and
I'd no doubts at all about who'd sent it.
Glancing at the envelope, I saw it was
postmarked Leeds. Mrs Pearson was as
careful as they come. Knowing Norris as well
as she did, she'd have realized what watching
the video would do to him. It had been
cheaper than hiring a hit-man, and the law
couldn't touch her for acquainting a father
with things he'd want to know. She'd caused
the death of her husband just as surely as if
she'd shot him with a gun.

When I rifled through the contents of the
other drawers, I found a bundle of passports
held together by a rubber band. They'd all
been issued to Eastern European men. Two
photographs made me pause. The guys who'd
harassed Velma, the guys I'd been reckless
enough to work over, were staring out at me.
Maybe Norris had some hold over the men
who did special jobs for him and keeping
their passports was part of it.

The middle drawer held a folder of newspaper articles about Summerfield Developments, and there were a few copies of high-class county magazines that contained photographs of Norris and his wife attending functions. One carried a full-page head-and-shoulders shot of his daughter in a ball gown. Carefully lit and posed, it made the most of her youthful freshness. It fell short of making her look beautiful.

A final trawl through the contents revealed a pocket-sized cash book that contained names, dates and payments. I ran my eye down the columns. Ben Bradley, the chairman of the planning committee, was mentioned more than once on most pages. Dennis Osborne, the chief planner, featured a couple of times. The other names meant nothing to me. I slid it back under the magazines.

There was nothing of any interest in the unlocked drawers to the left of the knee hole. Bottles of spirits, more boxes of cigars, pads of paper, envelopes, packets of cheap pens stamped with the Summerfield logo: all the usual office stuff, but no files or information of any kind. I pressed the drawer front back in position, then slid the drawers shut. A casual glance wouldn't reveal that the lock had been forced.

Rising, I rolled the swivel chair under the

knee hole, then rounded the conference table and strode on towards a door in the end wall. The key was in the lock. I turned it and stepped into what remained of the original hay loft. An open hatchway took up most of the floor, and a ladder descended to the stables below. Pigeons were fluttering around in the rafters, making cooing sounds. The floor was splattered with droppings. Peering out of the tiny window, I saw the sunlit yard was still deserted. When I looked across at the house, dark windows stared back at me, brooding and malevolent.

The cash book and the drawings with the bloody thumbprints had to be left for the police. I toyed with the idea of taking the video, then thought better of it. It was the sort of thing a man like Norris would procure if he became suspicious, and it wasn't likely to be traced back to Mrs Pearson.

The windows of the house were still glowering at me through the ivy. Should I go over and take a look around, or should I quit while I was ahead? If the office was the only place broken into, Norris would know someone was watching him. If the house was entered and turned over a little, he'd probably think it was a burglary. I glanced at my watch. It was almost 11.30. Norris would be in the chapel at the crematorium, being bored rigid by the vicar. The Norris and Pearson families had visited each other's homes; the two daughters were best friends. Norris would probably feel obliged to attend the meal at the Belmont Hotel. It would look out of place if he didn't, and the last thing he'd want to do is look out of place. There was plenty of time to give the house the once-over.

Heading back, I retrieved the holdall and descended to the garage. Before stepping out into the yard, I paused and listened to pigeons cooing and the faint drone of a tractor moving along the distant road. I couldn't hear any barking. The dogs were still comatose, but I'd no idea how much longer they'd stay that way.

I walked over to the house, put my shoulder to the back door and forced the sharpened end of the jemmy into the narrow gap between door and frame, just above the mortice lock. It took three attempts before the wood splintered and the door swung open.

A wide corridor led to the front entrance hall. I only had to open a couple of doors to realize Norris was a man of considerable means and his wife a woman with expensive tastes. Ceilings were high and ornate; carpets deep and mostly plain. Silk ropes tied back curtains that soared up to matching pelmets, and sofas and armchairs were large and well stuffed. The remaining furniture looked antique and carefully chosen. Oil paintings, large and small, mostly of landscapes and animals, hid a good deal of the boldly patterned wallpaper in the sitting and dining rooms. Occasional tables in the larger of the two sitting rooms were covered with family photographs standing in ornate silver frames. I crossed the hallway and pushed at a door beneath the stairs; looked into a kitchen not much bigger than a tennis court that was full of handmade units topped with black granite and polished copper.

I'd left the doors of a sideboard and the drinks cabinet open, but I needed to make it look more like a break-in, so I headed up the stairs and began to slide out drawers and empty them on the beds.

The sound of the front door opening, then thudding shut, echoed up the stairwell. I crept out of the master bedroom and looked over the banister rail.

An irritated voice was saying, 'Really darling, I'd no idea you'd be quite so upset. And we ought to have gone to the Belmont. Heaven's knows what excuse I'm going to give to Emma.'

'I'm sorry, Mummy. When I saw Nancy

crying, it really got to me. I mean, her father dying like that. And I'm upset about Andrew, too. I simply couldn't bear it any more.' The girl began to choke back sobs.

'Let's go into the kitchen,' Mrs Norris said. 'I'll make us both some tea.' She linked her arm in her daughter's. 'I know it's absolutely dreadful, darling, but you must try not to be so upset.'

I heard whistling and Norris shouting, 'Dark, Digger, Sting, Jet.' He was moving towards the back of the house, clapping his hands and calling out, 'Here boys; come on boys.'

He suddenly fell silent. He must have seen the damage. Seconds later, he burst into the hall. 'Out,' he snapped, then took his wife and daughter by the arm and hurried them towards the front door.

'Out? What do you mean, out?' Mrs Norris protested.

'Intruder. Back door's been smashed open. He could still be in the house. I want you to stay outside and lock yourselves in the car. When Bruce and Jimmy arrive, we'll search the place.'

The women's startled voices faded when they stepped outside. I wouldn't get another chance. Dashing down the stairs, I ran into the corridor that led to the back door.

'Hey! What's the hurry?' a Scottish voice growled. A mountain of a man in a double-breasted bespoke suit was blocking my way.

'Norris,' I said, trying to squeeze past. 'He's sent me to look for the dogs.'

'The hell he has.' An enormous hand grabbed me by the arm.

Jerking free, I shoved him against the wall and kneed him in the groin. He jackknifed forwards, gasping out beer fumes. I made a grab for the splintered door. When I pulled it open, a smaller guy was standing on the step.

'Sassenach bastard!' a voice snarled behind me. I half turned, then felt the blow, and suddenly three pairs of hands were grabbing me.

'Office,' Norris panted. 'Get the bastard up to the office. And tell Tony to go and find out what's happened to the dogs.'

17

He had a desolate stare. When I looked into his pale, almost colourless, eyes, they seemed dead.

'Where are my dogs, Lomax?' Norris's voice was as chilling as his gaze; his thin lips were pressed into a hard line.

'Didn't see any dogs,' I said. 'And how do you know my name?'

'You're the guy who's minding Velma Hartman?'

I nodded. I wished I hadn't. My ears were still ringing from the punch the guy called Bruce had swung at me.

'Every *Sun* reader knows your name, Lomax. And I want to know what this is all about? Why are you nosing around?'

I blinked. Pain was making concentration difficult and they'd bound my wrists so tightly my hands were becoming numb. 'Videos,' I said. It was all I could think of. 'I recorded videos. One of the disks went missing. I got worried when Pearson was killed, so I started looking.'

'What videos?' Norris snapped. 'And why did you expect to find videos here?'

292

I was crouching forward in the chair, trying to keep my weight off my arms. The giant called Bruce and the smaller guy called Jimmy were standing on either side of me. I glanced at them, then looked back at Norris and raised an eyebrow.

His gaze flicked up and he made a dismissive gesture with his hand. 'Go and find Tony. Help him search for the dogs.'

Feet shuffled on the boards behind me. When the door had thudded into its shattered frame, Norris repeated, 'What videos?'

'Of a meeting between you and Pearson in Pearson's office. You were discussing a new shopping mall opposite the parish church and a housing development.'

'You did this for Velma Hartman?'

'Why would she be interested? She's going to live abroad.'

'Who, then?'

I grinned at him.

'Don't piss me about, Lomax. Who?' he snarled.

'Dennis Osborne. Hired me a couple of weeks ago.'

Norris's eyes narrowed. 'The borough planning officer? That Dennis Osborne?'

Pain flared behind my eyes when I nodded.

'Why would Osborne want a video of me and Pearson?'

'No idea. I don't ask questions. I just do what the client wants. Osborne gave me the time and place of the meeting, and I set up the gear.'

'How many meetings?'

'Just the one in Pearson's office. Like I said, the disk went missing before I could deliver it.' I was making it up as I went along; trying to give him plenty to think about.

'This doesn't ring true, Lomax. Osborne's just a petty official; a grovelling little time-server. He wouldn't have the balls to hire a private eye to spy on me, and he'd be too tight to pay for one.'

'He didn't,' I muttered.

'Didn't what?'

'Pay me.'

Cold eyes studied me. Beyond the ringing in my ears, I could hear the rumble of distant thunder. Sunlight wasn't blazing through the tiny windows any more. The sky had darkened, the long gallery was filled with shadows, and the air had that oppressive stillness that precedes summer storms.

'You said just one meeting in Pearson's office. Where else did Osborne send you?'

'Made a video of a meeting at a house in Albert Street.'

His eyes narrowed. 'What meeting?'

'Osborne said it was between Pearson and

a woman. I don't know who. He just gave me the date and time, and I installed the gear. It switches on automatically when someone enters the room. I collected the disk and removed the equipment the next day.'

'What was on this disk?' His voice was menacing.

'No idea. He hasn't paid me, so maybe there was nothing on it. It happens.'

'You're a lying bastard, Lomax.'

'Check with Osborne.'

'I intend to. And you're going to tell me what was on the disk.'

'I do a lot of this sort of thing. I'm well known for it. If I watched all the videos I recorded, I'd do nothing else.'

'You're even better known for chasing benefit cheats. You've targeted a lot of blokes who work on my sites. The benefits agency are chasing me now. They're saying I've been employing illegals; paying less than the minimum wage. They're talking about big fines. Even my lawyer's worried. You've been nothing but trouble to me, Lomax. You're . . . ' He paused and his gaze moved past me. Feet were thudding up the stairs. After a respectful knock on the door, they were tramping down the long room towards us. Apprehension began to show on Norris's face. He was picking up the men's agitation.

295

It was the first time his features had displayed anything other than a chilling remoteness.

'Well?' he demanded.

'Your dogs are dead, Mr Norris.'

'Dead? What do you mean, *dead*? They can't be dead.'

'Found 'em in the bushes, Mr Norris, beyond that old summer house.'

'They're not dead, you stupid bastard, they're — '

'Dead, Mr Norris.' There was fear in the man's voice. 'They're stretched out in the bushes. Stone cold.'

Norris's eyes blazed at me. 'You . . . You've killed my dogs!'

'Didn't see any dogs,' I protested. 'I just climbed the gates and — '

'This was resting in a fallen tree on the far side of the wall, Mr Norris.' The guy called Tony, the one who'd been doing all the talking, walked past me and put the cool box on the desk. 'If you lift the lid, you can still smell the meat.' He was tall and vigorous looking, wearing a decent suit like the others, and his long fair hair was drawn back and tied with a leather thong.

Norris sent the box crashing against the wall. 'I loved those dogs, Lomax.' His voice was an anguished roar. 'They were like children to me.' He leaned forward and tugged something from his trouser pocket. I could hear keys jangling. He pushed one into the lock beneath the rim of the desk. When he tugged at the topmost drawer, the front came away in his hand. He looked stunned. It was as if he couldn't believe anyone would dare to kill his dogs, break into his home and wreck his desk. His shocked gaze was focused on the drawer front he was holding. Someone behind me was trying to suppress laughter. Norris's face became incandescent with rage. He hurled the drawer front, I heard a shocked intake of breath, then it clattered to the floor. Risking a glance, I saw Bruce wiping blood from his cheek with the back of his hand.

'Think this is funny? You think this is fucking funny?' Norris screamed. He leaned forward and tugged open the bottom drawer. When he came back up the gun was in his hand. He pointed it at me. 'I was going to kill you with this, Lomax, but that would be too quick. There wouldn't be enough fear; there wouldn't be enough pain for a miserable little shit like you.' He glanced at the men standing behind me. 'The basement excavations on the Warncliffe site; have they been back-filled yet?'

'Yesterday, Mr Norris. They did it yester-day.'

Norris frowned. He seemed to have

297

remembered something. He bent down, fumbled around in the drawer, then came up with the padded envelope. He peered inside to make sure the disk was still there, then tossed it back and slid the drawer shut. Glancing up at the men, he said, 'If there isn't a hole, you'll have to get a machine out of the compound and dig one. I want this bastard buried. I want him buried alive and fully conscious, his face and head protected, so he dies slowly, in the dark, his body trapped by the earth.'

'In this downpour, Mr Norris?' The thunder was no longer distant and heavy summer rain was pelting down on the yard. 'We'd never get a trench dug on the Warncliffe site. It's too sandy. The rain would bring the sides in.'

Norris rose and moved his nightclub bouncer's bulk around the desk. He came close. I could smell the deodorant he'd sprayed himself with, the newness of his suit. Without warning, a fist as big and hard as a couple of bricks smashed into my face. 'Dirty bastard,' he snarled. Then more blows punctuated the words as he said, 'My dogs . . . you . . . killed . . . my . . . beautiful dogs.'

The room was becoming darker and thunder was growling above the drumming rain. I felt myself sliding forwards, tipping out of the chair. From a great distance, a voice was saying, 'It won't rain for ever. When it stops, you can dig a bloody deep hole and bury the bastard alive.'

And then my face passed through the boards and I hurtled on down into the abyss.

★   ★   ★

The wooden floor was rough under my cheek, my body ached and I could no longer feel my hands. Lying there, in the gloom, I listened to the steady drumming of the rain, the occasional fluttering of wings. Then I heard what I thought was a woman crying. When I tried to lift my head from the floor, a searing pain lanced through me, so I abandoned the idea. I couldn't make out where I was. It wasn't just the gloom that made seeing difficult: my eyes were almost closed, my vision blurred by a sticky film of congealing blood. I tried saying, 'Help me,' but lips I could no longer feel wouldn't shape the words. When I let out a groan, the sobbing stopped.

Thunder was growling over hills that rolled up to the moors and I didn't hear her climbing the ladder. A pale face suddenly rose out of the floor, close to mine, and I realized I was lying near the hatch in the room beyond the office.

I heard a sharp intake of breath. 'Dear God, what have they done to you?' Shocked brown eyes stared at me out of a tear-streaked face. Her mouth, with its full, almost pouting lips, was hanging open.

I let out another groan.

'You're the burglar! Daddy said they'd thrown you out on to the road.'

'Privestigator,' I mumbled. 'Not buglar.' The words stumbled out over rubber lips made for a much bigger mouth than mine.

'Private investigator? Why? What were you — '

'Pearson: your father killed Pearson.'

'Daddy killed Andrew? That's ridiculous. They were friends. They . . . '

'He found out you were lovers.'

Her mouth snapped shut. Wide eyes stared at me. The rain was really pelting down on the roof now. I could hear it cascading over the gutters and splashing down on to the yard.

'That explains things,' she breathed. The words weren't meant for me. She was thinking out loud. 'I thought Daddy had gone all silent because he was upset about Andrew dying, but it was because he knew.'

'Untie me,' I moaned. 'I can't feel my hands.'

'What *have* they done to you?' she gasped.

She was seeing me again.

'Only what they did to Andrew Pearson before they killed him.'

That seemed to rouse her. She climbed the last few rungs of the ladder and knelt beside me. 'Can you roll over a little?'

When I tried, I almost blacked out. I felt her hands grabbing my shoulder, turning me so she could reach my wrists; felt pigeon droppings slimy under my cheek.

'Your fingers; they're black and blue!' She knelt astride me. I could feel her tugging at the cords.

Voices and footsteps approached beyond the door to Norris's office.

'Jimmy and Bruce!' she gasped. 'They'll tell Daddy if they find me here.' And then she was disappearing through the hatchway; climbing back down the ladder that descended to the stables.

She'd done something. Blood was pumping into my hands again. Every spurt felt like a sledgehammer blow. Somehow, I managed to roll on to my arms and conceal the loosened cords. The door opened and someone swung a kick at me. 'Up, Lomax.' It was the Scottish guy.

Groaning, I tried to roll on to my knees, then felt hands grab me and haul me up. My legs buckled. A wave of nausea surged up

301

through the darkness and I began to retch.

'Spew on this suit, you bastard, and you'll know about it. Untie his legs, Jimmy. He's too big to carry.'

I swayed and Bruce held me while Jimmy fumbled around my ankles. Feeling had returned to my hands and I gathered the ends of the loosened cords into my palms. Jimmy rose to his feet and gave me a shove. I staggered towards the door. When I almost fell, they grabbed me, dragged me through the long office, then held me while I stumbled down the stairs.

A white van had been reversed into the old coach house. Bruce and Jimmy heaved me inside, then climbed up and sat facing one another on rough wooden benches. The doors of the van crashed shut, boots scraped on concrete, then the hissing of the downpour became louder. Someone had opened the big coach house doors. The engine clattered into life. We lurched forward and rain was suddenly drumming on the roof of the van.

After I'd bounced around on its dusty metal floor for a while, Bruce grinned down at me, and said, 'How's Velma? How's the bonny wee lassie?' His Scottish accent was so broad I had difficulty understanding some of the words. Closing my eyes against the nausea and pain, I could hear him laughing. He

302

didn't want a conversation. He was amusing himself.

'No doubt about it, Lomax, she's a bonny woman. I was going to do her a service that night at the farm, but Jimmy here put me off.' He laughed. 'Jimmy plays for the other side, if you know what I mean. The sight of naked female flesh revolts him. His mother made him that way. What with Velma having hysterics and Jimmy screaming abuse and spitting all over her, it put me right off.' Glancing across at his partner, he laughed again, and said, 'You spoilt it for me, didn't you, Jimmy? You couldn't bear the thought of me having it off with the lovely wee Velma.'

Jimmy said nothing. He was sitting with his head resting against the side of the van, his legs stretched out, his shiny black shoes pressed against the wooden bench.

We rattled along for a while. My brain was beginning to clear a little, enough for me to string a sentence together, and I asked, 'Who worked Pearson over?'

'Speak up, man. I can't hear you.'

'Pearson: who worked him over?'

'Norris. The boss wanted to do the job himself.' Bruce laughed. 'Never seen a man as terrified as Pearson was that night. Pissed his pants. Norris wore a slaughterman's gauntlet over a leather glove; one of those chainmail things that protect hands from knives. We all piled into Pearson's office, Norris walked straight up to him, smashed him in the face, and said, 'That's for Sophie.' Never said another word. Just dragged him into the toilet and got stuck in. The boss was covered in blood when it was over. Had to put plastic sheets down in the car.' He glanced at his companion. 'We thought Pearson must have been trying it on with Norris's daughter, didn't we, Jimmy?'

Jimmy nodded.

'Norris dotes on the girl,' Bruce said. 'She's his wee princess.'

The van started to lurch and bounce. Bruce glanced through the back windows, then looked down at me and laughed. 'I've got good news and I've got bad news, Lomax. Good news is, we're not going to bury you alive. We couldn't dig a hole in this downpour. Bad news is, you're going to drown like a dog. A feeder to the town's storm-relief sewer is at the end of this track: four-foot pipe that should be running full after all this rain. Screens keep the big debris out, but rats and turds get through.' He laughed again. 'It was the boss's idea: let you drown in the cold and dark, fighting for life amongst shite and vermin.'

The van lurched to a stop. Bruce kicked

open the rear doors and jumped down; Jimmy followed. Hands grabbed my ankles, dragged me across the floor of the van, then heaved me into a sitting position. Beyond the curtain of pouring rain, I could see the driver, Tony, opening a door in an old red-brick building. Bruce and Jimmy linked their arms in mine, then hurried me down a path, and into a place where the roar of fast-flowing water echoed up out of the darkness.

They dragged me towards a near vertical stair. 'You go first, Jimmy.' Bruce urged. 'Make sure he doesn't fall. Boss said he's got to know what's happening to him when we drop him in.'

Jimmy grabbed the handrail and descended backwards, his free hand pressed against my chest. Bruce kept hold of the back of my jacket, and I began to stumble down rusting chequer-plate treads. Twelve feet below, Tony was standing on the concrete floor, grinning up at us.

Corroded bulkhead lamps, like barnacles on the slimy brickwork, intensified the shadows in a channel that crossed the chamber. The sound of rushing water roared out of it, bringing with it an acrid metallic stench that pervaded the dank air. The sloping concrete floor felt sticky underfoot. Looking down, I saw the telltale signs, the black slug-like shapes: it was smothered in rat droppings.

Bruce and Jimmy dragged me over to the channel, then held me. Jimmy was grinning. Tony, the driver, was grinning. Bruce was laughing and yelling something I couldn't hear above the roar of storm water cascading over twigs and rags and all the other debris that had piled up behind a massive iron screen. It was a six-foot drop into the swirling water. I could just see the top of the arch over the outlet pipe. The sewer was running full.

Acting on instinct, I jerked a shoulder free, swung a kick at Jimmy, then made a dash for the stairs. I wished I hadn't. Three pairs of hands grabbed me, gave me a good slapping around, then dragged me back to the brink and pushed me over. I got my knees up to my chest, pulled in a lungful of air, and forced my wrists apart against the cords. The instant I hit the water its force possessed me; swept me down into the darkness.

How long can you hold your breath? Until every beat of your heart makes lights flash behind your eyes, until you think you can no longer bear the pain, until your lungs begin to congeal? That long, and longer. I struggled with the cord around my wrists. When I shook it free, I rolled on to my back and kept my head close to the crown of the pipe, my hands skating along its slimy surface. Suddenly there was no pipe and my head was above water. I took in a lungful of foul air, and then my face smashed into a wall. I was in a manhole for inspecting the sewer.

The force of the water dragged me on. Body suspended in the torrent, I clung to edge of the brickwork, but there was no way I could haul myself back to the air-filled chamber. I let go, allowed myself to be swept on, tried to keep my face just beneath the crown of the pipe while I prayed for another inspection place. It didn't arrive. I thought it was all over; that I'd have to submit to instinct, to open my mouth and suck in water. And then I felt air against my cheeks and took great greedy gulps at it. I was rushing along with my face in a pocket of air and there were furry things swimming and squeaking in the blackness beside me. A rat's instinct for survival is as strong as a man's.

Without warning, the air pocket ended and I was choking on fetid water. I braced myself. I had to be ready when the next inspection place came. Air began to rush past my face, but my hands could still feel the slime at the top of the pipe. Then my ears cleared the water, and I was deafened by a roar that began to boom and echo. Suddenly the pipe was gone. I was in a chamber.

I tried to stand, but the force of the torrent was too great and my face and chest were hurled against a wall. My feet were slipping. I was being dragged along. Arms flailing, hands groping in the blackness, I touched a hoop of metal, grabbed it and managed to cling on. I don't know how long I was hanging there, breathing in the foul stench, spitting out water and slime. Furry things were scuttling up my arm, fighting one another to share the projecting metal step with my hand. The rats were in need of a resting place, too.

Cold and noise and exhaustion were beginning to overwhelm me. I knew that if I didn't get free soon, I'd die. Tightening my grip, I hauled myself out of the water and groped with my hands and feet for more of the metal hoops. My fingers touched one, I pulled myself up higher; then, sensing the way they were arranged in the wall, began to climb. I felt vibrations and, above the roar of rushing water, heard the rumble of a passing lorry. I climbed higher, the shaft narrowed, and then my head thudded against something hard. When I reached up, my hand brushed across rusty metal.

The noise of passing traffic was louder. I heaved as hard as I could against the massive

308

cast-iron manhole cover. It didn't budge. Climbing higher, I got both feet on to one of the step-irons, pressed my hands against the other side of the narrow shaft, then settled my shoulders under the rusty metal. It could have been in the middle of a road. I didn't care. I just wanted to get out of the stinking darkness.

Straightening my legs, I applied all the force I could. When nothing happened, an angry desperation seized me and I began a frenzied heaving at the cover. Lorries were roaring past only inches away. I could feel the chamber shaking, hear tyres hissing through pouring rain. And then the rust suddenly released its hold and the cover lifted. The sound of traffic was deafening now and I could see lights moving through spray. Hooking my hands over the frame to stop the cover falling back, I clung on, and sucked in the clean air while I tried to gather some strength.

My legs were shaking. The lights were becoming blurred. If I lingered, I'd drop down to the rushing water. Hunching my shoulders, I gave the metal cover a last desperate heave. It lifted clear of its frame. When I shifted my body to the side of the shaft and straightened my back, it dropped clear. Dragging myself over the rim, I crawled on to the grass of a central reservation.

The darkness of the storm had deepened into the darkness of the night when I heard voices. A man was saying, 'Christ, what a mess. It's not a hit and run. The poor bugger's had a right beating. Lift him; lift him now.' And then I was on a stretcher, being hoisted into the soft light of an ambulance.

Doors slammed and a green-uniformed paramedic bent over me with a hissing mask. Pushing it away, I mumbled, 'Where are you taking me?'

'Barfield General. Don't talk. Let me put this on.'

I turned my head to stop him fixing the mask. 'Police,' I said. 'I've got to talk to DCI Foster. Only Foster; no one else. Call him for me. He's on secondment to Barfield CID.'

The man laughed. 'You're persistent. If you wear the mask, I'll call him on my mobile. OK?'

18

If I remained still, there wasn't any pain. The hissing mask had gone. I felt clean and warm and comfortable.

My eyes wandered around the room: hardwood doors, magnolia walls, curtains half drawn along chrome rails, winking lights on equipment stacked on trolleys. They came to rest on a big, dark, untidy shape. I tried to focus. They must have had me heavily sedated; the face had finally lost its power to shock.

I heard some throat clearing, then a gruff voice said, 'How are you feeling, Lomax?'

'Better.' Memories were surfacing like mountain peaks through a mist. 'Did you . . . '

'Arrested them all,' he growled. 'Dawn, day before yesterday. Alan Norris, Bruce Haggart, Jimmy Levine, Tony Spencer. Did a second trawl early this morning and rounded up the hangers on. By the time I get back to the station, they'll have suspended four officers on corruption charges.' He rose from his chair and ambled over to the bed. 'Blood on the drawings was Pearson's,' he went on. 'The

311

thumbprint belonged to Norris. Found Norris's chainmail glove in a bucket in one of the stables. Careless bastard. And forensics have matched the spit on Velma to Levine.'

Velma. The name triggered more memories. 'How's the land sale going?'

He began to laugh. It wasn't much more than a chesty wheezing. 'Planning meeting was held last night. Bradley got his fellow committee members on side, Osborne submitted a very convincing report, an estate agent called Charles Allot sent a banker's draft for the deposit to Velma's solicitor, and they went ahead and gave themselves planning permission. Almost two hundred acres.'

'Will she have to sell?'

Foster shook his head. 'Rex Russel's a crafty old devil. He waited until five, then returned the banker's draft; said it wasn't the amount agreed by Miss Hartman.' They couldn't get to the bank; they couldn't withdraw the report from the committee; so they risked it and went ahead.' We grinned at each other.

'I suppose they'll reverse the planning decision?' I said.

Foster shrugged. 'Very persuasive report to Committee. If Osborne backtracks now, he'll be seriously compromised.'

'Velma's going to be a wealthy woman.' I closed my eyes and tried to think. 'How long have I been in here?'

'Four days. I came in yesterday and the day before. I need a statement, but they wouldn't let me bother you. I'll probably send someone in tomorrow.' He nodded towards a vase of white chrysanthemums. 'The blonde, Melody Brown, brought those in. Comes in every day, sits on the bed for most of the afternoon and evening.'

I rolled my head over, saw a mass of red roses on another table. 'You bring those?' I asked.

He chuckled. 'Velma. Came in a limo. Didn't stay long because the press were chasing her. Had a little weep, gave you a kiss, then buggered off.'

'What about Tarquin's mother?'

'Awaiting psychiatric reports. Dalton's resigned as Home Secretary. Wants to spend more time with his family.'

My chest hurt when I laughed. 'He's not got any family. Son's dead, wife's in the slammer.'

'We can't all be winners, Lomax.' He laughed heartily at that, then said, 'Do you want a kiss? Everyone else has given you a kiss, and you're as ugly as I am now.'

'I'll pass on that,' I said.

He lumbered over to the door, then glanced back before he stepped out into the corridor. 'The blonde was pretty upset when she saw you, Lomax. Cried her eyes out. Maybe you should forget the advice I gave you.'

'Advice?'

'About not letting your dick do all the thinking.'

★ ★ ★

'You've been tidying up.' Melody stared at the exposed leather top of the desk and the pile of refuse sacks.

'It's the new me,' I said. I gazed up at her. Her colour was high, her hair was pinned up and a few stray curls had broken free. She looked very fetching. The red woollen dress was seasonal, its softness flowed over her, and her red and gold shoes had probably cost more than most men earn in a week.

'The new you?' She laughed. 'You're only just beginning to look like the old you again.' She stacked my cup and plate on the tray.

I relaxed back in the chair. 'Missed you at lunchtime,' I said.

'You missed your lunch, you mean. You didn't miss me. Christmas party. I took the girls to the Sheraton.'

'Bit early,' I said.

Long lashes flicked up and big blue eyes held me in a reproachful stare. 'Tomorrow is Christmas Eve, Paul. Christmas day is on Friday.'

'Didn't realize,' I mumbled.

She nodded at the two cards on top of the filing cabinet. One a nativity scene from her; the other a big art-house reproduction of Velma's *Adam and Eve*. 'Who sent you that?'

'Velma Hartman,' I said. 'Take a look.'

Melody unfolded the card. Eve was on the back, Adam was on the front and the crease ran through the big red apple. 'Was this the picture she . . . ?' Words seemed to be failing her.

I nodded. 'Could have been you and me on there. She was keen for us to pose.'

'She was keen for *you* to pose.' Melody laughed, then her face became serious, as she murmured, 'He was unbelievably handsome.' She folded the card and stood it back on the filing cabinet. She hadn't bothered to read Velma's letter telling me about her new home and studio in Italy, about the bill I'd never sent her, and the cheque she was enclosing. Velma had been generous way beyond extravagance. But then, I had helped to make her a very wealthy woman.

'Marry me, Melody,' I said.

315

She let out an exasperated sigh and picked up the tray. 'You're not still going on about that, are you, Paul? And why do you want to marry me this time?' She threw the question out as she was heading for the door. Beneath the red wool, her posterior sway was electrifying.

'Because I love you,' I said softly.

It stopped her dead in her tracks. She just stood there with her back to me for maybe a dozen heartbeats. When she turned her face was deadly serious. 'What did you just say, Paul?'

'Because I love you.'

She slid the tray on to the desk, walked round to my side and touched my knees. When I pressed them together, she sat on my lap and wrapped her arms around my neck. Our faces were close. Her blue eyes seemed huge and suddenly very bright.

'I wish you'd not said that, Paul.'

'What's wrong with me telling you I love you?'

'It changes things,' she murmured huskily. 'And I liked them the way they were.'

She closed her eyes, drew my head down and kissed me. Her trembling lips were hot, almost feverish. When she opened her eyes again, she gazed at me for a long time, then the tears began to fall. I passed her my best blue silk handkerchief; Velma had legged it with the red one.

'How much do you love me?' she sniffed.

I tried to hold back a smile. I seemed to have passed the *why* test, and now we were moving on to *how much*. I thought of Pearson's battered body in the toilet; Velma's lover lying bleeding on her kitchen floor.

'Beyond reason,' I said. 'I love you beyond reason.'

'Beyond reason! That seems an awful lot.' She tried to smile, but her face crumpled and she leapt up and dashed into the tiny washroom at the top of the stairs.

After waiting quite a while, I went and tapped on the door. When she opened it, she snapped, 'Don't look at me. I'm an absolute mess,' then swept past me and went back into the office. She'd washed her face. The lipstick and eyeshadow had gone.

'I thought we might have dinner together tonight,' I said.

'It's the day before Christmas Eve, Paul. Everywhere's booked solid.'

'I meant come to my place. I've got a frozen chicken, a few sprouts, a couple of paper hats.'

She was laughing again. 'It might be better if you come home with me. You can keep me company over Christmas; tell me how much you love me.'

'Is that a yes?'

'What do you mean, 'Is that a yes?' '

'Yes, you'll marry me?'

'No, it's not a yes. Don't even class it as a maybe.' Picking up the tray, she called over her shoulder, 'I'll go down and lock up. Then you can drive me home. I didn't bring the car in today.'

The tap-tapping of her heels grew fainter as she descended through the empty building. Sighing, I slid open the top drawer of the desk, found the tiny red-leather box and flicked up the lid. Points of light flared and sparkled: the diamond, big and brilliant, was ringed by sapphires, almost as blue as her eyes. *Don't even class it as a maybe.* I closed the lid, reached out to drop the box back in the drawer, then had second thoughts. Season of goodwill, wine with a turkey dinner, a few mince pies, a couple of brandies. If I managed to pass the *how much* test there was just a chance Melody would warm to the idea.

We do hope that you have enjoyed reading this large print book.

Did you know that all of our titles are available for purchase?

We publish a wide range of high quality large print books including:
Romances, Mysteries, Classics
General Fiction
Non Fiction and Westerns

Special interest titles available in large print are:
The Little Oxford Dictionary
Music Book
Song Book
Hymn Book
Service Book

Also available from us courtesy of Oxford University Press:
Young Readers' Dictionary
(large print edition)
Young Readers' Thesaurus
(large print edition)

For further information or a free brochure, please contact us at:
Ulverscroft Large Print Books Ltd.,
The Green, Bradgate Road, Anstey,
Leicester, LE7 7FU, England.
Tel: (00 44) 0116 236 4325
Fax: (00 44) 0116 234 0205

Other titles published by
The House of Ulverscroft:

CRIPPLEHEAD

Raymond Haigh

Private eye Paul Lomax never wanted the case. Checking on errant wives wasn't his scene, but keeping an eye on Rex Saunders' ex-fashion-model wife, Mona, promised to be all profit and no pain. How was Lomax to know that foxy old Rex was keeping so many secrets? And then there was the problem of Lomax's budding relationship with the irrepressible Melody Brown. Taking the case didn't help the romance along, especially when Mona dumped her inhibitions. Now Mona is terrified by sickening threats and the local morgue is filling up fast. When a hit man moves in and the police don't want to know, Lomax and Mona find themselves on their own.

DARK ANGEL

Raymond Haigh

The Prime Minister and the Home Secretary are scared — very scared. Terrorists, riots, the plague sweeping over the country, these are not the cause of alarm. Their concern centres on the documents held by a biochemist, which implicate the Government in a grave crime. Now, the biochemist is missing, as well as his wife and child. Government agent Samantha Quest is searching for them — but soon she is also being watched and hunted. A trail of death follows. Can Quest find the missing family and protect them from powerful men who will stop at nothing to conceal their crimes?

THE BODY IN THE VESTIBULE

Katherine Hall Page

Seeking an epicurean adventure in the French provinces, caterer and minister's wife Faith Fairchild decides to throw the perfect dinner party. But after the last guest has departed her gastronomical triumph, she encounters something neither expected nor welcome: a dead body lying in her vestibule. Unfortunately it doesn't help her credibility when the corpse vanishes before the local gendarmes arrive. But Faith realizes that, though the police refuse to take her seriously, a killer just might. And if she doesn't get to the bottom of this fiendish French conundrum, Faith's recent successful feast could end up being her last.